Desolate Paths

Erin Unger

F
Ung

Printed in the United States of America

Cover Design by Serenay Daphn

Edited by Cheryl Grey

All scripture is taken from the New King James Version Bible

First Edition

This book is a work of fiction. Names, characters, places, and incidents are made up or are used fictitiously. Any resemblance to actual events, locales, or persons is a coincidence.

ISBN-13: 9781790322336

Dedication

For Michael, my husband, my rock, my biggest
cheerleader.

Proverbs 3:6 In all your ways acknowledge Him,
and He shall direct your paths.

1
Brooke

I almost killed someone. It stunned me into reality, and I decided I had to change. That was why I ended up at the center—but my wobbly knees urged me to run in the opposite direction.

I just had to go forward. I stood at the train station and struggled to gain my bearings—and my senses. A sign announcing *Carrick Living Museum and Rehabilitation Center* flashed in green digital letters. What was a living museum? In one short train ride, I had left the modern world and gone back in time. Hadn't I signed up to recover at a facility where *worry-free recuperation* and *slower paced stays* were in quotes on the website?

Women dressed in what looked like ball gowns swooshed past me. They had to be hot in all that material. *Wait a minute...* It started to make sense as another lady walked past me. I had seen pictures of the old dresses in the header of the website. The place was a kind of museum and rehab center.

The men? Had I gotten sucked into an historical novel? Their muscles bulged below rolled-up sleeves in shirts like the costumes from my favorite Charlotte

Bronte-based movie as they loaded and unloaded cargo and what-not. One in particular paused to check me out. And I actually thought my headache paused long enough to let me take in his perfect sculpted cheeks and tanned skin. His sandy blond hair was only a shade darker than my own. I grinned—but only for a split second—as my headache shocked me back to reality.

With a tip of his hand to his temple, the guy saluted me. He called out over the noise of the tourists moving around me, "The name's Kyle."

I spun around. Rehab wasn't for ogling great looking guys. It was exactly the opposite. *Don't even let him into your brain matter.*

Disorientation replaced my cute-guy radar. Where did I go from there?

As one woman eyed me, I wrapped my arms over my too-snug T-shirt. For some reason, my skinny jeans seemed to cling tighter than I remembered. I dropped my arms. Since when did I care what people thought about the clothes I wore?

I pinched the bridge of my nose. Why hadn't I read the whole website and application I'd signed online? The dull pounding of my head echoed in my ears as I looked back to the train, already groaning in its struggle to accelerate out of the depot and away from the strange world I had just been plunked into.

Tears ebbed in the corners of my eyes. *Please don't let this be like the other place.* I lowered my achy head and looked down at the wooden planks of the arrival and departure zone, and then back up to the busy depot.

"Miss…"

"Yes?" I swung around and glanced down at the arrival entrance. No familiar faces, no more comforts that I'd taken for granted most of my privileged life. And I was hours from home.

"Over here, Miss." A rangy teenager threw his arms open wide. "Welcome to rehab. I'm here to pick you up and take you to Mr. Carrick. He said I'd better hurry, so let's get goin'. I don't want to get another demerit." He trudged toward me and grabbed a suitcase out of my hands. The movement pulled the corner of his shirt free from his knickers. I wanted to snicker at the gap between his weird half-pants and high socks, where knobby knees protruded.

"Shh. Not everyone needs to know why I'm here."

He knit his brows together. "If you're here," he made a broad gesture with his empty hand, "everyone already knows why."

He was about to get a fist in the nose. I lowered my voice and pointed at the sightseers circling the depot. "They don't. So hush."

He hiked up one of his socks and tried to tuck it under the bottom of his knickers. Smudges and dirt splotched his shins like a schoolboy after a skirmish in the mud.

His voice rose like a little girl as he beckoned me. "Come on."

I rolled my eyes at the sharpness of his tone. Biting my tongue, I fought the urge to retort. He didn't want to make me upset today. I counted to five and blew out a breath. "I'm Brooke Hollen. You are…?"

"I know who you are. Who else would have suitcases at that arrival zone?" He paused, then looked back at me before moving full steam ahead. "Now let's go."

I almost bumped into the kid as he came to a sudden halt. I say kid, but he wasn't that young. Maybe seventeen. It was his attitude and squeaky voice that threw me off. "Whoa. Your name would be nice. Who are you?"

"Bret. Climb aboard."

I stopped staring at him and blinked hard in the direction he pointed. "A wagon?" What had I gotten myself into? A gigantic horse turned its head, ears forward, as I took a cautious step toward it. Its thick legs and large body shifted, and I backed away a couple steps. I glanced behind me. The train was gone. I had no way to make a quick escape. I thrust my hands in my pockets and rubbed the used ticket in the right one. "You're kidding, right?"

He cocked an eyebrow. "How else would we get around here? This place is big."

"Oh." I pursed my lips.

The wagon had seen better days. Its green and yellow paint peeled away at the edges, but the wood looked solid. I edged toward it as Bret tossed my luggage into the back bed.

"Hey, be careful with that." My face heated and fists tightened. "I'm going to throw *you* if you do that again."

"Yep, you do need a few sessions with Mr. Carrick." He cupped his hand on one side of his mouth and whispered, "Anger issues." Winking and laughing, he grasped the side of the wagon and hoisted himself onto the seat.

Anger issues were only the beginning of my problems. And he came very close to finding out what my anger could unleash. Let him say one more word…

2
Sarge

Crowds hid dark deeds. What better place to feed Sarge's cravings? What better place to do so much? A quick caress. A stroke of the hair.

Hide.

Blend.

Act.

Repeat.

Nightfall made it even better.

Sarge thrust another box of canned vegetables onto his dolly and waited for a cute brunette to step into his path. She wouldn't even notice how close he got to her with all the people lining up to get their tickets.

But instead, a lady with two inches worth of hair roots showing at her scalp stepped on his foot as she backed up to snap the millionth photo he'd seen her take. He grumbled under his breath. Those tourists knew how to rile a sheep into retaliation.

"Oh, sorry."

I bet you are. He slathered a gushy smile on his lips. "No problem, ma'am."

She backed off when he didn't manage to disguise his squinted gaze in time.

Someone's hair tickled Sarge's arm as he turned to lift another box. The sudden contact sent a thrill of shockwaves all the way to his booted feet. A young woman slipped so close between him and the brunette that her arm brushed his. A new resident to the center or another pesky tourist? Something in her hand bumped one of the boxes of vegetables and made it teeter. He reached out to steady it, giving him one more chance to touch her. What a beauty. As he scratched his head, he tried to pull his gaze from her but couldn't. "Hello."

She gave a dismissive wave and bolted down the exit ramp. *No, she didn't just do that.* He bit his tongue hard. How dare she. The loading dock of the train depot buzzed even louder with sudden activity, as if a hoard of cicadas had flown there to infest the area. Sarge marched into the crowd of people. Which way had she gone? For once, all the people became too much of a shield.

There she was. When she scooped up a couple of the suitcases, his heart began to pound in his ears. No tourist. A resident for sure.

Her hair swished in the breeze and moved against the middle of her back in a provocative flow. She seemed so confident, somewhat feisty with the tilt of her defiant chin. He moved out of the crowd and pressed his back against the harsh brick wall as he watched her. Yes, feisty described this blondie—and haunted too. The red, puffy rims of her eyelids showed her poison of choice. He'd had the same facial cues not so long ago.

She turned and checked behind her for a brief moment. Sarge smirked. Yes, he was up to a new challenge. He just had a few things to tie up with someone else first. Then he'd approach her.

Tourists blocked his view again, and he strained to peer around an old man in tube socks and Velcro sneakers. Didn't those stop selling in stores thirty years ago? A growl emanated from his mouth as he flexed his hands into fists.

When he tried to spot Blondie again, she'd caught up to the nitwit, Bret. She had to be on her way to see the owner to sign away all her rights. Didn't every resident have to get their marching orders before they could even breathe their first breath of confinement in that place?

He pulled at his mandarin collar as he exited the depot and looked around. People shifted around close by but ignored him. All of the tourists annoyed him, but there was no better place to be for what he desired. The center made everything he wanted so easy to attain. Life. Death. Who'd miss a girl or two with the kind of history those addicts had? Residents ran away all the time. Or at least appeared to.

He let the powerful surge of energy course through him. No one would stop him from getting what he wanted, and what he wanted was the blonde.

3

Brooke

Did Bret want me to relapse right in front of him? Because I came so close to giving up as I stood and stared at the wagon. Another mark against that place.

How was I supposed to climb up the side of a wagon on my own, when I'd never even seen a real one before? Add a bad headache and the shakes, which started making my muscles limp as old celery. My fingers fumbled to get a hold on the wooden side. I shifted my grasp to the top ledge of the wagon bed as he had, watched the horse, and then tried my best to jump up unaided. As I landed in the seat, I raised my chin. The horse twitched its tail and turned to eye me. Ha, I did it.

Bret shook his head and chuckled one last time, then snapped the reins. "Yah."

He'd better stop laughing at me—

The horse moved forward, making me lurch in the seat. If it wasn't for the rigid backboard, I would've toppled over the hard seat into the bed of the wagon.

I harrumphed. No way would I even glance in his direction.

He trotted the horse down a side street and returned to the main road as I bounced with each footfall and kept my face trained with the best bored look I could muster. The further we went, the more each building and the activity around it caught my attention. He didn't need to know I cared one bit about the old town we moved past. But I couldn't keep my fake-bored glower when a young woman stepped out in a bonnet and floor-length skirt with a high-waisted jacket to match the hem of the dress.

"Yep. It's so weird, isn't it, having to wear these crazy costumes? You read about it, right? We don't get to change into regular clothes at the end of the workday, either." He shook his head. "Rules, rules."

What? I started to answer, but shut my mouth.

Bret interrupted my thoughts with a whistle between his teeth. "Just wait 'til you see all the paperwork. You assumed you filled it all out before you arrived? That wasn't anything."

We passed street after street, and the buildings grew older as we went. More people strolled along with guide maps and camera cases.

Bret stopped the horses, and I lurched forward with a yelp. Somebody needed to take his carriage license—or whatever they called it—and burn it. He pointed to a building on the right. "Mr. Carrick's office is behind the check-out counter and down the hall in there."

I grabbed the side of the wagon to steady myself.

"Git on, now. I got things to do."

"Fine." He didn't even blink when I nailed him with a death glare. It took a second to coordinate my balance enough to jump down and land without face-planting into the wooden sidewalk. I grabbed the wagon wheel and begged my breakfast bar to stay down.

Something cool and mushy caked the hand I used to steady myself. I pulled it away and stared at the brown manure smooshed between my fingers, which emanated a disgusting odor. My gag reflex worked just fine. I began to retch beside the wagon, but somehow the tiny bit of breakfast managed to remain in my stomach.

"Ew, ew, ew." Tears stung my eyes. I didn't care anymore who saw me cry. The morning had started out horrible and everything continued to stink up my day, like the manure in the crevices of my fingers.

Where could I wipe my hand?

"Well, there you are."

I turned toward the tinkle of a bell from the front door. Another antiqued woman strode to the side of the wagon. Her outfit matched the same type I'd seen another lady wearing at the other end of the street. And her perfect bun pulled so tight her eyes squinted. She looked like someone I wouldn't dare mess with.

"You won't be needing ninety-nine percent of whatever's in those suitcases. Didn't you read the what-to-leave-at-home section of the website?"

Not again. "Um, I'm sorry."

With a shake of her head, she turned from staring at the back of the wagon. And I trembled a little more when her scrutiny shot right through me.

"My name's Dara Carrick, co-owner with Mr. Carrick, my brother." The woman thrust her hand toward me. "You can call me *Ms.* Dara."

I gulped and grasped her hand. "Uh, hi."

Oh, no. Wrong hand.

Dara dropped my fingers and looked at her palm. Red blossomed on her cheeks.

"Um, I'm so sorry." I bit my lips together and winced. "I put my hand in something... uh..." I pointed at the wheel. "I think it's poop... uh... manure."

I might as well pack my stuff and get back on the old train.

4

Sarge

So what if having a cell phone on the premises broke the rules? It wasn't the only thing he kept hidden. Sarge pressed the tiny cordless earbud into his right ear and touched the screen of his phone to start a downloaded song. He scanned the street before returning to his mission.

Bret drove a little too fast to keep up with, but Sarge had gained time while the wagon made an arc around the street. He strode at a clipped pace and barreled toward the general store.

Blondie couldn't keep her eyes off the other residents coming and going. That same rich wheat-colored hair he'd admired at the depot fought against the wind and whipped at the faded seat the new resident leaned against.

Who was she?

Had her name already been tagged on her work station or the schedule kept under the counter of the general store?

He'd almost caught up to them when Ms. Carrick stormed out of the store and stopped short in front of Blondie.

15

Sarge abandoned his original path along the storefronts and skirted to the side of the general store. Great. That woman didn't miss anything. Almost.

But he just had to have one more minute to watch Blondie. Maybe the women would share a little introduction and he'd hear her name.

Ms. Carrick looked over Blondie's shoulder straight into his eyes. A growl threatened a wild escape from his throat. Now he had no choice. He'd have to act as natural as possible and walk right past them. No more chances to study her in her natural state—as he liked to think of it.

The co-owner eyed Sarge again and waited for him to pass.

Man. Privacy policies were a drag.

Oh, well. He'd find another way to memorize every detail about her. He'd start with her suitcase. It was handy to have access to the keys for the storage lock-up. He'd be in and out before anyone noticed him. And he'd take a memento from it. Something small and insignificant to her. Something more unique than the last time.

5
Brooke

Good grief. I hadn't even made it an hour at the center. I squeezed my eyes shut for a second and waited to get kicked out of rehab on my first day.

Dara shook her hand in the air. "Let me take you to the wash room, and we'll get you cleaned up. I'm glad to see you made it with no problems along the way—I hope. Entering rehab is more than daunting. I congratulate you on taking the first step."

Her jovial voice matched the smile on her round face. Not what I expected at all from the squinty eyes. Good. Now I had another chance to *not* screw up everything.

A sudden chill ran through me. I glanced around and fidgeted as my scalp prickled. Was someone watching us? How silly to think such a thing. The street and sidewalks crawled with tourists. I forced my shoulders back down a bit. I'd seen paranoia on the long list of detox symptoms when I'd done an online search. Of course, I'd have that one too. *Stop being so crazy.*

Ms. Carrick paused and waited for some of the people to pass us.

"I'll show you around since Mr. Carrick has some business to complete. But he'll be back to run through the rules and regulations with you in a bit."

I glanced up at the sign with *General Store* painted in yellow letters as I followed the co-owner into the building. The smell of old leather and fresh apple pies engulfed me as I noted several girls who stood in long dresses helping customers. Funny poofs held out each side of their dresses. Some type of colonial style?

I lifted my nose and pointed at one of them. *Oh, please no.* "Uh, Dara, I don't remember agreeing to wear one of those. At least, that's what Bret said was the dress code. He's wrong, isn't he?"

"Please call me Ms. Dara or Ms. Carrick. Respect is very important here. You need to refer to all of your superiors as miss or mister." She scolded me. "And yes, when you agreed to enter this facility, you agreed to follow all codes and rules. That is the dress code. Once you've been here awhile, it won't seem so strange. You'll even have a chance to pick the material and style you want for more dresses if you need them. You'll get used to it."

Her cheery voice began to grate on the few nerves I had left.

We walked around barrels of goods, stepped behind the main counter, and then headed through a door and down a hall. Dara pointed at the different doors, then stopped short in front of one of them. "Here's the break room, and just beyond it is the restroom. At the very end is Mr. Carrick's office."

I followed her into the restroom and scrubbed my hands under the water. For once in my life, I had to stick to something. I hadn't come all that way to turn and run as I always had before. I would wear the dress. Period. Even if I looked like a frumpy marm from the past.

"Now let me show you the town." Dara scurried out of the bathroom, and I stayed close to her side.

The rack on the wooden counter quivered as she whipped out one of the maps, unfolded it, and shook it to straighten it. "See here? This is where we are." She pointed at a little star on the diagram. "Now, if we go out here to the left, you'll see the milliner's shop, and down further a restaurant with authentic time-period cooking, and…"

The doorbell jingled on our way back to the street.

"A what shop?" She might as well have been speaking Chinese.

"A milliner's shop. They make women's hats. And there's the dress shop and tea shop." She started to walk down the planked sidewalk. "Now, as you gain our trust, and you meet the goals we outline for you, you will be given the opportunity to work at one of the other stores. Maybe even the Somerset farm down the road. Of course, at first you must start at the general store."

The sun beat down on me as a spring breeze cooled its intensity. I covered my mouth as I concentrated on the woman's words.

I need a drink. I pinched my wrist and winced at the sharp pain. Those kinds of thoughts had to stop.

"Down that way is the hotel, and in that direction is the boarding house for the women." Ms. Dara pointed to her right. Tourists ambled past us as she talked and walked. "The men's quarters are at the opposite end of town, just past the train station."

I scuffed my designer sneaker on the ground and hooked my thumbs on my back pockets. We went to so many places, but I didn't remember most of them by the time we returned to the general store.

"Here comes Mr. Carrick." Dara paused in her lecture, then motioned for him to join us.

He lifted his head and gazed in our direction. What

height he lacked he made up for in sheer presence. His swift gait slowed, and his long suit jacket settled around his legs as he halted in front of me, giving the illusion of a Dickens character. I couldn't help but wonder if there was a movie crew just around the corner. One quick glance into his eyes made me want to hide as he stood and appraised me for a moment.

"Hello, Ms. Hollen. I'm Nathan Carrick, and I'll manage your case during your stay. Let's go to my office and get started on the paperwork. If you have any questions, I'll answer them after we go through the regulation booklet. And you may always come to me or Ms. Carrick if others come up later." His sharp eyes held mine.

I squared my shoulders. Why wouldn't he stop looking through me like he could see my soul? I followed him down the hall to his office while Ms. Dara stayed behind to help a customer.

Mr. Carrick rounded the side of his desk and sat in an old winged-back chair. He reached for a file folder. "I'm sure Bret gave you the lowdown about the paperwork." A stack of papers landed between us on the desk. "Please take a seat."

I needed a comfy seat after the ride from the station. I perused the room and checked each seat before choosing the one on the left. With the toe of my sneaker, I turned the empty leather chair beside me and propped my feet on it. Wow, he didn't tell me to take my feet off the furniture. "You're kidding, right? You want me to fill all that out too?"

"We have to make sure that everyone's on the same page, so yes, you have to fill it out. And here's the rule book." He pulled it free from a small pile of documents and held it out for me to take. I thumbed through it as he began to speak again. "As you know, there will be no alcohol, no drugs, no smoking, no explicit materials, and no food allowed in your room. Now let's go over the demerit policy. Oh, and give me your phone."

"But…"

"Policy."

I half-gasped. *Not* my phone. The only thing that would protect my sanity while I stayed there for months. With one last look at it, I handed it to him and gulped.

He guided me through each page and read aloud. With each word, my body threatened to get up and bolt out the door on its own accord. How did he expect anyone to live by the rigid rules set forth in the book?

"On Sunday, we all attend religious services. There are several churches you may choose from once you don't need a guide. But you must have your logbook signed by the pastor to show you were there for the allotted time. There're devotions each night, and your housemother will lead those. Once again, your logbook has to reflect that time as well. It's required."

Not the church thing. "You're not for real, are you? And someone's going to follow me around, like everywhere?"

"Yes. It's all a part of this program. And as I understand it, you chose to be here." He stared me down, and then shoved a paper in front of me. "When you sign this, you agree to all of our guidelines."

I rolled my eyes and crossed my arms. No way. I couldn't sign it. I just couldn't.

…But I owed it to the kid I almost killed.

He stood. "If you've changed your mind, now is a good time to see yourself out of my office."

The blood heated in my veins. My nostrils flared as I struggled to fight it. No one had ever been so direct with me. Not even the director of the other place. I flicked my long hair over one shoulder and tapped my toe against the ancient rug at my feet. I had to sign it.

His gaze swallowed me again. "This is something you have to do for *you*. I'm not going to hold your hand or bend the rules for you. You're a grown woman, twenty-two, right? You choose." His voice softened. "You have to really want this."

The quiet strength of his voice riveted me to my seat. My eyes left his for a moment, all anger deflated like a pierced soccer ball. "I … I do want this. I'm sorry."

"Apology accepted. Now let's get back to this paperwork." He sat back down and pulled the chair closer to his desk.

I signed them and listened as I turned over each one. With every page, my throat tightened and the pen grew heavier. Could I do it?

"As you know, there are two payment methods. You may pay by cash or credit once your insurance company disburses their portion. You do have insurance?"

I nodded. As long as Dad didn't kick me off his policy while I was in there. And I wouldn't put it past him after my blow-up before I left home.

"Good. There is another option. You can work here for three extra months to repay your debt. The last step in your rehabilitation plan is to help others, so I suggest you stay for the extra time even if you can afford the cost. Oh, and the work you do while you complete your plan will pay some of the cost down as well. We take a certain percentage for that.

"Here are your copies. Please keep them on hand. You need to memorize the demerit system and the chore requirements. We'll give you two weeks to put it to memory. Did Ms. Carrick talk to you about your roommate?"

Was he crazy? He expected me to share a room too?

"Well, all new patients to the program have to have what we like to think of as a guide, if you will. As I mentioned earlier, they will keep an eye on your progress, and will help be strong deterrents from rule breaking.

"Now, let's talk about your therapy. You and I will have one-on-one sessions every morning at eight."

"Whoa, that's way too early."

He tilted his head. "We're trying to form better habits. One of those is not sleeping in so late. And you'll meet every night for group therapy."

"Anything else?" I blew out my cheeks, but the pressure made my headache surge. I tried to steady my tone, to control the emotions that built in my abdomen, but an explosion threatened my sanity. I might as well be a caged hamster swinging from the ceiling bars, desperate to escape.

"And I'd be glad to set you up with one of our other therapists, if you feel you need extra private sessions." He raised his eyebrows. "Of course, you'll be on an anti-anxiety medication for one to three weeks to help prevent the possibility of seizures during your detox period. You've been clean for how many days?"

"Two." My hands began to shake as if on cue. *Stop. Please stop*, I begged my body, but it refused to listen.

"Well, we don't want you to have those too severe symptoms that can occur between forty-eight and seventy-two hours after your last drink. It's imperative that you show up at the clinic every morning and evening at your appointed time to get your meds.

"Let me direct you to Ms. Carrick. She can show you where to go. Then she will lead you to your room, and of course look through all your belongings."

"If I admitted myself, why would I bring contraband?" I made air quotes and huffed.

"Regulations." He rose and straightened a few things on his desk. His arm rested on the back of his chair. "Brooke, we're all here for you. I believe you can do this. I have faith that God can change you, make you a new person."

His soft words left me breathless. Had anyone ever believed me capable of change? Tears stung my eyes, and I blinked. Not even my own mother cared enough to believe in me.

Did Mr. Carrick really understand me? His eyes held something I couldn't put my finger on as he watched me from across the room. "Now, let's start your first session."

By the time we finished talking, I wanted to crawl into a cave and not come out for the rest of my life. Wasn't therapy supposed to make people feel better? Well, I didn't. Not yet. But one thing I did understand, for the first time, was that I was mad—I mean really mad—and it had created the root to what made me drink in the first place. But why?

He straightened the tie thing at his neck and ushered me out of the office and down the hall to the store. "Ms. Carrick, Brooke is ready to go to the medication station and detox center."

"I had a quick question for you." Ms. Carrick pulled him aside for a moment.

She returned and ushered me out of the busy store. "Let's get you to the clinic. Now watch your step. You wouldn't want to smell like a barn again." She pointed to a pile of horse manure, and I looked around at quite a few mounds along the road. No need for a repeat of earlier.

Dara picked up her skirts as she stepped over another pile. She skipped a little and walked with briskness even though it winded her.

A few buildings down, Dara pushed through the door. "This is where you pick up your medication. And if you get sick or hurt, they can treat minor things, but otherwise patients are sent to the hospital." She held the door for me. "The detox center is in the rear of this building."

She waved to the lady behind the small window in front of us. Its bars reminded me of jail.

"Nurse Marlene, this is Brooke Hollen. She should be on your detox and new medication schedule."

"Hello." The woman moved as close to the window as she could and swooshed her ponytail over her shoulder. "It may be tough at first, but we'll take care of you."

My heavy sigh rustled a sign-in paper on the small counter between me and the bars.

The nurse marked the documents in front of her and unlocked the medicine drawer at her side. Her voice cut through my musings. "Here's your first round of pills."

"Okay." I swallowed them, acrid taste and all, and took the small paper cup of water the woman offered. Anything to get my racing heart to slow down would be great.

The nurse's attention returned to the sheets in front of her. "Let me know right away if you have any unusual side-effects like difficulty breathing, vomiting, or numbness."

I bristled but nodded. Good grief. The cure might kill me faster than any major seizure had a chance to.

"Open your mouth and let me see."

"Huh?"

"I have to make sure you swallowed the medication."

I rolled my eyes but did as she asked.

"Great. Now go to that door on your right. I'll buzz you in. Then you can take a pee test."

Dara waved to my new drug dealer and plodded out of the building.

I crossed my arms tight over my abdomen and looked to the floor. *I can do this. I can.*

What horrors waited on the other side? Too many TV shows depicted dark views of rehab. Patients who hurled everything, including their bodies, against their cell walls and doors as paranoia consumed them. Even going crazy as the treatment fought against the body. Cries and screams. Would this hold up to television standards?

6
Brooke

My three days spent in the detox center was a lifetime when anyone had been through what I had. I would have kissed the ground my first day out of the place, if I wasn't so drained from the ordeal. Cloudy brain. Thick tongue. Body aches. I had the works. But I was clean—*truly* sober—for the first time in years.

Ms. Carrick hurried past me. "Now, let's get to the boarding house. I'll bet you're hungry. There should be some soup and a sandwich saved for you once we finish our tour."

How many horror stories had been told about institution food? My stomach gurgled in protest. I hadn't eaten enough in the center to know how bad it tasted. "Please tell me it's not bean soup."

"Maybe." She grinned at me, her lips pulled tight against too-straight teeth. "Anyway, I'll make sure you're taken care of."

Dara halted her mad stride a few blocks north. She smiled as she looked from the large dwelling in front of us to me. "Here we are. Isn't it beautiful? We work hard to make all residents comfortable in their new housing."

The house in front of us stood close to the road,

surrounded by expansive side gardens. Stalwart would have been a better word to describe it. But it seemed to fit into its surroundings well.

At the left side of the house, a teenager dug at the ground. She stopped working for a second and stared at me. "Hello."

"Hey." I could barely see her face as the huge brim of her straw hat swooped with each jerky movement she made. Her light eyes watched me for a moment before she turned her attention back to the plants.

I hooked my fingers in my pockets. Good. She asked no questions. My business was my business.

Dara stepped onto the porch and threw the door open. "Now this is the main living area that you'll share with the other girls. I expect you to clean and cook as everyone else does. There's a list over there." She walked through the large space, sunny and open to the dining room. "I'll make sure you're added to it by tomorrow. Each patient rotates when they sweep, wash dishes, or do other tasks."

"Oh? There're no maids? I mean, I've never done chores before."

"*Not here.* We want all of you to learn how to function on your own. Life skills are important."

Dara walked to the kitchen and smiled at a woman whose hair showed so shiny it looked like strands of silver.

Sleeves rolled up in huge wads of material, the woman sliced some apples with so much fervor that I cringed. I had too wild of an imagination. It took a lot to keep an image of her finger in my food from taking hold. "This is Ms. Anna. Ms. Anna, this is Brooke Hollen."

Anna stopped chopping for a moment and wiped her glistening forehead with her sleeve. "Hello, I'm glad you're with us."

I gave a short wave. All I cared about was not seeing someone dismember her own finger—and a nice nap—not small talk. I looked into the sweet face of the housemother and stopped the attitude. Exhaustion made me grumpy, but she didn't deserve to be on the other end of it.

"Ms. Anna helps with the cooking and makes sure chores get done. And she does some of the counseling with the women. She lives on the premises. Now, let's go see your room." Dara left the kitchen and clutched the stair railing with splayed fingers big enough to wrap almost all the way around it as she climbed a steep set of stairs.

Sun poured into the upper hallway from two tall windows on each end. "There's another floor that has six rooms, but you'll stay on this level. The main level has no electricity since it is part of tours sometimes, and we're trying to keep it as historically accurate as possible. But the top two floors have power for everyone's safety. Here we are." She stepped into a room. Several shallow breaths rattled through me from the exertion of getting up the stairs. "You have to share the bathroom with your roommate and the two girls in the adjacent room." She pointed in the direction of a closed door. "All four of you are responsible for its cleanliness."

The throb of pain in my head began to stop all assimilation of information as my stress level climbed. *Not more work.*

Dara ran through the rules again, and added lists of things I had to do every day. Then she crinkled her mouth into a smile. "You may lie down for a bit … if you'd like. I have to go through your belongings before I leave, though."

I looked at my mangled suitcases in the middle of the

floor and waved for the woman to do her job. Why fight it?

Bret had a five-hundred-dollar replacement bill headed his way, since he hadn't bothered to listen to me about being more careful with those.

Dara continued to talk as she pulled everything out of them. She set a few items aside along with all my clothing, other than my jammies. "I have to take these, but you may retrieve them when you leave the center."

I held my breath. Some of my makeup landed in the contraband pile. If only I could pull a Yoda move and get back those much-needed items.

Dara rested her hand on the doorframe after she finished. "Let me know if you have any more questions. Your guide should be here soon."

"Fine." I huffed, too tired to stop my bad manners.

"Be in the kitchen by five o'clock to help with dinner." She gave a short wave and walked away with my suitcases, still mostly full.

My conversation with Mr. Carrick—when had we talked—oh, yeah, days ago … Well, it stuck in my craw as it had every night I lay in detox, unable to fall asleep. What was with my attitude? Even Ms. Carrick got a piece of it before she left.

The bright sun sheering through the huge windows pierced my eyes, and I sauntered sluggishly to them and pulled the curtains closed, then lowered myself onto the bed. If I napped for an hour, maybe I'd feel better. The quilt fell over my legs as I pulled it and lay as still as possible. At least I was there. And I'd made it through the first several days.

I rolled over to get away from the thin slit of light as much as possible. Sleep needed to replace the pain. In more ways than one.

30

7
Brooke

Sunlight smacked me in the face. It seared into my eyelids as if someone held a blow torch close to my face. I braced against the sudden pain and tried to cover my face with the blanket, but it lay twisted around my body. A hand pushed at my shoulder. It was close enough to bite.

Whoever had flung open the curtain hovered beside me. "Wow, why are yah asleep in the middle of the afternoon? It's a beautiful day, don't yah think?" She yanked at my quilt. "The name's Willa, and I'm your new cell mate, ha ha. I've been waiting for you to get here. We have so much to do. Come on now. Get up."

I squinted through one half-open lid at the way too cheery face above me.

A young woman held out her hand, brown tendrils of hair bouncing.

I tried once more to wrench my blanket free.

She scurried around the room and straightened the desk and her bed. "I'm also your new shadow. They call it 'guiding' here. If you need help with anything—or even if you don't—I'm here to watch out for you. Keep you out of trouble… that sort of thing."

I rolled my eyes and tried one last time to turn over and ignore the young woman prancing about the room as if she were in a Disney movie—and making way too much noise. My stomach gurgled in a bad way. Uh oh. If my body had its way, I'd have to dash for the bathroom—forget the now pounding headache.

"Come. Time's wasting. You're going to learn quick that it takes so much longer to do everything around here. We have to do it all by hand. We need to help Chris in the garden, and then there're the chickens to pluck. Fortunately, Josh came over and killed them for us. And—" As she spoke, all of her o's were elongated in a funny way, giving a humorous tinge to her conversation. What part of the States was she from?

"Chickens? *Killed?*" My too-vivid imagination accelerated the squall going on in my stomach. "I think I'm going to be sick." I struggled to free myself. *Please let everything stay inside until I get to the toilet.*

"Oh, look at yah. Ms. Dara must've forgotten to bring your costumes." She turned to the closet door and flung it open. "Yep, she did. You need to run down to the tailor shop and pick them up. I don't have time to go with you. Just hurry. Meet me in the back yard by the barn when you get back. There's a coop out there." She hurried away, managing to straighten her bun and reset a few stray pins in her hair.

Was she from Wisconsin or something?

One last upheaval in my midsection sent me scurrying to the bathroom. Detoxing was not for wimps.

Before I made it all the way to the toilet, someone bowled right into me.

"Watch out. I gotta go and I can't hold it." Red curls floated around the young woman's freckled face.

I didn't move. "Hey."

"I got six sisters at home. I don't much care if you stand there. I'll just go anyway and you'll be the one embarrassed, not me."

I hurried out and lowered myself to the wooden planks of the floor as I leaned against the doorjamb and squeezed my eyes closed. Could I hold it in? Whose idea was it to make four people share one bathroom—at a rehab center? "What is wrong with you people?"

One minute later, the curly head popped back through the door. "I'm Jade. Sorry 'bout that." She pulled at her dress and yanked at the collar. "You're Brooke, right? Once had a rat named that. Gotta go. See you around."

She disappeared as fast as she'd come.

I didn't wait a moment longer. With a quick peek through the other door to make sure no one else wanted to fight me for the toilet, I closed and locked it.

Moments later, I brushed my teeth and changed into a different shirt. The last one hadn't made it. How smart was it to go out when I felt this bad? But I had to get with the program. Literally.

I held the town map in my hand and headed back to the store. At the entrance, I paused and rested against the door for a moment. My stomach hadn't given up on its war against me. And the time warp going on in the place made me dizzy. Eyeing the rows of goods and the counter, I spied Dara in the far corner with a customer. My foot tapped as nervous waves flowed through me. When she turned, I held up my hand. "Hey, Dara, I mean Ms. Dara. Willa said you forgot to give me my uniforms."

"You're right, I did. Just go to the dressmaker's shop and get them. I'm too busy to do it now." She pointed at a building on the map. "It's right there."

I walked out the door, looked in each direction, and then returned my attention to the map. How many streets between where I was and there? Had I even gone in the right direction when I went left? I headed down the planks and counted the number of streets I needed to cross before I had to make turns, like a Candy Land board game. The sudden impact of something against the paper in my hands sent it fluttering to the ground and stopped me in midstride. Huh?

Someone steadied me before I bounced backwards onto the sidewalk. "Gotcha."

"I … I'm sorry." I looked up in time to see Mr. Carrick's eyes flicker. "I didn't see you. That blasted map doesn't make any sense to me. I can't seem to find my way to the dress shop."

"It's okay." He bent down, retrieved the map off the ground, and handed it to me. "I need to take some paperwork over there. I'll show you where it is."

I gave a mental pump of my fist in the air. With his help, I wouldn't lose my way. "Thanks."

"Hold on one minute, and I'll be right back." He didn't give me a chance to answer as he disappeared and then returned.

I spun around and checked my surroundings. A few tourists passed, lost in their own maps of torture. I folded the map and shoved it into my pocket, then leaned against the side of the building. The birds screamed their welcome. The breeze whistled too loud. Everything resonated at ten times its normal volume in my head. I put my hands over my ears.

Down the dusty street, Bret struggled to pull a large trunk through the door of a brownstone building. I grinned. He had to be the best comedy show the place offered. He mumbled something as he tugged and pulled. Then his feet slipped out from under him and he fell to the ground. Some colorful terminology left his mouth.

But he jumped up and looked around as if a magic demerit slip might fall from the sky. I turned away, not able to hold in the laugh that erupted. At least he was far enough away not to hear. Guilt replaced my laughter. He didn't deserve to be my comic relief while I waited.

Mr. Carrick returned. "It's this way." He quickened his pace. "How do you like your living arrangements? Have you met your roommate yet?"

He and Ms. Dara hurried way too much for my liking. I shrugged. "I'll get used to it. And, yes, I met her."

"Good."

Another group of residents passed us, their arms loaded with material bags full of something. I turned and walked backwards a few steps before facing forward. "Everyone's in such a rush around here. I don't know if I can get used to that."

He raised his eyebrows but kept silent.

I looked through the windows as we passed several historical buildings, and then went across the street.

"It's not always so busy. But you'll adjust soon enough."

Several turns later, Mr. Carrick and I walked under a row of trees. He stopped in front of a cute little building and then headed into the cooler interior. "Here we are."

A voice muttered from behind an old mannequin. "Hello, Mr. Carrick. It's good to see you. Did you bring the paperwork?"

I scanned the room but didn't see anyone.

"You must be here to pick up the uniforms." The words slurred together. When the woman stepped out from behind a mannequin, she managed to grin with pins protruding out of her mouth. One dimple dug into her round cheek. I loved the intricate style of her hair, with braids and a bun in gorgeous perfection. "Oh, I didn't see you. You must be the new resident."

Yikes. What if she swallowed that slew of pins?

When she pulled them out of her mouth, she set them in the patterned material which hung on the mannequin. "I'm Stacey Ward."

I waved to her.

He set the papers on a long wooden counter. "Call her Ms. Ward, okay, Brooke?"

"Yes, sir." Why did I feel like a toddler in trouble even though I hadn't said anything?

Ms. Ward scurried out of the room and returned with a handful of outfits. She smiled and held them out for me to see. "These should fit just right if you sent accurate measurements with your application."

Oh, boy. Not good. None of them were wide enough in the waist from what I saw. I tried not to wrinkle my nose at the awful prints. I'd have better luck pillaging through Grandma's closet to pick out her gaudiest dresses.

"Now this is your corset." Ms. Ward whipped out a cream-colored thing.

Mr. Carrick pivoted on his heels so fast he knocked a pile of material off a nearby table. A red tinge climbed up his neck and face as he moved toward the door and tried to avoid looking at me and the corset Ms. Ward held.

"Oh, I'm so sorry, Mr. Carrick. I didn't think." She pulled me aside and showed it to me.

Why was he so embarrassed? I studied the clothing item. "Please tell me it's not part of my uniform?"

Ms. Ward looked back at Mr. Carrick.

"I … I think I'll just step out for a minute," he stuttered as he rushed out the door.

I balked at the undergarment. It made a great torture device for sure. "Please, no. Don't make me wear that thing."

"Well, we try to be as authentic as possible, and this is part of your clothing, so you do have to wear it." She gave a tight smile and pulled something else out of the assortment of dresses. "Now these are your underskirts, basically slips. They are called petticoats. You wear all of them together. First, this one, called a shift. Then this one." She held up a cream-colored skirt. "It's the under-petticoat. And the top one is the petticoat."

I pursed my lips and tilted my head to one side. "But summer's almost here. It's going to be hot in all that. I don't think I've ever worn that much clothing at the same time in my entire life."

"Once again, it's part of the outfit. You'll be surprised how quick you get used to it. Oh, and I almost forgot. See this?" She held up a purse kind of thing. "This is a pocket. It goes between the under-petticoat and petticoat. You're going to want to wear it every day or you won't have anywhere to store things. Now, go get Mr. Carrick for me, please."

Separate pockets? Different. I took in the seamstress's own clothing. The bodice and gathered skirt, which touched the floor, looked uncomfortable. But it was the most elaborate one I'd seen so far. I wouldn't mind dressing in a similar outfit, the way it showed off her tiny waist.

The seamstress folded the underskirts and corset and wrapped them in brown paper, then tied them with twine as I called Mr. Carrick back into the shop.

His face still held splotches of redness. He sure was easy to embarrass. "Thank you once again for the fine work you've done, Ms. Ward. Will you have the next order completed today?"

Ms. Ward handed the bundle to me. "Sure. Some of

the women are doing very well. Their work on the aprons and hems shows great improvement from a few weeks ago. It shouldn't be a problem to have the older outfits adjusted."

I reached for the pile of dresses that lay on a large table, where the seamstress had set them. They slid between my fingers, but Mr. Carrick grabbed them before they hit the floor. "Thanks."

"Glad to help." He turned to Ms. Ward. "See you later." He held onto the dresses instead of handing them back to me.

"Bye." I held my stomach as round two began to make its debut.

Up the road, the general store came into view. I sidestepped a large group of tourists on a guided tour. Kyle—the hot guy from the train depot—stopped, mouth open as if to say something, then wiggled an eyebrow at me as I passed him.

No. No. I wasn't there to sample the clientele. *Keep your eyes forward.* But his gorgeous smile sent waves through my already upset stomach.

Mr. Carrick glanced from Kyle to me, and I hunched a little more. He didn't need to have us on his radar, either. "My new roomie wants me back like now." And I needed another quick potty stop too. "I better hurry."

I held out my hands and waited for him to set the dresses across my arms.

"They're pretty heavy."

"It's okay. I can handle them." He paused, and I remembered my manners. "Thanks for your help."

Even if I managed to survive rehab, all the syrupy sweet "thank you's" and "misses and misters" was going to send me to the loony bin.

8
Brooke

Potty dance, potty dance. I hurried down the street and ran up the stairs, then trotted across the porch. With my elbow, I knocked. *Please let someone hear me.*

Anna pushed open the door and held it while I rushed past her and straight up the stairs.

"You're welcome." Her tone said a lot as she called after me.

Good grief. I missed another pleasantry.

I slowed as I ran down the hall. What was the room number? To make sure I had the right one, I peered in at the unmade bed. There had better not be two rooms with the same mess and quilt. I started into the bathroom and dropped the clothing in the middle of the floor.

Minutes later, I cursed the awfulness of the day. I almost had to crawl back to the clothes on the floor. How much trouble would I be in if I skipped putting on the horrible costume? I lifted one flower-printed dress and fake gagged. A groan escaped as I yanked out the petticoats and plunked them back onto the rug.

Better not tempt fate. To get better, I had to follow all the rules.

Twenty minutes later, I hadn't gotten any closer to

being ready than when I'd started. I slammed my fist on the rug beside the mounds of material and the corset thingy.

"Oh, well." I tossed the corset aside and put on the shift. It bagged around my body like some woman in an old-fashioned movie. I took the dress. There didn't seem to be a zipper or buttons. How did anyone get into the bewildering thing? I pulled it over my head and struggled to get into it, but it wouldn't budge once I put my arms through the armholes. I tugged. A tiny ripping sound stopped me. What now? My arms flailed in the air and I stumbled into the desk, then righted myself before I fell. Something crashed onto the floor.

"Why, why, why?" I tumbled onto the bed. I needed something to get me through this horrible day.

Shame hit me in the abdomen. I would've covered my face if my hands hadn't been stuck straight up in the air. *That kind of thinking is what put me here.*

I sat still for a moment. Could the day get any worse?

The squeak of the door stopped my pity party, which was in full swing.

"What kind of a mess have you gotten into?" The onslaught of Willa's rebuke caught me off guard.

My cheeks began to burn as much as Mr. Carrick's had. "I'm a little stuck, but *don't* bother if it's that much trouble to you."

"Oh, really?"

I pulled my arms down a couple inches. More tearing sounded again.

"Stop, stop." Willa rushed over to me. "I'll help yah. There's no other option."

Once she'd released a few hidden buttons, the dress slid over my head with ease. "Thanks." I could tell my hair stood up in odd angles, frizzing around my face.

Willa snickered.

"What?"

"You might want to take a look in the mirror, and while you're at it, hurry up."

I watched her cross to the bathroom and then peered down at the dress. Where had those buttons come from? The flap that had covered them lay open. I sucked in my breath as much as possible and tried to rebutton the bodice. It was like a tourniquet around my chest. "What's wrong with this thing? It's the wrong size."

Willa left the bathroom and checked her reflection in a mirror at her desk. "You'll get used to it."

"It's way too hot for long sleeves. I never wear more than a tank top in the summer."

Willa smirked. "Well now, go ahead and complain about that, too, while you're at it. Come on. We need to get down to the kitchen. I already had to bring in the chickens without you."

What happened to a chance to warm up to things in this place? I had to look like a stuffed sausage as I walked toward Willa.

She eyed me up and down and then huffed. "You didn't put the corset on, did you? I can tell." She didn't wait for a reply. "It's not going to fit right if you don't wear it." She rummaged through the clothing on the bed and pulled it free. "Come on, let me show you."

I drew in my breath and held up my index finger. "No way is another chick going to help me with something like that." I challenged Willa with a stare and pulled myself up to my full five-foot height.

"Fine." She tossed it aside and crossed her arms.

I tried to put my arms straight down, but to no avail. "Whatever. Get over here and help me."

"I don't know what you're worried about. That slip

covers more of you than the clothes you came in, I'm sure."

I had to think for a moment. True. I allowed Willa to help. I had to watch every step so I could do it myself the next time.

"There. Now let's go. Don't worry, in a few weeks everything is going to fit way looser." Willa turned on her heel, marched to the door, and flung it open.

I took a labored breath and moved my arms. "Why?"

"Well, you know, all the walking and work you're not used to is going to help you drop a few pounds." She scowled at me then continued out of the room.

Should I be insulted or not? *Just let it go.*

In the kitchen, Willa pointed to a rack of aprons. "Make sure you put one on. You don't want to have to wash your dress every time you work in the kitchen."

"*You mean I have to do laundry?*"

Willa laughed. "By hand. So be careful how you treat your clothes."

I balked. No way. "I've never washed anything before, let alone without a washing machine."

Anna flitted across the kitchen. "Hello, Brooke. There're some fresh vegetables you can clean and cut for me."

Willa pointed to a wooden bowl. "Now, wash those carrots and potatoes well, and set them over here when you finish."

I stumbled as my skirt caught under my shoe. This dress sucked big time. And sweat already began to make circles at my armpits.

I scrubbed the vegetables and grumbled and cursed under my breath. A couple times I had to cover my mouth to keep from barfing everywhere too. They didn't expect me to eat this stuff, did they? "Where's the nearest fast food restaurant?"

I only got a laugh from the other women. Oh, right. I was in prison.

When I finished the task, Anna showed me how to cut the vegetables. "Slice them into thin pieces."

I seized a carrot and sliced it. The first one shot across the table onto the floor. I grabbed it and hoped no one saw my blunder. With it set aside, I cut a second piece, but it jumped off the table as well. Grr. I held my hand over the knife and carrot, and managed to keep the rest on the board.

Someone slammed an unseen door. "Show me where you want me."

I turned. The redhead from the earlier bathroom debacle tied an apron around her waist. She gave me a quick smile.

"Wash those for me, please, Jade." Anna pointed at the chickens. She returned to a cast iron stove and poked at the wood burning inside it. I stuck my tongue out and tried not to look at the birds, which had been alive two hours ago. No way was I eating them.

I finished slicing the potatoes. And without adding a piece of my finger to the bowl. "Where would you like this? I can't remember what you said."

"Over here, please." Anna pointed at a pot that sat on top of the cast iron stove.

I checked around for a real oven. "You're cooking on that thing?"

"Yes, ma'am. I use the fireplace too."

"No..." Not possible. Boy, did I wish I'd paid better attention in home economics and history class in high school.

"Yes, that's how we do things around here."

Hmm. How did it all work? I took the bowl to the older

woman and watched her dump the mixture into the pot. Heat emanated toward me from the stove.

A few more girls ambled into the kitchen and grabbed aprons.

It had to have been two hours before we all headed to the long table, platters and dishes in hand, and sat down. Chatter filled the room as the women passed the dishes, but I watched them in silence. My hand trembled as I took a small spoonful of the stew and dumped it into a bowl. Had anyone noticed? A sigh shuddered through me. They were too busy with the food. Good. I stared back at the food. It smelled okay. Nothing too gross bobbed to the top.

I caught Jade's eye. "What?"

"You're gonna starve if that's all you plan to eat."

"Mind your own business." My sharp remark halted the other women's conversation but didn't stop Jade's scowl. At least my tremors had gone unnoticed.

Jade held her spoon halfway to her mouth. "I guess you don't want me to tell you someone was looking for your earlier, 'cause that would be me getting in your business."

I pursed my lips. "Who?"

"Don't know. I've seen him around. That's all."

Not much info to go on. "What did he look like?"

"Blond. Tall. Looked like every other junkie around here."

Our conversation got Anna's attention. "We don't refer to residents by *junkie*."

Jade mumbled a *sorry*.

I dipped my spoon into the bowl and scooped up a piece of chicken.

So a man had come looking for me. Should I be impressed? Was it the Kyle guy?

My stomach threatened to heave as a piece of chicken bobbed to the top of the soup.

Anna cleared her throat. "Let's pray."

Everyone bowed their heads—except me. The center was affiliated with a religious organization, but shouldn't all practices be relegated to church on Sundays?

I was about to get stuck praying with these people, whether I liked it or not. "Dear Lord, thank you for this bounty of food. Bless the hands that helped to prepare it. And thank you for sending Brooke to us. Please help us be a blessing to her today. Amen."

I opened my eyes and looked at Anna and her gentle smile. That wasn't so bad. Kind of nice, really. I returned my attention to my bowl and focused on the vegetables, but avoided the pieces of chicken as if they carried swine flu.

Willa passed a basket of bread to me and lowered her voice. "There's a bonfire tonight, and the guys are going to be there."

A titter of girlish giggles filled the room even though most of the women were at least in their mid-twenties and thirties.

I smirked. "And…"

"Everyone's going. And since I'm your guide, so are you, 'cuz I won't miss it."

I shrugged. Their idea of fun needed a facelift by two hundred years.

Jade chewed with her mouth open. "You too good for us?"

"Maybe." I rolled my eyes and then challenged the redhead with a hard stare.

"Ladies, that's enough." Anna folded her hands in front of her, elbows resting on the table.

"Sorry." I sighed.

Jade's gaze lingered, one eyebrow raised.

I glanced over to Willa. Her pursed lips said a lot. Awesome. Load me with guilt.

I didn't even get to finish the last few bites of my vegetables when a couple women I hadn't met sprang up and removed food platters and empty bowls. I tried to ignore them as I chewed on a slice of homemade bread.

Willa stood and tapped her foot when I didn't hurry any more than before. "The world doesn't revolve around you. Now let's go. It's devotion time. We had to switch around our schedule because of the bonfire." She pointed to the front of the house. "Everyone'll be there in five minutes. You might not want to make them late for the event. They've been looking forward to it for weeks."

I took one last, deliberate bite and rose. The women buzzed around like bees as they put away the food and rinsed the dishes. My attitude needed an adjustment, but it wasn't getting one that day. Sickness and exhaustion had a much tighter grip.

Willa took the bowl out of my hand and set it on the counter with the others. "We need to get our log books."

I headed up the stairs to grab mine for devotional time. Willa stayed on my heels like a puppy begging for treats.

In the living room at the front of the house, there were no empty seats. I walked in between the girls and found a shadowy corner. Maybe I could take a nap while I hid back there. I sat down and draped the layers of skirts around my legs.

Anna broke through the hubbub. "Let's pray."

Again?

She paused. "I see you hiding in the corner, Brooke. Come out and join the rest of us, please."

I opened my eyes and glanced around the overstuffed chair beside me. With a deep sigh, I grabbed at my skirts and moved into Anna's view. As the older woman talked, I played with the hem of my dress until the tremors in my fingers stopped me and the pain in my abdomen overtook all thoughts.

Anna folded her hands in her lap as the Bible teetered on her knees. "I want you to always remember that God loves you. He may have to discipline you sometimes, but He always loves you."

What did she mean? *God loves me? How could He? Who was He anyway?*

"He wants to be a part of your lives."

How did this woman think He loved me? He didn't even know me. None of it made sense. She had to be doing her own drugs in secret. No one loved me.

Another shock of pain erupted from my stomach and squelched all other thoughts as Anna talked.

Anna closed her Bible. "Just remember, God is interested in everything you do. Think about Him. Pray to Him. Consider His ways before you make decisions."

Everyone rushed out of the room, not all beaming with joy. Too many of them mirrored my own confused expression.

I rose from the floor and dusted off the back of my too-tight dress.

Willa strolled my way. "Come on. Let's go." She stopped speaking and cocked her head to one side. "What is it?"

"Nothing." I smoothed my dress again and eyed the entrance.

"You can ask me. What's bothering you?" Her funny twang flavored her words.

I looked at her and then down to the floor as I pinned my arms behind my back. "I never went to church before, and I don't understand what Anna was talking about.

What does she mean, God loves us? How does He know me?"

"Oh, He knows you, all right, and everything you've ever done too."

I smirked. "You're sure?"

"Yep. But don't worry. Once you accept Him into your heart, He'll forgive you no matter what sins you've committed."

I stared at her. "It's like you're speaking another language. What do you mean, 'once I accept Him into my heart'?"

"Seriously, you've never heard about Jesus? That's a first. Oh, I'm sorry. I've blown this whole conversation to smithereens, don't yah know."

I stopped her. "Of course I've heard of Him. I just don't know much about Him."

She gave a brief, really strange explanation.

"I still don't get it."

"You know you sin, right?" Willa tapped her shoe against the floor and put her hand on her hip.

I shrugged and picked at a nail.

"When we go to church tomorrow, the pastor can tell you in a better way. I just bungle up everything."

She threaded her arm through mine. I tried to pull away. We weren't best friends or anything. But she wouldn't let go. "So, are you ready to head to the bonfire?"

Jesus, sin, dying? Something unsettling awakened in me. And it wasn't the thought of being hijacked by a bunch of hormonal ladies out to rubberneck the men in that place.

9

Sarge

Fire danced its dangerous little circles around Sarge's stick, and he waited for it to catch a flame. The bonfire was hot, but Sarge refused to pull back. He noticed Blondie on the other side of the flames. She looked almost sad. But in an instant her expression changed like a bipolar rabbit as she jumped up. He took a step back to follow her movements.

At a picnic table, she grabbed some marshmallows and returned to the other side of the bonfire. She punctured two of them and thrust her stick close to the fire.

He rubbed his hand over the scruff of his chin and adjusted his hat. His rough cotton pants irritated him as they lay taut against his knee. He tried to ignore the sensation, to focus on her and the angelic glow the flames reflected on her. Maybe tomorrow he'd try to talk to her.

A few young women sat on the log next to his. He inched away and grumbled. Couldn't they see he didn't want anyone near him? This was *his* side of the bonfire.

He almost got up, but something they said stopped him.

Their heads bent together. "You should've seen the look on that new girl's face."

They laughed. "What's her name?"

"Brooke something. And Willa's her guide. Lucky her." Sarcasm etched one woman's words. She batted at the air. A hoard of gnats? The bugs were everywhere already.

"Brooke," he said under his breath. He liked the way it rolled off his tongue. If Willa guided her, he didn't have much of a chance to get close to her. He sneered. The insidious woman. Her sharp tongue had cut him more than once, and he refused to be in her presence. It was like she saw straight through him. A dangerous thing for her.

He got up and paced. No. Better keep his distance for the moment. Later there would be time.

The bonfire roared as a spark shot toward him. He squinted at it and followed the jagged slice of the flame. His heart began to race as if he'd downed a whole pot of coffee. If he didn't do something soon, all that black energy was going to consume him.

He fought to gain control. Time to leave. A project awaited his attention and he needed to go.

No, he would stay for one more minute—and watch.

10
Brooke

Something cold shot through me even though I stood mere feet from a gargantuan bonfire. Like earlier that day. I checked around me. A shiver sparked my tremors to start again. The apprehension had to be a side effect of detoxing. Just my paranoia again. Had to be.

I tried to ignore the uncomfortable sensation and focused on the warm fire.

Flames flickered and leaped at me as I coerced a couple marshmallows onto a stick. I thrust it over the flames and took my eyes off it. A pack of gossipy women moseyed past me like a gaggle of geese waddling to the pond. Where was my guide, anyway? Shouldn't she be *babysitting* me? There she was. If I avoided eye contact, maybe she'd stay over there and leave me alone.

Flames began to climb my marshmallow skewer. I jumped into action, but muscle cramps stopped me. There was nothing worse than burnt marshmallows on a half-charred branch. And I'd better extinguish them before I burned my hand. I swished it back and forth.

Willa laughed at my predicament and continued to talk with a couple other residents.

One last shake sent it flying off the stick and up into

the air, where it disappeared on the other side of the fire, out of view. A yelp followed. *Oh, no.*

"Sorry," I yelled as I hurried to the innocent bystander, who had to have been scorched.

My marshmallow hung precariously off the fingers of my victim as he tried to shake it free.

Kyle. The delicious guy from the station. "Can I help you?" I batted at it with my blackened stick, but only managed to smack his good hand. "Sorry."

He backed away to avoid me, then continued to shake his hand free of the gummy, hot mess. "It's quite okay. I'll get it."

He winced as it slid off his hand and onto the ground.

I dropped my stick and twisted my hands together. "Really, I'm so sorry. It just jumped off my stick."

"Don't worry about it." He grimaced at me. "You're the new resident."

"Yep. I'll be right back." I threw the stick into the fire and rushed to the drink table. Bottled water lined one side. I scurried over to him with one in hand and twisted off the lid. He let me pour it over the already visible burn mark. "Let me find a napkin for you. It's the least I can do."

At the table, I grabbed a handful and hurried back to him.

"Thanks." He cocked his head to one side.

I hesitated. "I'm Brooke Hollen."

"Kyle." He tipped his hat at me.

"You said as much at the station." I gave him a small smile as I glanced at his attire and returned my attention to the redness on his hand.

He kept shaking it as if to cool the hot burn. "So, how'd you get stuck here?"

"Look, I don't tell complete strangers my life story." I squeezed my eyes closed as soon as the words left my mouth.

Kyle began to turn away from me as he shook his head.

"I'm sorry. That was harsh." I paused and considered my words with way more care. "I misunderstood the whole living museum thing when I chose this rehab, but now that I'm here I'm going to make it work."

He watched me.

I shrugged and crossed my arms tight against my abdomen. "Sometimes you just have to admit that you can't get clean by yourself. One night a few days ago, I woke up on my bathroom floor after this big party. I'd blacked out—had no memory of how I got there. But... that wasn't the worst of it." I cringed on the inside. With a wave of my hand, I looked at the ground. What about the kid I almost hit and killed? "Anyway, I realized I didn't want another drink. Or anything else, for that matter. But to know it and to do it are two different things. Now I'm here."

He raised his eyebrows. "That takes a lot of courage. I wish I'd been as smart, but some of my buddies had to force me to get help." He stared at the burn on his hand. "This place isn't so bad once you get used to it."

"So everyone says." I rolled my eyes. I didn't want to hear one more person make the comment. My curiosity was piqued, though. "Why are you here?"

He sat on the rough-hewn log behind him. "I hurt my back cutting down a tree, and I had to get surgery. But after the surgery, I couldn't get rid of the intense pain. I started to take pain pills. It didn't seem like such a big deal at the time, right? The doctor gave them to me—it was legal and all. But then one wasn't enough. I should have recognized I didn't need them for every little discomfort. Maybe I could have prevented this if I had. I started to take more and more, and it got out of hand." He grew quiet for a moment and then continued. "You know, I never thought it could be me, but it happened."

I wanted to stroke the soft-looking stubble that had grown on his jawline and tell him it was going to be okay, but I knew what a crock that would be. It was never fully okay with us addicts. It only took one slip-up—even after years of sobriety—to put us right back in our addictions. He might even be less than twenty-four hours from a relapse. Me too.

I tried to concentrate on the conversation and not the depression that sprang up out of nowhere. "Oh, I knew it would happen to me. My dad and grandfather were drinkers. My mom liked her own cocktail mix every night. And the weekends at my house … you don't even want to know. Even as a kid, Mom gave me a sip of her drinks now and then. She deserved a perfect mother award, right, getting her kid hooked on alcohol so young?" I laughed even though there wasn't one single funny thing about it, and settled on a log next to the one he occupied. "I just didn't realize that I'd ever want to quit until that night on the bathroom floor."

Kyle's gaze didn't leave my face. "Alcoholism. But you're so young."

Did I want him to know about the drugs too? They'd been only for social use, but still. "I guess, but Mr. Carrick says family history makes me very vulnerable to it. And there's more to it than that."

"More?"

I raised my shoulders. "Well…"

Kyle raised his hands. "I get it. I won't ask any more questions, for now anyway."

I lowered my eyes a little. "Yeah, maybe another time. So how's your back now?"

"I learned that I could live without the pills after being

here a couple months. It's still hard sometimes, though. My back still bothers me, but I deal with it. Although ice is my best friend."

I laughed.

Willa sidled over to us. She kept her gaze on me as she spoke. "You want to roast some more marshmallows?"

I laughed. "Oh, no. I already tried that and failed miserably."

Willa quirked her eyebrows. "What?"

I winced and gestured toward Kyle. "Ask him."

Willa stared at him. "Go ahead. Tell me."

He related the story to her, but she didn't seem to think it was that funny.

Willa eyed me as she pulled at one of her curls that'd fallen loose. "Well, how about a game of hoops?"

"Yeah, sure, I can do some major damage on a court."

Willa laughed. "Not that kind. It's called hoop trundling. Come on, I'll show yah." She gestured to Kyle. "How about you? Want to join us?"

"I don't know. I need to get some things done." He pointed behind him.

"Come on, you can work any time."

I tripped on my skirt as I hurried to keep up with Willa. My face grew warm as I righted myself. What a relief that dark covered my bumbling all over the place because of that dreadful dress.

"Do you need some help?" Kyle moved toward me but didn't offer his hand.

Well, I guess it wasn't dark enough. And what was with him not trying to help me? Not that I needed it. "Um, no, I think I've got it."

"Sorry, but we're not allowed to have physical contact unless, of course, there's an emergency. Rules. You know, me being a guy."

"Of course. Is there anything there isn't a rule about?"

He rewarded my sarcasm with a smile.

We found Willa on a well-worn path at the edge of the park with a bunch of other people. "Come on, Kyle, just one game."

He nodded. "Fine."

I studied the two large wooden hula-hoops Willa held. "What are you going to do with those things?"

Willa showed me two short sticks in her other hand. "Well, you take one of these and you use it to roll a hoop like this." She demonstrated. "See?"

"And what's the point?" I crossed my arms.

"We'll race each other. We can even make up an obstacle course."

"That sounds so stupid—like a child's game."

"Girl, when you don't have anything else to do on your free time, you learn to like these kinds of games. Come on, it'll be fun."

I shrugged. "Whatever."

"We'll go first so you can see. Come on, Kyle. I'm going to whip you."

They lined up beside each other. I called, "Ready, set, go."

Willa whisked past him, whooping, but it wasn't long before he passed her. His hoop almost collided into hers. On the trip back, Willa managed to get ahead, but Kyle thrust his stick through his hoop and sent it reeling over the finish line as he grabbed his back with his free hand. Only a foot separated the two.

"You didn't have a chance against my trusty stick." He kissed it and shook his straight blond hair out of his eyes. "Good thing my back didn't give out, either."

"It's only a matter of time before you're mine." Willa huffed. She joined me on the sidelines and tried to hand over the hoop, but I refused to take it. "*Your* turn."

"Oh, no. I don't think so." They both looked at me. "Haven't you seen me trip over this dress all night?"

"All the more to entertain ourselves with." Kyle laughed.

I refused. "Isn't there something else to do around here?" I shook my hand to rid myself of a tremor and tried to ignore my pounding heart. At least the stomach pains had subsided.

Willa shrugged. "We could play quoits."

"And what's that? Not another ridiculous game."

"It's like horseshoes."

"That sounds okay." Together we walked around the bonfire, skirted large groups of people now gathered around it who roasted marshmallows and talked, and headed to a few logs with metal rods that protruded out of their center.

A half hour later, I tossed my last metal ring and missed the wooden stake by ten feet. The other two laughed at me—my insides bubbled to the point of eruption. *No one laughs at me.* But somehow, I kept calm. "Yep, this is not a game for me, either."

By my usual standards, the night would've just started. But I'd do anything to get some time to myself and a long sleeping binge. "I'm ready to go back to the boarding house."

"You're right, we have to be up by dawn." Willa placed the metal rings beside one of the stakes. "We should head home."

"No way. I won't get up that early. I don't care what the Carricks say." Many nights I'd just crawled into bed as the sun began to rise.

Willa chuckled. "I'm kidding. We actually have to be up at six-thirty. Unless we have kitchen duty."

That was no good, either. I turned to Kyle. "I'll see you later."

"Yeah, so much for that project I planned to finish. It's awful late. Maybe I'll see you tomorrow." He disappeared behind a crowd of people.

I left Willa at the bottom of the boarding house stairs and hurried to my room. I laid down with care not to rock my muscles into spasms. My bed mattress wasn't for the princess in *The Princess and the Pea* but it wasn't horrible. Ripping sounded at my side and I grumbled as I tried to find the new tear. I should've been honest about my dress size for once. How was I going to make it for months in these clothes?

My mood didn't improve as I struggled to release the ties on the corset. I'd have to be an octopus to take off the thing. When it finally loosened, I threw it on the floor and scavenged for my comfy jammies. At least Dara hadn't taken those from me.

Sweat dripped down my back. Someone needed to turn on the central air system. I mashed the quilt as I kicked it to the bottom of the bed.

Willa changed and dropped into her bed across from me. It wasn't long before quiet snores filled the room, but they weren't mine.

I tossed and turned, but sleep refused to wrap its comfortable arms around me. Tendrils of hair stuck to my clammy skin. It had been five whole days since I took my last drink—and as many sleepless nights. Would I ever sleep again? Tears threatened to cascade down my cheeks.

I rolled onto my stomach and pulled out a blank notebook and mini reading light from my duffle bag under the bed. The pen unsnapped from the side of it. Writing in my diary always made me feel better. And that night, too many emotions warred inside me which needed to come out.

I glanced over to the bed across the room and watched for any movement, but Willa slept hard. The last thing I needed was another loud opinion from her. And thanks to her, I had questions burning to be answered. The God thing… It kept circling in my head. "God, are you there?"

The room remained quiet and oddly blank. Oh, well.

I smiled as I recorded the incident with the flying marshmallow and the ridiculous hoop game.

Willa stirred but didn't open her eyes, and I covered the light with my hand when she rolled over. I continued to write once my roommate lay still again, and when I wrote my last thought, I drew a frowning face over the period and closed the notebook. With it tucked under my mattress, I squirmed around to get comfortable. My stomach was still at it. It threatened to tighten with pain, and a cold sweat began to dampen my tank top.

"Would you please lie still? I'm trying to sleep here." Willa's groggy, muffled voice floated from under her pillow.

"*Sorry.*" Not really. It wasn't fair that she enjoyed complete sleeping bliss while I lay there in pain and exhausted hyper-awareness.

Lack of sleep did crazy things to the mind. Like make the shadows move in human-like forms. I hid under my quilt. *It's my wild imagination. That's all.*

When another shadow moved toward me, I cried silent tears. What if it was real? Like something coming after me for all the bad things I'd done.

11
Brooke

Dad always said the church would collapse if a Hollen stepped foot inside, but there I stood and looked up to the rough-hewn rafters. Everything remained in place. I even ducked as I entered and fanned myself with a paper bulletin. The air smoldered and I couldn't breathe. How did these people live without central air? I twitched and watched the different groups of residents. Some sat quiet, their heads down, while others bantered back and forth in small groups.

The empty seat on the back row looked like the most inconspicuous spot to sit, and I sat with a sigh. If the sermon would just start so I could hear about this Jesus person, it would be great.

I turned at Kyle's voice. What now?

"If you want some free demerits, by all means, stay right there. Otherwise, you might want to sit on the far side."

I followed the point of his finger. What was he getting at? Men littered the row of pews in front of me. *Only* men. "Huh?"

"As you can see, this is not your designated area." He grinned. "As much as I'd like to sit with you, the girls sit

60

on one side and the guys on the other."

I huffed and exited the pew. "You're kidding, right?"

He raised his eyebrows. "Nope."

I laughed a sarcastic harrumph, but inside I really wanted to rebel against the millionth rule I'd been told since my arrival. *Yet another ridiculous, old-fashioned regulation.* I scooted to the other corner. As I took a seat, the piano player began to play a slow song and the other women filled the rows of wooden pews.

Willa flitted over to me and sat. "Here, I got you a Bible since I doubt you have one."

I rolled my eyes. But the assumption was accurate.

Why hadn't she warned me about the seating arrangement? "Thanks for telling me where to sit."

Willa covered her mouth and sniggered. "Oops, sorry. I'm used to it. I didn't think to say anything."

A large flat fan protruded out of the hymnal tray in front of me. *Nice.* I grabbed it and worked overtime to cool myself.

The pastor climbed the narrow steps up to the dark stained pulpit and stood on the tiny raised platform surrounded by an ornate railing. "Welcome. Let's sing a song."

I leafed through the songbook and sang as quiet as possible. What a relief when the song ended.

I ducked my head and flipped through the Bible to find the place the pastor said. Where was John? Willa grabbed it from me and turned to the right page. When she handed it back, pointing at the right verse, I glared at her, even though I should've been glad for the help.

It wasn't easy to follow along. But every word he preached riveted me to my seat. I could well imagine the scenario he described to the congregation. I listened harder than I'd ever listened before. Even the unwanted quiver of my nerves and the sweat on my brow hadn't swayed my attention.

The pastor moved his hand across his Bible. "When Jesus said, 'He that is without sin among you, let him first cast a stone at her,' they knew they were guilty. No man is sinless except Jesus, God's son."

Was that what Willa had tried to tell me last night? Everyone sinned?

The pastor's words interrupted my thoughts. He studied us for a moment. "He loves us so much that He wants us to be in Heaven with Him. The problem is, God can never look on sin. Something had to happen to redeem us from our sins."

He stepped down from the podium and stood near the first pew. "Jesus, God's son, came to be the Redeemer. He went to the cross to die for us." The pastor smiled at everyone, and I held my breath, waiting for him to continue. "And three days later, He rose from the grave. All of this was foretold in the Old Testament, and Christ fulfilled Biblical prophecy to prove he was God's Son."

"Can you imagine … He did it for you … and for me?" His eyes held mine. Then he returned to the podium and studied his papers.

"When we think of love, we sometimes put conditions on it, don't we? But He didn't. He loved everyone. He would have gone to the cross, even if there was only one person in the world who believed in Him."

Something within me stirred, as it had the night before. God loved me? I fought the tears that threatened to spill down my face. My throat tightened. I wanted that kind of love so much, but there wasn't anything lovable about me. Were my sins even forgivable?

As he continued, I just knew that his words were true, that no amount of alcohol or drugs would ever fill the void

I always felt. Could Jesus?

As the pastor closed, I squirmed in my seat. "Anyone can receive Christ into their hearts. Salvation is a free gift. Please come forward."

Everyone bowed their heads and closed their eyes as he requested. I climbed out of my seat and headed to the front. I wanted this Jesus. There was no sense in holding back.

Later, when I exited the sanctuary, Willa left her group of friends. "So…" My roommate crossed her arms and tapped her foot. "How'd it go?"

"I did it. I got rescued." I had the dorkiest smile on my face, but I didn't care.

"What? Oh, you mean saved." Laughter escaped her lips.

I furrowed my brows. "Yeah, that."

Willa squeezed my arm. "See, I told yah the pastor could say it better." She shook her head. "I can't believe it. I thought it was going to take so much longer."

"What?"

"Well, for you to accept Jesus." She shook her head again.

Willa kept staring at me. I tucked the new Bible under my arm. "Let's go help with lunch."

Her mouth fell open. "Okay."

For the first time, I couldn't wait to work. How had that happened? How had God worked on me so fast?

In the kitchen, the assigned girls made the food while the others set the table. When we all sat, Willa raised her hand to quiet them. "Guess what happened today? Brooke got saved."

Most of the girls cheered and congratulated me. Embarrassment hit me in the chest. I didn't want all of them ogling me the way they were. But then again, was it so bad that they wanted to encourage me?

Jade pulled on one of her red curls and made a face at Willa. "Guess you lose."

What were they talking about?

The leftover chicken from the night before had been turned into chicken salad sandwiches. And a fresh lettuce salad sat in the middle of the table. I gulped and scooped some of the meat onto fresh bread, but tried not to look too closely at it.

One of the girls waved her hands. "Hey, I thought I'd add some garlic to the bread dough, so tell me how you like it."

Several of the girls gave her a thumbs-up sign as they ate their lunch.

I took a bite of the bread. "This is really great. You made this?"

"Yep, and you will too some day."

I raised an eyebrow. I couldn't cook a piece of toast. "Me?"

Our housemother said, "Every Monday is bread day, and each week a different set of ladies help bake. You'll have a turn soon."

The old Brooke would've complained, but now I nodded and kept my mouth shut.

"I hope you don't help on my day," Jade teased.

I started to react but stopped and looked down at my plate. I was a new person, according to the pastor. I had to stop letting every little thing get to me.

I finished my lunch and put my plate on the counter by the sink. The whole conversation between Jade and Willa seemed off. What did Jade mean, that Willa lost? As I pulled at my scratchy Sunday dress, I bit my lip.

Willa tapped me on the shoulder. "Come on. We have things to do."

I jumped a foot.

"What are you all worked up about?"

"Nothing. You just scared me."

"Well, let's get to work."

Something didn't seem quite right to me. I leaned back against the counter. "What did Jade mean when she said you lost?"

Willa waved her hand in the air and averted her eyes. "Nothing."

"Oh, really?" Hands on hips, I waited for her real answer. She definitely had done something wrong.

"Okay." She pulled me down the empty hall to a private spot. "We all made bets about how long it would take for you to … settle in."

"And…"

"Well, I lost."

Hmm. Betting was taboo around there. "Isn't it against the rules to bet and gamble?"

"Yeah. *So?*"

I grabbed her arm. "You should know better, then."

Willa jumped into action. "You won't turn us in, will you? I mean, I know it was wrong. I'm sorry."

"Yeah. I'll go straight to Ms. Anna." Not really. I took a step away from her and tried to hold in a snigger.

"No, no, you can't."

"Don't worry. Of course I wouldn't." I laughed as I pushed at the sleeves of my dress with no success. Oh, for the day when I went back to wearing real clothes again.

Willa put a hand to her forehead, but then her face fell. "Gambling is one of my addictions. I just can't seem to stop."

I shrugged and put a hand on her forearm. "I understand, but you need to let your counselor know. Isn't that what they keep telling us? They can help."

My hand trembled and I yanked it back and hid it in the folds of my dress. Easier said than done.

12

Sarge

The white church loomed behind Sarge like a judgmental minister as he worked his way down the hill to the men's boarding house. He tossed the wrinkled church bulletin onto the ground, and didn't care that he would be the one to clean it up the next day. Sarge's hand raked through his hair again and again as he kicked every rock on the path.

What a miserable morning. All Sarge wanted to do was escape. He needed to think, get control. He stomped around the corner of the boarding house and punched the brick wall. If he could've gotten a little time out in the fields, things would be better, for sure. But no, it was Sunday, and there would be questions if he'd missed the church service. There were chores to do too.

He yanked at his suit and adjusted his cravat, took off his hat, and then leaned against the wall. The sun heated his light hair and drained more color out of it. A bit of dust marred his legging and he brushed at it, but it didn't want to wipe clean. He scrubbed it so hard it hurt. It had to come off.

The pastor just couldn't stop meddling in his life and he was sick of it. What right did he have to tell the congregation all about Sarge's mistakes? Sweat trickled down his neck, and he paused in his ravings. He had to admit, the pastor hadn't called him out by name, but still … it was obvious that the pastor gossiped about him.

Someday that man would answer to Sarge for using him as an example to the congregation. And that day might be sooner rather than later.

On a good note, Brooke looked provocative—perfect in her tight-bodiced dress. He wanted her more with each passing hour. Maybe he should pay her a visit again.

13
Sarge

Hard work kept Sarge's mind from things it shouldn't think. But his crazy pace that day hadn't blocked any of the images he wanted to forget.

He wiped his brow as he studied the heavy cabin beam at his feet and looked up to the rafter line, where it had to go. He had cut the notches into two perpendicular beams where it would sit, but it was going to take more than one strong back to get it there.

Sarge turned to the men who helped him. "Hey, guys, let's get this in place."

He gestured for them to grab the other end, and they hoisted it up and guided it in. As it hit against the ridgeline, he hurried up a rickety ladder and pounded it with a heavy wooden mallet, settling it into one of the notches.

Back on the ground, he tied a rope onto the next beam. "Come on, let's get this done. I don't want to be here any longer than I have to."

His gruff voice sent the other men into action.

Once the second beam was in place, he called to them, "Take this stuff and lock it up." So what if his tone remained sharp. He didn't care. Sarge wasn't about to do the menial work the other men were fully capable of doing.

A tourist popped his head into the cabin. "Looks like you're doing good work."

Yeah. So? He ignored the man and grabbed his large lathe, used to shape the wooden beams.

The others gathered up the tools, threw them into the horse cart, and left him standing in front of the cabin.

As he watched them disappear up the road with the tourist, he rested against the cabin and spit. No one remained to watch him or question him. For the first time that day, he relaxed. The solidness of the doorframe at his back braced him, and he closed his eyes. If he wasn't so tired, he would follow through on his original plans, but the ache behind his eyes forced him to reconsider. There was plenty of time. He didn't have to rush anything. Yet he just wanted to be done with the old business.

He pushed off of the frame, shuffled from the cool shelter of shade into the hot sun, and turned back to study his work. Sarge couldn't believe the speed with which they had put the replica together, and soon it would be time to daub the spaces between the large beams. Perhaps he could convince his boss to let him do it on his own. He preferred things that way. He was sure he could work faster without the others hanging over his shoulder anyway.

With one last look, he meandered down the path toward town, wiping his brow again. The sun began to lower, casting longer shadows, but he didn't hurry. What about the list of chores that grew longer every day? If he didn't get to them soon, Carrick would be breathing down his neck. *No more excuses*. He was going to have to suck it up and do them. That meant there wouldn't be time for his woman. But then again, she was exactly the reason he'd gotten behind.

A frown crept across his face. She had begun to make him mad with all of her demands. She didn't deserve his time and attention, especially now that Brooke had arrived. His pulse quickened. Yes, he definitely wanted to move on.

At his boarding house, Sarge headed straight for the woodpile and stacked a bundle in his arms for the kitchen stove. The cook would be glad to see he had restocked the pile in the lean-to by the kitchen door.

He checked the chore off his mental list and then turned his attention to the broken latch on the door. With a few nails, he tweaked it back into place and repaired it. The old iron cooled his palm as he rubbed it. Fixing things always calmed him. He hadn't minded taking charge of the maintenance at the boarding house. It gave him time to think.

The dinner bell tolled, and he returned the hammer to the shelf above the woodpile. At least he hadn't had to cook that night.

He seized one of the plates lined up on the counter on his way to the dining room, and found a chair at the end of the table. As he kept his head down and studied the meal, the steam hit his nostrils as he dug the fork into it, eating with deliberation.

He still needed to replace a pane in the kitchen window. Where had he put the new piece of glass? It had to be in the basement. The last bite slid down his throat and he pushed away from the table.

The basement door opened with a little reluctance as he headed down the stairs. One tug on the light cord sent it dancing in the glow of the single bulb. At his workstation, the tools were lined up just the way he liked it. He would know if one thing was out of place.

Sarge grabbed the glass pane and a small putty knife and turned to leave. But the small wooden box where he kept screws—and more—begged to be pulled out. Underneath a cardboard square, his little treasures lay hidden. He set the glass pane and putty knife aside and gingerly pulled out the container. If only he had time to look through it. Soon he wanted to replace some of the items with new ones. He tapped the top and put it back before returning to the glass project.

The sun set as he sculpted new putty around the window. Sarge couldn't wait to go to his room. He hurried to put everything away, scuffled up the stairs, and headed to the bathroom to wash off the filth of the day. Then he lay in bed as still as possible.

The creak of the bedroom door made him hunch a little more under his thin bedsheet. His roommate grew instantly silent when he entered the room. At least Ryan knew his place.

Sarge turned to face the wall and cleared his throat— a little warning he was still awake. Sarge waited for Ryan to stop shifting around. There was no way Sarge could sleep with all the noise he made.

Just once, he'd like the silence of the night to bring him sleep instead of memories. An hour later, he rubbed at his temples. Flashbacks of boot camp bombarded him. So much for what his therapist said about taking a few deep breaths. It certainly hadn't calmed him that night.

He thrummed his chest with his fingers. He would never forget the day he got the nickname Sarge. The other men had taunted him and oppressed him. He took it for awhile until he exploded. Did they get a hint? No. They just kept pushing him. When they had cornered him one morning, he attacked them like a viper—pushing, punching, and ripping at them. The commotion alerted their sergeant, who meted out sharp discipline. His diffusion of the situation turned the men against Sarge even more.

From that day, they'd called him Sarge. The nickname became a part of him, a signature of who he really was. They intended it to shame him, but it stood for the true man inside, the one who would take control and deal out punishment at will. They thought they'd won. But the scars some of them would carry for life because of him would always be there. No one could take his new name from him. He had the control to decide who called him that and who didn't.

Perhaps someday he'd let Brooke in on his secret name.

14
Brooke

If anyone had told me I'd work so hard all day *and* deal with debilitating withdrawals—at the same time—I'd have laughed in their face. But I was pulling it off. And it took almost more patience than I had to not let grumpiness snap me into diva mode.

The counter gleamed at the general store, but my arms ached from scrubbing and wiping oodles of fingerprints from it. The doors would open any minute, but fatigue might lay me out on the floor to be trampled by the oodles of tourists. I looked up at the hand-wound clock. Only three hours ago the wake-up bell had startled me out of a fitful sleep, but it seemed like an entire day had passed at breakneck speed.

I rubbed the wrapper in the colonial-style pocket tied around my waist. Someone had left a candy bar with no note in my mail slot. Kyle for sure. It wasn't a surprise I fell for that trick. I had a thing for guys who brought me presents. He must have gone to the town twenty minutes away to get the little gift. What next? Maybe some flowers?

Dara bustled over as I bent and straightened a few maps on one of the bottom shelves. In a sing-song tone, she said, "Good morning."

"Good morning to you. Boy, I have a new respect for the early Americans. I never imagined what they went through every day. No wonder they weren't fat the way our generation is." I caught Dara's eye. "Uh, sorry, I mean overweight."

"Looking back can always teach us things." Dara started the register and placed the money in it for the day's transactions. "It's Memorial Day, so it's going to be hopping in here today."

I laughed at her use of words and set the rag down behind the counter on a shelf. "What should I do next?" Not that I really wanted to know.

Dara rifled through some paperwork and handed me a booklet. "Here you go. These are historical facts about this general store. You need to memorize it all, because you'll give speeches about this building to groups. It will really help you become familiar with all of the products here too. Some are from local authors, artists, and musicians. It helps to give them publicity and us sales if we can tell customers about their work."

I thumbed through the book and shook my head. How did anyone memorize so much at one time? School hadn't been my thing. Under-achiever should have titled the "most likely to…" page of my yearbook instead of "hottest party girl" under my name. Well, at least I had the candy to keep me happy while I read.

Dara walked to the door and flipped over the *Closed* sign. Her heels clicked on the wooden planked floor. "Please turn the cider pot switch on for me."

As I straightened a few items beside the cider, the bell tinkled over the main door. I glanced up at Kyle, who stuck his blond head in and waved.

"Hey." He looked around. "Come here." He waited for

me to hurry over to him. "You want to meet later after dinner at the park during free time? I'm sure Willa will come with you."

I glanced over my shoulder. Was I about to get in trouble with Dara for talking to Kyle during work hours? "That's right, my shadow." I smiled at him. "Okay, I guess so."

"See you then." He grinned at me and closed the door before Dara noticed him.

What was I doing? I swatted a strand of hair out of my face. Why couldn't I resist his gorgeous blue eyes and quirky smiles? No matter what, we had to stay friends. I couldn't let it turn into something.

I fingered the candy again. Oops. Why hadn't I remembered to ask him about it?

Several customers strolled in, and a man with a huge paunch called to me. "Hey, lady, what's this thing?"

I looked around for Dara, but she helped another customer at the other end of the store. I slowed my pace as I moved closer to him.

"Hey, I said I need help." The impatient tourist scratched his upper leg, and then crooked his finger at me.

"Yes, sir—"

Dara cut me off and got between us. "I'm sorry, sir, how can I help you?"

Phew. It wouldn't have been good for me to help him, considering his attitude. And my nerves. At least the tremors had begun to subside, and my stomach had settled a little.

Dara talked to him and then brought the item to the counter. "Can you please bag this for our customer?" She pointed at the paper on a rack.

I wrapped it with care and put it in a paper tote.

By lunchtime, my feet ached to the point of throbbing.

I hobbled to the break room and sat down with a sigh. When had I walked so much? At least the workday was almost finished. I wanted to break down in tears. The previous night had been another almost sleepless one, and my therapy session had only added to the misery. All my old inner wounds I'd opened yesterday were still running over into my nightmares. It had been the first time I'd talked about the poor kid I had come so close to hitting on one crazed night of drinking and driving.

As I did the math in my head, I counted my few broken hours of sleep. Three hours. The tremors in my hands showed the most when I was tired. At home, I could sleep half the day away to make up for the night, but not at the center. As I laid my head on the table, a familiar voice echoed down the hall. *Ugh.*

"Brooke? Hey, where are you?" Willa peeked through the doorway. "Let's go down to Daisy Cakes Delicatessen and have some lunch."

"The tea shop? I don't know if I can move." I lifted my head and peered at her.

"Come on. You can do it. It won't be long before you'll get used to it. Now, let's go. Besides, no one but Ms. Daisy can make such a fabulous meat pie."

"Don't we have to cook lunch with Anna?"

"*Ms.* Anna, you mean." Her pursed lips didn't hide her smile. "We're not on the schedule to cook today so we can go out to eat if we want. If we don't hurry, we'll be eating on the edge of the sidewalk because there won't be any tables left."

I pushed myself upright with all the willpower I possessed and limped toward Willa. "Okay, but you may have to carry me."

She sniggered.

Those new shoes might fit the historical role, but they

might as well be made of wood. "By the way, Kyle wanted to know if we'd meet at the park tonight."

"Really." A comment, not a question.

I tried not to let on how much I wanted to see him. Just as friends. That was all. "He left a candy bar for me, I think. I need to thank him."

"Hmm." She put a finger on her chin. "You know the rules. There better not be anything going on."

My hands flew up. "No way."

"I'll do it if you'll wash the dishes for me … or something."

"Hey, that's not fair." I elbowed her. "Look at the condition I'm in." I pointed at my aching feet, but she only held her chin a little higher and gave a half-smile. "Okay, if that's what it takes to get you to go along, but don't think the door doesn't swing both ways."

"Oh, don't worry. I won't be asking you for any favors." She stuck her tongue out at me but quickly retracted it when Mr. Carrick stepped into the hallway.

"Uh huh. You say that now, but we'll see." If her game included favors, I knew how to play.

15
Brooke

Did I really want to owe Willa or anyone else? Favors were dangerous. Even if I knew how to misuse them.

When we entered the Daisy Cakes Delicatessen down the street from the general store, my mouth began to water. Coffee, danishes, and stewed meat blended into a wonderful meld of deliciousness. Large doilies and multi-colored tablecloths covered the café-style tables scattered around the room in a cozy blend of hominess and comfort. We hurried to the counter to place our orders as tourists followed us into the restaurant.

"Ms. Daisy, this is the new girl, Brooke. Can you set up a tab for her, please?" Willa pointed toward me as she spoke.

"Nice to meet you." Daisy straightened a glass platter of little cakes. "I'd be glad to. Now what can I get for you today? The meat pie is ready to be served."

"That's exactly why we're here." Willa looked at the cakes. "And we'll take two of those as well."

I didn't need her to order my food. I huffed but Willa ignored me. A tart remark tasted sweet on my lips but I repressed it. And good thing. I needed to work on acting nicer. Maybe Willa or the pastor had good advice on how to talk to God, because I needed His help with my attitude, and I didn't mind admitting it.

The door to the tea shop opened and a group of colonial-clad men laughed their way to the counter. They surrounded me. At one time, I wouldn't have minded them checking me out, but not anymore. For once I appreciated my very conservative dress.

"Hi there. My name's Jason and this is Wes."

My shoulders tightened, and I pressed against the counter. "Hi, I'm Brooke."

He leaned in to speak to me over the noise of the people. "You're new, so we just wanted to say hi. Not everyone here is so friendly, so we nominated ourselves to greet you."

I let my guard down some and smiled. If they knew the way I'd grown up, in the best private schools full of the meanest kids in the state—because they could be— they wouldn't think anyone there was very bad at all.

"Hey, guys, introduce yourselves." He motioned to the others and several waved. Two Sam's, a John, Richard, Shelley, Amber, and several other names I'd already forgotten said hi Most of them turned away before I had a chance to reply.

"I'm Eric." I almost couldn't hear the guy beside me over the noise. Unlike the others, he reached out and took my hand in his warm palm.

"Hello." The word wasn't all the way out of my mouth before he disappeared.

He could rival Kyle in the looks department. His thin beard highlighted his wide jawline, and tendrils of curly hair shone with sweaty wetness.

Then Kyle joined the hubbub around me. "Hey, I didn't know you were having lunch here today. How's your day going?"

Willa waved at him and he gave her a nod.

I eyed a couple other people who said hi. "Exhausting."

"This place is tough. Wish I could tell you something awesome, but really it's all about taking it one moment at a time and deciding to keep going no matter how hard it is." He moved very close but didn't touch me, and smoky wood plus masculine musk scents reached me. "I have to go, but see you later. We're meeting tonight, right?"

"Yep."

"Well, I'll be at the park waiting." He drew out the last word.

"I'll see you then."

He went to the counter and grabbed two large paper bags of food and left with a backwards grin at me.

"Hey. Thanks for the—" Never mind. He'd left before I'd finished speaking.

Willa grumbled all the way to a table near the back. "He's so self-absorbed." She lashed out, and then went on a rampage about the crowd of people. "Isn't it annoying being bombarded by all these people? I couldn't stand it when they wanted to meet me."

I didn't get a chance to say, one way or the other, what I thought about the greeting.

She grabbed a cup of tea for me and herself. "Now, don't yah worry, we get a discount, and the cakes are heavenly."

"Thanks for ordering." The words stuck in my throat. But why? How often had I been appreciative of anything? I got what I wanted when I wanted it. And I'd ignored Dad's attitude when I refused to be grateful. But starting that day, I had to be more thankful to others. I sat across from Willa and took a sip of tea.

Willa grinned at me and played with one of the tendrils

of hair that refused to stay in her bun. "What's this about Kyle? It's Kyle everything with you."

I looked away. "Oh, nothing."

Willa sat back in her chair. "You know there's no fraternizing here, right?"

"I'm sure I read it somewhere in the endless list of rules." I watched Willa for a moment. "Don't worry, we're just killing free time. That's all." I repositioned my bun and tried to get the loose strands back in it.

"Right, but just so you know, I've never seen him with any girls, just a few of the guys in his boarding house."

I shrugged. I wasn't about to make a big deal about an innocent friendship.

When the waiter brought our food, I managed to eat half of it. My appetite had begun to return.

The chatter around us created happy white noise.

Willa paused with her fork hovering over her plate. "See, I told you how good the meat pie was."

I nodded with a mouth full of food. Fast food restaurants and high-end coffee shops were my norm, not homemade meals. Dad almost never got home in time to cook or eat with me. I set down my fork. "This food is the best home-cooked type meal I've ever had."

"Yeah. You don't get that at your house?"

"Ha ha. No way, no one's ever there to do it. How about you?"

Willa looked away for a moment. "I guess."

My eyes crinkled. I didn't want anyone knowing my problems, so I wasn't about to question Willa about hers.

Willa eyed me. "You know I don't talk about it much, but … I went into foster care when I turned twelve. At first I got moved around, but when I turned fourteen I went to this one family that kept me for three years. Then, out of the blue, poof, I returned to the shuffling game."

She looked down and blinked. "It's hard to stay in one place when you got a mouth on you like I do … but that's okay."

I'd had a close call with social services once, but Dad and Grandma had been able to lie enough to get them off their backs. "Life stinks sometimes."

"You could say that again." Willa laughed, the sadness erased from her face. She grabbed her cake and took a large bite, then swallowed a gulp of her tea. "We better leave, or they'll come looking for us with some demerits in their hands." She wiped her mouth with a linen napkin and stood.

How had I avoided an armload of demerits so far? And why break my good-luck streak?

I followed her up the sidewalk, our shoes clunking against the wood. We waved goodbye when I entered the general store.

We weren't in rehab to get boyfriends. Quite the opposite. But it still made me smile all afternoon to think I had Kyle's attention.

Kyle refused to stay in his friend box in my mind the rest of my workday—no matter how much I tried to convince myself it would end in a bad way for sure. Two addicts were a dangerous mixture.

…But if God was in it, might it work?

I filled wrapping orders and watched Dara use the cash register as closing time seemed to get further away. We weren't allowed to touch any money or tourists' credit cards, which was fine with me. One less thing to have to learn. Between trying to help customers, I read a little from the booklet I had to memorize.

The store quieted at last. I walked over to the bolts of material that occupied one corner of the store and picked through them, pulling out a deep purple one. It would make a nice dress.

Wait a minute. No way. Mr. Carrick and Dara would fix me and send me on my way too fast to need more of the dreadful dresses.

Or so I hoped.

16
Brooke

Kyle had the calf muscles of a runner. And the white stockings he wore below his knickers showed them off so well I almost tripped over a picnic table as I stared at his languid body resting under a huge oak tree, with its fresh new leaves covering the view to the sky. Those colonial clothes might have me in a dither, but they did wonders for the men.

Willa and I walked across the lawn. I slowed to give myself more time to take in the rest of him. Nice brown long jacket with brass buttons on each side. A vest against his tight abs. Even a funny triangle hat at his side. Yeah, he was a tall glass of something.

"So…"

"Hey, you up for a game of quoits?" He stood, fiddled with the stick in his hands, and glanced around at the other people who strolled along the garden paths.

My feet had been pounding with pain, but for a minute I forgot about it. Still, I'd better get a seat before they threatened to fall off. An arbor covering a bench had the perfect bit of privacy. "Wanna sit over there for now?"

"Your feet are killing you, I bet." He shook the hair out of his eyes.

"I've never worked so hard before."

Willa and Kyle flanked me. We strolled onto the brick path that led through some flower gardens to the arbor. The flowers stood out in stark contrast to the green lawn. "Wow, it's beautiful here. What are all these different types of flowers? Do either of you know?" I touched a delicate petal. "Who takes care of all this?"

"There's a head gardener, but the residents do the majority of the work." Kyle walked with his hands behind his back.

"Oh?"

Willa looked like she'd rather be anywhere but in the garden. "Don't worry. No one makes you do this job. But you can choose it if you want."

I didn't have a green thumb. In fact, I had never cared for a plant or animal my whole life.

"Why? Are you interested?" Kyle plucked one of the puffy flowers at his elbow and handed it to me.

Heat climbed my cheeks. "Thanks." I ran a hand along the sprigs of tall orange, pink, and yellow blooms. "Um, I don't know. Do you work here?"

"No. I prefer livestock and horses. Sometimes I'll volunteer down at the Webster farm on Saturdays."

"Not me." Willa moved ahead of us. "Yah wouldn't catch me near those nasty pigs and stinkin' cows."

I settled on the end of the bench and laughed. "That bad, huh?"

Willa sat on the other side, leaving the center for Kyle. She made a funny face. "Yeah."

Kyle stretched out on the bench, much as he'd been under the tree, crossing his ankles and resting his arms on the back of the seat. "Well, I like it." He gave Willa a quirky smile and turned back to me.

If only I could pull off my boots and rub my feet or

prop them up somewhere. A tired headache settled between my temples. As I leaned back, I looked up into the abundant spray of leaves and miniature roses that covered the arbor.

"You feel okay?" Willa didn't look at me but concentrated on the leaves above us. "I remember how rough coming off stuff was those first few weeks."

"I'm fine." I rubbed my temple and closed my eyes. I didn't want to admit to the headache.

"Hey, did yah notice Jordan wasn't at dinner tonight? And I didn't see her at her usual place at work, either."

"Jordan? Who's that?"

Willa dropped her gaze to mine. "You know. The girl who's always working on the flowerbeds at the boarding house."

I vaguely remembered seeing her on my first day. "Oh. Her?"

"Anyway," she changed the subject, "tomorrow's going to be a crazy day."

"Yah, yah." Kyle copied Willa's accent.

She made sure no one saw her, and then reached over and punched him in the arm.

He pointed and laughed. "Hey, female violence is not permitted here."

Willa shook her head and turned, resting her head on the back of the bench.

Kyle rubbed his chin. "Have any trouble with customers today?"

"Oh, yeah." I didn't elaborate.

"They are demanding." He smirked.

"Well, you know, it's so hard to not go into attack mode when people are rude to you, but I managed to refrain from dropkicking the worst customer." Only a few weeks ago, I would have had some choice words—or worse. But … things were different somehow.

Kyle raised his eyebrows. "Yeah. I've helped my fair share of demanding tourists. There was this one that I 'accidentally tripped'." He made air quotes. "I almost got kicked out for it, and it took a month to get rid of my demerits."

Our eyes lingered on each other a little too long. The willies, which crawled up and down my skin, wouldn't take a break, either.

17

Sarge

"Stop or I'll kill you." Sarge threw his hand over the woman's mouth as she tried to scream. He encircled her waist with his other arm and squeezed her tight against him. His voice remained quiet, but she got the idea. She went slack in his arms. He'd seen the fear in her eyes the millisecond before he'd grabbed her. She should have been afraid, he had warned her, but she wouldn't listen to him. "This is the way it's going to be. You don't come looking for me. I will talk to you when I want."

"I … I didn't."

"I've watched you, so stop the lies."

The way-too-thin woman looked sideways and strained against his arms.

What was she trying to do? All he wanted was to talk to her and end everything, but she didn't listen. He hated the fear that reflected in her eyes. So like the others. "Hold still."

She jerked backward, eyeing the garden where they stood.

"Oh, no. *Don't* do that." His sharp tone lost its restraint. Heat burned through his muscles. He struggled to control the searing anger, which struggled to take over. Too late…

18
Brooke

Jordan never returned. I chalked it up to dropping out of rehab. But everyone else seemed way more worried. I didn't know her, so maybe I should keep my opinions to myself. But when a girl goes missing from rehab, why make such a big deal? Addiction could pull the strongest person back to it. The girl had a better chance of returning to her drugs than a table tennis ball to a cup in a game of pong.

"Jordan Magnus has been missing for two days." Anna stood in front of everyone.

The women murmured amongst themselves as I shrugged at Willa's wide-eyed stare.

Anna lifted her hands. "We believe she left of her own free will, but there's a certain protocol that we follow. If any of you have information about her—maybe you saw her or talked to her—please let one of the leaders or counselors know."

I watched her as I played with my fingernail. Only the day before, Willa had commented on Jordan. I finished the last bite of oatmeal in my bowl. My stomach somersaulted. I had therapy in twenty minutes. I had better hurry. Mr. Carrick would be waiting for me before my shift started at the store. My skirts caught underfoot and I almost fell as I hurried to the kitchen with the empty bowl. *Not again.* I wanted to jump up and down and throw the new dress across the room. Oh, great. I hadn't checked the chore chart yet. Better get to it before I left. Running my finger along the list, I found my name. Dish and bathroom duty. Oh, great.

I did the chores in record time, but it still made me twenty minutes late.

I grabbed up my skirts and rushed out the front door past a group of teens who protested as I scurried between them.

I tried to shove down the mounting agitation which refused to subside, even though other withdrawal symptoms had. Would I ever stop being so volatile? I had to admit it didn't feel good to be on the edge all the time.

Mr. Carrick opened the door at my knock. He glanced at his watch and then at me, raising an eyebrow.

"*I know.*" I looked away and bit my lips together. He was the last person I should lash out at. He ushered me into his office, closing the large windowed door. If I just took a deep breath, maybe I could focus my attention.

"How has your first week gone?" He took out a file and poised his pen above an empty piece of paper.

I tried to sit still, but my racing pulse made me want to skitter like a jumping bean. Where did I start?

He looked at my hands folded in my lap. "Tell me some of your symptoms." He shuffled through the paperwork and grabbed a different sheet of paper. "Tremors…"

"Yes, but they're almost gone."

"Insomnia, irritation…"

I rubbed my left wrist. "Yes."

"Depression?"

"No." *Maybe*. He ran through the list. Wow, I had way too many symptoms still.

When he finished, he looked up, and I wrung my hands together. I studied his professional blank stare. There was a hint of compassion in his eyes, though. "Is it ever going to get better?"

"For the most part, over time, you should see the symptoms diminish, especially the tremors. But it's only going to happen if you realize you cannot live life controlling your addiction. No one controls addiction. It controls you. Do you understand that? That's why you are here, to get it totally out of your life, right?" He waited for me to answer, and when I nodded in full agreement, he continued. "Look, I understand how hard it is, but that's why we're here to help you through it." He leaned back in his chair, then sat forward and took out a pamphlet. "Remember the twelve-step plan I gave you on the first day? We'll personalize it together to overcome your specific areas of struggle."

I took it from him and looked at it. *Forgiving others* splayed in bright letters close to the top of the list. Couldn't I skip that one?

"Back to your weekend. I heard you accepted Christ into your heart." He cracked a smile.

The one good thing I'd done. "Yes, I'm … happy about it. I wish someone had told me about God before."

"I'd be glad to discuss any questions you have." He reached into a drawer and pulled out a tiny book. "Here. These are simple prayers to help you talk to God."

"Thanks." I took it, more thankful than he could know. "It's making a difference already, for sure. Like yesterday, I wanted to slam this guy in the store, but somehow I managed to beat my emotions into submission."

"That's God working in you."

I looked at my fingers. "I didn't realize how much anger I had. But now I can see it. And it's really hard sometimes not to give in to it." He smiled and nodded but didn't interrupt. I told him everything I'd felt and how I'd reacted. When the flow of words stopped, I winced. I hadn't meant to say so much. The only thing I'd left out was Kyle.

"The first step to dealing with your anger is to recognize it. Well done."

Then we talked about my childhood. I found myself punching a fist into my other hand. Weird. I'd started doing it without even realizing it. By the end of the session, the usual anxiety rested in my chest. Therapy still didn't work. Why bother to come?

He stood and waited for me to follow suit. "I want to talk about the orientation of your anger this week. I'll give you a couple days to dig deep and really figure out why you think you get so angry."

I left his office with my arms wrapped tight around my chest. If only I could punch a wall. I hated therapy.

I headed to the shelves, where Dara straightened some candles.

"Reporting for duty." I almost saluted but stopped.

I might also hate work, but at least it kept me from thinking about the one thing Mr. Carrick wanted me to concentrate on the most. 'Cause at the moment, I had no intention of jumping into that black pool of memories intent on drowning me.

19
Brooke

Fluffy clouds scuttled across the sky. Kinda like my brain fog. I wanted to be up there bouncing on them as if they were puffs of cotton candy—minus the sticky part—not down here trying to block thoughts of the therapy session that morning. As I picked at my lunch, dark gray clouds blew in and ate up the fluffy ones. *Not a storm.* Please don't let it hit until I returned to the store.

Willa stretched and bundled up the empty bag from her lunch. "You know how they were talking about Jordan leaving on her own?"

"Yes." I stopped running my hand through the grass and waited for Willa to finish her train of thought. *Not this again.*

"I don't believe it. You know, she struggled, but I think she wanted to get better." She avoided my eyes. "One time I tried to talk her into covering for me and she wouldn't even do that. She said she wasn't taking a risk for anyone anymore."

I listened without voicing an opinion. It almost took a muzzle to keep quiet.

"Do you think they checked all of her stuff? It's not likely she would have left without it." She looked away.

"I did see some police here yesterday."

Five minutes later, Willa hadn't shut up about Jordan's departure. She lowered her voice and checked around us. "Let's go see for ourselves."

"They said she dropped out. So leave it alone." Besides, we didn't have time. I couldn't afford any more demerits.

"Come on." Willa pulled me to my feet and headed to the boarding house.

There had to be a rule against what we were about to do. We hurried up the back stairs and went to the top of the house on the third level.

Willa looked around and waited for a few women to leave, and then she pulled me into one of the rooms. She pointed at the single desk in the room. "You look over there, and I'll look under her bed."

I glanced out the door and then pulled the desk drawer open. If they caught us and thought we were stealing, Willa would pay big time. Beads of sweat formed on my forehead. Why go along with her crazy plan? It wasn't worth getting in trouble. Yes, I actually cared about being in trouble.

What did she want me to look for? My body trembled—not from detoxing. Only blank paper and a few pens lay in the top drawer, but the rest were empty. I moved to the center of the room and looked around. Now what?

"Check in the dresser drawer." Willa spoke in an exaggerated whisper.

"Which one?"

Willa let out a sharp breath. "I don't know."

I grabbed each drawer handle and pulled them open. "There's nothing in these."

She joined me at the closet. "This is her favorite dress,

but I don't see any modern clothing in here."

She rifled through the other set of drawers.

Where had the brave life-of-the-party part of me gone? I wrenched my hands together.

Footsteps echoed through the hall. I jumped toward the bathroom, stumbling on Willa's foot. As we got our bearings, we hid against the wall behind the bathroom door. The clicking heels disappeared down the hall. I threw my hands over my face. "This is crazy. I've done way worse than this, yet I'm shaking like I committed a major crime."

Willa laughed. "Stop worrying. I'll make up an excuse if anyone comes."

"Seems like you were just as worried when you hid beside me."

Willa waved her hand. "So? Come on. Let's finish what we were doing."

As we reentered the room, I scurried to the other closet and looked inside it. A purse hung on a hook and a few dresses lay scattered on the floor. "Willa, is that hers?"

Willa followed my pointing finger. "No, I don't think so. You know that girl Raquel? She was Jordan's roommate. I heard she moved to another room a couple days ago, though. I've never seen Jordan with that, so it has to be Raquel's."

I edged toward the door. "What's your conclusion?"

Willa walked out of the room. "I guess she did leave on her own."

As we headed down the stairs, the clock chimed two. I put my hands onto my cheeks. "I'm definitely getting demerits now. I was supposed to be back five minutes ago, and this is the umpteenth time I've been late."

"Stop worrying. I've had plenty of them."

"The point is to *not* get them." I rushed out the door.

"Are you satisfied with your investigation now?"

"Yeah, I guess."

At the store, I waved to her and ran inside, almost toppling over a customer. "Sorry." I'd apologized more in the past couple days than I had in the whole year.

"Are you all right, honey?" A lady with the whitest hair I thought I'd ever seen put out her hand to steady me.

"Yes. May I help you with anything?" Maybe if I looked busy, Dara wouldn't notice my tardiness.

"No, I'm just moseying around enjoying my afternoon in this store."

Dara looked up from the cash register, crooked her finger at me, and then returned her attention to the book in front of her.

I dropped my chin to my chest and headed to the counter. *Here it comes.*

"You're late. That's five demerits." She spoke without looking up from the account book as she rested her hand on her ample waist.

"I'm sorry—" Not another apology. "Willa needed help with something."

"And?"

"I needed to help her." I twisted my hands and bit my lip.

"Don't let it happen again. Now, that shelf needs stocking. You'll find the items back there." She pointed to the rear of the building.

The last thing I wanted was to lose free time, or to have extra bathroom duty. Even worse, one more demerit meant not seeing Kyle.

I put my hands in my pockets and touched a plastic wrapper. Good grief. I still hadn't thanked Kyle for the candy bar. Had I fried too many brain cells to ever remember anything again?

20
Sarge

If one more person bumped Sarge, he'd go ballistic, and he'd lose more than his temper. He pressed into the cluster of residents and tourists crowding the general store right before closing time. *Keep your focus.* There she was. Brooke headed toward them with an armload of merchandise. Everyone shifted. Perfect.

He moved with them, only inches from her as she restocked a shelf. He ran his hand along the small of her back, a millimeter from actual contact. Shockwaves whizzed through his fingertips. If only...

She stepped back, and he bit his lower lip as he made contact with the cotton material of her bodice. Better not let her see him. He ducked into the crowd.

When she looked around, someone else stood where he'd been. She smiled at the resident and said something he couldn't hear.

How sweet a moment it had been. Did he dare go back and get the smallest whiff of her hair before he headed to the boarding house?

In one swift movement he pulled away from the crowd, but not fast enough. She was gone.

Next time. Maybe he'd even take a lock of her hair.

21
Brooke

I gasped and tried to breathe. Why hadn't I listened? A white cloud of flour floated around and filled my lungs. Coughing didn't help. And anger had no shot at making the situation better, either. *Welcome to breadmaking day.*

Anna set logs in a small oven at the side of the kitchen fireplace and stoked it. "Honey, I told you not to drop that bag on the counter."

I clenched my fists for a moment, and then wiped my face. For once I wanted to stop jumping from zero to angry in two seconds. But with the flour dust littering the air, I couldn't take the two or three calming breaths that Mr. Carrick had encouraged me to use. Flour continued to fall to the already littered countertop.

Anna hurried to the water pitcher with a glass and filled the cup. "Here, here."

I grasped it but dared not speak, afraid to start another coughing spell. Several swallows later, I croaked, "Thank you, Ms. Anna."

The older woman patted me on the back and smiled. "Are you ready to get to work?"

As I nodded, I set down the glass.

"Can you grab a dozen eggs and some olive oil for me?

The other women should be here soon, but we'll get started without them." Anna turned to the oven.

I returned from the pantry with the items and waited for her next order.

"Now I need yeast, which is over on that shelf." She pointed, and then took a large wooden bowl off the shelf under the island table. "And get the salt out of the pantry."

I searched the shelves for a moment, noting the neat system of organization, then lifted the salt tin and returned to the kitchen. "Anything else?"

"Over on the stove is a pot of warm water. Bring it here." She patted the counter beside the bowl and waited patiently for me. "Pay attention, now. This is how it's done." Anna started measuring out the flour and oil. "Make sure you learn these measurements because you're going to be doing this a lot." The yeast went into the pot of water as Anna spoke. "Go ahead and start cracking those eggs."

"All of them?"

"Yes, ma'am."

Over the past couple weeks, I'd become very proficient at measuring and mixing ingredients, but hadn't finished an entire recipe by myself yet. As the egg whites and yolks fell into the bowl, I paid attention to Anna's sifting.

We mixed the ingredients together in order.

Anna smiled at me, keeping her attention on the bowl. "Go ahead, get your hands in here with mine; there's plenty of room." I reached in and gingerly pushed the dough, squeezing it with my fingers. It oozed and stuck to my hands.

"Now's a good time to get all of your aggressions out, because the dough doesn't care if you pummel it. Here, take this piece." She pulled a large clump loose and tossed

101

it onto the countertop. "Now roll it like this." Anna demonstrated. "And push it with the palms of your hands. Then roll it again, turning it."

I grimaced. It looked easy enough, but it wasn't. As I rolled the piece and pressed on it, it stuck to the counter. "No."

Anna poured more flour over it as I struggled. "Don't worry. Keep adding flour until it doesn't stick anymore."

Anna paused before returning to her own dough ball. "How's it going around here for you? I noticed you've been sitting closer to the front during devotional time. I'm proud of you."

"You know, I look back at the way I was before, and it seems like a different life, a different person. I never want to be that person again."

Anna patted my arm and left a flour print. We both laughed. "When I got saved, it was the same for me. But it doesn't work that way for everyone. Some people take it slower and grow in their Christian faith over time." She pulled the dough into eleven balls and placed a towel over all but one of them. "Have you heard from home?"

"No." I punched at my dough.

"I know how hard it is these days. No one writes anymore."

"I don't expect them to anyway." I didn't meet her eyes.

"Just let that bread know how you feel about that." She swung her arm in an arch, fist in the air. "Like that."

I smiled as I rolled the dough. The way it gave under my palms released my tension one turn of the dough at a time. "You're right. This does help."

Maybe I'd punch more dough and less people from then on.

22

Brooke

Darkness claimed every corner of my room and the outside world in a creepy way. I couldn't stop glancing to the yard below. The streetlamp a block away did little to illuminate our lawn. I crumpled the piece of paper in front of me and threw it into the trashcan. One last try, then I'd give up. I'd never written a letter to anyone before. Texting? I was a queen of it. But not writing. There were too many other forms of communication in the world. But there were no phones and no email accounts at the center. I set the pen against the smooth paper and began again.

Something moved down below. I sat ramrod straight and looked again. Nothing. Maybe a rabbit. I'd seen a few out there early in the mornings. I trained my gaze across every space around the spot. Just my imagination. The center had to be the safest place to be.

With a shake of my head, I went to put the pen back on the paper, but I slashed a mark across it when another movement startled me. I crushed it and walloped it into the trash beside the three other papers.

Had Dad even noticed that I'd left? I'd told him about the program, but he'd been too wrapped up in his work to even send a nod of acknowledgement. Oh, well. I was an adult. I didn't have to answer to him anymore. I tapped my chin with my pen. Would he pass my letter on to my grandparents? They didn't care either, or at least they'd never acted as if they did. But someone should know where I was.

I shoved the letter into a matching envelope and sealed it.

More shapeshifting caught my eye. In the bush across from my window. I clicked the tiny light switch to my reading light. No way could anyone see me with that bit of illumination. Not possible. Yet I hid in the dark, not moving a muscle.

I stared so hard my eyes hurt, frightened beyond belief of what I might see. Yet more afraid to look away. For like five minutes.

Nothing.

I let go of the edge of the desk, which I had gripped tight, and shook out my arms. *Stop being silly.* My paranoia had returned. That was all. But I might as well go to bed, or I'd be drained tomorrow.

With one last look out the window, I pulled the curtain closed.

My body begged for a drink. And I despised myself for it. Writing Dad had started a completely new set of withdrawal symptoms. What a betrayal to all the work I'd done. I clenched my hands tight together. "Thank you, Jesus, that there's nothing here to tempt me. I don't know if I'm strong enough yet to squelch the cravings on my own. Please take away this obsessive thinking."

Where was the prayer book Mr. Carrick had given me? I needed every kind of prayer I could think of.

The book lay in a mound of junk at the end of my bed. I pressed it to my chest and got up to pace. "God, why do

I have to go through this?" But I knew why. I had to pay the consequences of my actions, Mr. Carrick had said. Withdrawals were a part of it. A hot flash came and went, leaving me clammy. Maybe I should go for a walk, so I wouldn't wake up Willa. No, it took way too much work to redress.

I climbed into bed and curled into a little ball, wrapping my arms tightly around my form as a few tears slid down my face. *Please let it be over soon.*

"You finally going to bed? If I had labored over a letter that much, I could've written ten pages." Willa peered over the pillow stuffed under her arm.

"Whatever." I turned toward the wall and wiped my face.

"Oh, don't be gettin' all mad. I didn't mean any harm."

I let the anger subside. "Good night."

"So who are you writing?"

I turned back to her. "Does it matter?"

"It would be good to know, so I can tell Kyle you have a boyfriend already."

I threw my pillow at Willa, but it landed just in front of her bed. "I don't have a boyfriend. And even if I did, I wouldn't have to answer to Kyle about it."

"Really? Because I think he would disagree."

I rolled my eyes. "You told me yourself there's no fraternizing here."

"Okay. Just checking."

I rolled the corner of the blanket into my tightened fist. "I was trying to write a letter to my dad, but I had nothing important to say. Or at least anything he would think was important."

"Things are bad with him?"

I looked away from Willa's darkened form. "Yeah, he never really cared about me."

"I doubt that." Willa paused then said, "At least you have a dad."

"What good is it when he cares more about the bottle of alcohol in front of him and his work buddies than his own daughter?" Years of frustration began to escape.

Willa grabbed the pillow off the floor and threw it back at me. "Go ahead. Pound that sucker to death. It'll help."

I let out a scornful laugh. Hadn't Anna said something similar? I gave it a few punches and then smashed it against the bed.

"Wow, I was just kidding, but if it helps, go for it."

I didn't know if I should laugh or not.

When I sat still for a moment, Willa said, "Is that how you got your liquor? From your father's stash?"

I squeezed my eyes closed. "Yeah, when I was older. And the sad thing is he never even noticed." Oh, how I'd wished he had taken notice, had acknowledged my existence. "So, I figured I'd just take whatever I wanted. Sometimes he left his wallet on the hall table, and it was so easy to take money out of it whenever I wanted to party with my friends."

"You honestly think he didn't notice?"

"Willa, the only time he noticed anything is when I got in his way at his parties, or if I didn't clean up after one of his drunken fits. Then the screaming would start. My grandparents would take his side and accuse me of being a slob, a lazy nothing." I looked down at my hands. "They always defended him. He was their baby. Me? I was just an inconvenience. Once my grandma said she wished my mother had taken me with her when she left." The memory flashed painfully through my mind.

"Wow, that's cruel. Why didn't you go with your mother then?"

Tears stung my eyes even though I tried to convince myself I didn't care about Mom's abandonment. "Well, how could she find some guy to take care of her if she had a bratty kid with her? I really didn't need her then, and I don't need her now."

"Yep, we're two of a kind, you and me." Willa got up and came to sit on the edge of my bed. I took her outstretched hand and squeezed her fingers.

For once, I dropped my defenses long enough to suck in her reassurances. But a minute later I pulled my hand free and gave a false chuckle. "Go back to bed and leave me alone."

23
Sarge

Most people beat stage fright by picturing the crowd half nude, but Sarge saw them in a much more sinister light to calm his nerves. Tourists knew how to set Sarge off, and that day they were in top form with dumb questions. He got into the zone and blocked out the relentless beat of the sun on his back and the crowds of people asking hundreds of questions about the historical accuracy of the cabin. He wiped the sweat from his face then pulled his shirt away from his drenched chest. Once he placed one more log section onto the gable wall, the roof would be ready to prepare for the cedar shakes.

Tourists sat on stumps and watched him work as a comrade gave a demonstration talk on the building of the cabin. His co-worker drawled, "You see these pieces of wood, how thin and long they are? We call them cedar shakes. They work the same as shingles on houses today. Once they dry, they'll last for a couple of decades, maybe longer, on the roof of this cabin."

Sarge pulled at the timber he'd propped on two finished logs and began shearing the bark off it, smoothing the wood with a large wooden planer. It was time consuming but it gave him an opportunity to think.

The words of his therapist kept biting at his last nerve, and he mulled them over and over in his head. How dare the therapist accuse Sarge of being manipulative and compulsive. He'd spent months trying to overcome those shortcomings.

He grated the hand planer across the wood so hard that a chunk clogged the blade. Just great. It took twice as much work to release the splintered wood. Getting angry always cost him. He needed to stay focused and vent in more productive ways. If he couldn't satisfy his therapist, then he'd focus harder on being quiet—keeping his true feelings to himself. He'd slipped up with the therapist anyway. Sarge had thought if he just told him a little, the counselor would help him squelch some of his cravings. That idea turned out to have been disastrous. Proof once again that he could trust no one.

Everyone began to disperse and head to the next housing exhibit, but he didn't bother to acknowledge any of them as they left.

"Hey."

Sarge looked around for the man who'd called him.

"Could I get a better look at that thing you have?" The man moved into Sarge's personal space.

Sarge turned sideways and took a deep breath. How would the jerk like it if he got all up in *his* face? He moved away from the man, then held the planer out for him to see. The man didn't seem to get the hint and he moved closer still, eyeing Sarge.

"Don't I know you from somewhere?"

Sarge wiped his brow and tried not to gulp. A telling sign of stress. "No, I don't think so. I'm not from around here."

The guy squinted and pursed his lips in a fish-face kind of way. "Probably just saw you around town."

The hairs on the back of Sarge's neck stood up. Not good. "I guess." His voice sounded guarded even to his own ears. "Sir, I need to get back to work."

He turned away from the man and grabbed his tools. When he spun back around, the guy shrugged as he walked toward the group headed to the next exhibit. Minutes later, no recollection of ever seeing the guy had come to mind. Acid burned the back of his throat. Was it time to bolt?

Sarge followed the man's every move until Ryan rounded the corner and blocked his view.

Ryan's gaze remained averted as he spoke. "What happened to the mallet?"

Sarge barked, "The tools are over there where you left them. Look, go do your work."

Ryan's retreating form said it all. He wouldn't be pestering Sarge for the rest of the day. And good thing the building foreman wasn't around to report his aggressive nature back to the head honcho.

He turned to the stump and sat down on it as he scraped the bark, but no matter how hard he tried, he couldn't put his full concentration on the work. He had never seen the guy before. He would've remembered his strange bulbous nose. But his stomach lurched anyway. Maybe he should keep an eye on him the rest of the day, follow his group to make sure he didn't talk to anyone about Sarge. If he did…

24
Brooke

Why was it so hot? I flickered awake as I pushed at the sheet, which stuck to my sweaty skin. I stretched and threw my leg over the side of the bed. Wait. The sheets weren't my silky soft ones. I touched the blanket bunched at my side. Not my thin fleece summer one. My eyes flew open. Right. I was at the Carrick center.

Wait. What time was it? I'd slept through the night? *No way.*

Fewer aches in my body. No headache. I almost squealed. *Best wake-up ever.*

A glance at the sky told me it was around five forty-five in the morning, not too late to spend a little time reading the Bible as the pastor had encouraged me to do.

I looked around for my hairbrush and then swept my hair up into a ponytail. It took a minute to find a clean enough dress. The ugliest one I owned lay on the floor of my closet, which explained why it was still clean. I pulled it over my head. It went on with more ease than ever before. I spun from side to side and looked at my figure. It was surprisingly noticeable that I'd lost weight. More amazing news. And I'd finished my last round of detox medications too.

Thank you, God. I wanted to fall on my knees in sheer gratitude. As quiet as possible, I made my bed and fished under the pillow for my Bible. Where should I start? I thumbed through it and stopped in the Gospel of John. The pastor had mentioned beginning there. Willa stirred but didn't wake up as I quietly sat at the desk.

Twenty minutes later the wake-up bell startled me.

Willa pulled her head up and looked at me through squinty eyes. "What are you doing awake already?"

"I thought it was time I started getting to know God better." I held up the Bible, and then put it back under my pillow.

"Oh, good thinking. Just don't expect me to join you that early in the morning." Willa sat up and ran her hand through the hair plastered to the side of her face.

"I'm going to gather eggs. I'll meet you in the kitchen." I didn't wait for a reply but hurried out the door.

Willa met me at the stairs as I returned from the coop. We worked together scrambling the eggs and frying bacon while a few other girls made a fruit salad for breakfast.

Once, I would've stayed in bed until noon or later, and then only gotten up to find my friends at the mall, but the center had showed me there was so much more to life. My daily routine had become important to me. As weird as it was to think, I had actually begun to enjoy the work.

Willa bent over the large skillet on the cast iron stove and flipped the bacon. "Laundry day."

I rolled my eyes. "Let me guess. You want me to get the buckets of water."

"You learn fast." She chortled.

It was too great of a day to ruin with a fight. "Fine, but it's your turn next time."

After we ate breakfast, we gathered our sheets and dirty clothing, and headed to the scullery to start hand-washing our clothes in the homemade lye soap and water mixture. As the pot of clothing heated over a small fire, I stirred it.

Hours later I hung the clean linens on the line outside. Willa hummed an unrecognizable song from the other end of the line.

"Hey there, how's it going?" Kyle popped his head around the sheet I was pinning.

I startled. *Oh, no. He might see my underwear.* "What are you *doing* here? You're going to get me in trouble. Quick, meet me over there."

I pinned the edge of the material then scurried out of sight before Willa spotted us.

"Do you have time to start a little project with me?"

Project? I fanned the heat out of my face—or so I hoped. He looked so incredible in his navy-blue colonial jacket. I whispered, "Okay. What do you have in mind?"

He picked up two shovels and some yarn from the side of the house.

"What's that for?" I checked again to make sure Willa hadn't noticed us.

"Do you remember our first trip to the garden? You asked about working there."

"Yes … I remember."

"Well, I talked to the head gardener, and he gave me some books about English gardens. He wanted to start a new section just past the oak tree. So I suggested that you and I could work on it together."

I grinned. "Obviously you forgot the part about me not having a green thumb."

"I don't either, but we can learn how to garden together. Besides, it'll give us an excuse to work together without Willa. Although the gardener was grumbling about having to waste time keeping an eye on us."

I looked down at my nail cuticles. He wanted to spend more time with me? No amount of breathing exercises stopped my cheeks from burning. But what about the dangers of jumping into a relationship in the middle of rehab? It went against every addiction recovery rule. "No chaperone, huh?"

He rested his hands on the top of the shovel, and his eyes sparkled as he watched me. How could I deny that gorgeous face?

Even looking away from his gaze, which begged me to agree, didn't stop the shocks of excitement running through my veins. "As if you could keep our old chaperone from following us everywhere."

"Well, I can try." He continued to stare me down and then began to make googly eyes at me. A small smudge of dirt accented the narrowness of his jawline.

I backed away in a ploy to break the frissons bouncing between the two of us. *Think of something—anything to say.* "Uh, you've got something on your jaw."

"What?" He lifted his hand and rubbed at his face.

"You got it. Looks like you've already been working in the dirt."

He smirked. "Must have been on the shovels."

I watched him for a moment and then turned away from his handsome face. "Let me take my basket in."

I hurried to the laundry line. "Willa, I'm done. I'll be back in a while."

"'Kay."

I followed the path to the kitchen door and flung it open.What should I do? It was in my rehabilitation plan that I couldn't get involved with anyone until I had successfully passed all the steps—including living on my own for a certain amount of time. Surely he had a similar plan to work through.

The basket caught on the handle, and I stumbled as it stopped me in mid-step. Refocusing on the task at hand, I pulled it until it jerked free.

Jade had her own load of laundry in the scullery when I got there. She bent over the pot of clothing and bed linens, her red curls springing even tighter from the rising heat.

"Here's an empty basket for when you finish." I left before Jade had a chance to comment.

At the side yard, Kyle absently picked at a blade of grass in his hand. When he saw me, he pushed away from the side of the house he had rested against and dropped the grass. "If you see any straight sticks, grab them. We need them to mark the outer edges of our garden."

Our garden. I moved just in time to avoid getting whammed by the shovels Kyle flung onto his shoulder. "Careful. You almost took off my head."

He put a hand on my arm, then pulled back as if he'd touched a hot stove burner. But his eyes showed his regret. Deep regret.

Good thing the rules kept us at a distance. I needed to hold onto them because the fireworks going on between us could only lead to trouble.

I bit my lower lip and walked beside him. We headed to the park side by side, and I smiled up toward the sky. "For the first time since I was a kid, I slept the whole night. I feel amazing."

His mouth quirked to one side. "Yeah, it takes a while. How's your plan going?"

"What plan?" Willa hadn't told him about our sneaking around and nosing through the missing girl's things, did she?

"You know, the twelve-step plan we all have to do."

Oh. I dropped my shoulders. He didn't need to know my snooping woes. "It's going well. Better than I thought possible. You know Mr. Carrick. He's good at getting people to talk. I didn't realize how much I bottled up, and then redirected to anger. But sometimes I don't think therapy is working."

"You can talk to me too." He gave me a sideways glance.

"Of course." I looked away and tried to slow down the racehorses in my veins. I spotted a few sticks as we passed under the trees lining the sidewalk and scooped them up as we went. Sweat trickled down my temple. Weeks of suffering in the heat had paid off. It didn't seem so hot anymore. Besides, there was no escaping it.

As we entered the park, he steered me to the rear. "See that spot over there? That's where we're going to start."

Did the new garden have to be located where we would be in utter seclusion? The real danger wouldn't be the outside heat.

Kyle dropped the shovels and pulled out a small book from his coat pocket. He flipped it one way, and then another, until it was right side up. "Okay, this is what we're doing."

I couldn't see the book without getting super close to him. I braced myself and moved just out of touching distance. My knees wobbled a bit.

How he kept his cool, I'd never know. He pointed to a picture, and then flipped pages to different shapes and designs. "Which one of these do you like?"

I looked at them and took the book, but my fingers ached to linger on his palm as he let go of it. "Are you sure you want to attempt any of this with me?"

He lowered his head but trained his eyes on me. "For

116

sure."

"This one." I studied the lines of the drawing. Its clear-cut angles looked simple but elegant.

"That's my favorite too." He set the book down and turned back to the area where we intended to work. "Let's start over there."

"Are you sure you can handle this kind of labor with your bad back? Shoveling looks hard."

"I'll stop if I need to." He reached for the sticks in my arms.

I handed him one.

He tied the string around it. "Okay, if you could take the string."

I abandoned the other sticks and took it from him.

We worked to check and recheck the angles of the outline we'd set up with the strings. How long would it take to dig and plant such a big area?

The gardener brought us a wooden wheelbarrow. He worked a short distance from our new plot of land and glowered in our direction every few minutes. No doubt he regretted accepting the supervision arrangement.

When Kyle handed me the shovel, I wished I'd said no to his plan. Wasn't there anything else to do together, which didn't involve dirt and worms?

He stood bent low. "Does it look like the picture?"

"It's hard to see right now, since we only have the outside marked." I backed up to a nearby tree and eyeballed it once again. "It's pretty close, though." The heat seemed to radiate up from the ground. I fanned my face with my hand. Why hadn't I brought a hat with me? Sunburn must be making my face glow.

"Do it like this." Kyle used methodical movements to dig the grass in straight lines, only shoveling away the grass and all the roots but leaving the rich dirt.

He refused to let me take the first load of grass to the dumping site. After the third load, I stopped him. "You don't have to be macho around me." Even though I really liked it. "I insist on taking every other load to the pile." Would I regret the demand? "I mean it."

He wiped the sweat from his brow and took a huge cleansing breath, a hand anchored on his lower back. "I need to get the fertilizer when we finish this part."

"What fertilizer?" I kept digging and tried not to let him see my trembling muscles, which ached like I'd been wrestling with a sumo wrestler.

"Aged Horse manure from the Webster farm."

I put my nose up in the air. "Eww, yuck. You're doing that part, right? Because I'm not touching it."

"This is our project, so you have to help." He glanced at the gardener before brushing at a loose strand of my hair.

I blinked and held in an ugly teenage-like giggle. "Uh…"

"No worries." He retracted his hand in time to avoid the hundredth frown the gardener passed us. "I'll give you gloves to use and it'll be fine." He grinned at me and resumed digging.

"You really just want to see me get dirty, don't you?" His sly smile said a lot, and I laughed.

I thrust my shovel hard into the ground and pulled the clump of grass up. The fresh scent of wet dirt wafted upwards. As I went to chuck it into the wheelbarrow, I stopped. A glint of metal shone up at me. "Look at this."

Kyle dropped his shovel and walked over to me with a stiff step. "What did you find, a treasure?"

The object came free from the grass where it had lain embedded. "It's a silver necklace. Look at the blue stone in it. It's beautiful." Whoever had dropped it had to be upset. It looked very expensive. "I'll take it to the lost and found." I slipped it into my pocket and picked up my gardening tool. Hmm. Something about it seemed familiar.

25
Brooke

Kyle. It was his fault I couldn't stop thinking about him. The hard knots in my stomach refused to loosen. I buried myself in the tub of hot water. My shoulders ached, and arms drooped by my sides. But they didn't bother me nearly as much as the drumroll going on in my veins and the mental distress of knowing I couldn't fall for him. I had to stop it from happening. I *had* to stick to my plan. *Lord, please help me to do the right thing.*

The towel on the chair nearby fell into my hands as I climbed out of my comfort zone in the tub. After I dressed, I tiptoed to my bed and reached under it for my diary. It only took a few minutes of journaling as I tapped my chin with the pen, and then jotted down a few thoughts to complete my entry, ending with a Bible verse I'd read earlier.

As I sprawled across my bed, I took one last look out the window toward the waning moon. At home, the city sky was barely visible over the orange hue of lights that glowed all night long. Here, one could see the stars as bright as crystals, and they reminded me of the small stone inlayed in the necklace I'd found at the park. I reached into my pillowcase and pulled the silver necklace free. The small amulet that hung from the delicate chain rolled back and forth between my fingers. No matter what, I had to show it to Willa in the morning, and then give it to Anna, but for now I studied it. How had it come to be in the grass at the park? It was untarnished for the most part and couldn't have been there very long. Maybe if no one claimed it, I had a chance at getting it back. Too many tourists trampled the center every day. The likeliness of anyone returning for it had to be slim.

I stuffed it back into my pillow and closed my eyes. It would match my favorite sweater back home. *Please don't let anyone claim it, Lord.*

Was it a selfish prayer? Something with its value had to be keeping someone else awake with worry. But who?

26
Brooke

If Mr. Carrick stared me down one more time at my absentminded lack of attention, when I should've been answering his questions, then I'd lose my extracurricular time for sure. But Kyle's muscular form bent over his shovel had me undone. For the past two days. I sat forward and cleared my throat. My knee refused to stop bouncing up and down. If my free time remained intact at the end of the day, perhaps I'd go work on the new garden at the back of the park and get rid of all the nervous energy flowing through me.

I tried to refocus on what he'd said. "You're right, I do feel less anxious." At least the detox anxiety—but not the building attraction to Kyle at the worst time possible.

"Have you been using those relaxation skills to control your anger?" Mr. Carrick placed his hands on the desk in front of him.

My gaze snapped to his. "Yes."

"Is it helping?"

I blew out my cheeks. "Yes. There was this one tourist…" I stopped in midsentence and stared out the window behind Mr. Carrick. My hands went clammy. Had someone just been watching me? Or was it real at all? Not another paranoia attack.

Kyle's head popped up and then disappeared again, and I almost fell out of my chair.

Mr. Carrick frowned and began to turn.

"Um … Wait." I put up a hand. "It worked that day."

When Kyle's head reappeared, he made a ghoulish face and disappeared again. I bit my lips together and held in a giggle.

Mr. Carrick studied me and furrowed his brow. "What is it?" He looked behind him just as Kyle's head disappeared again.

"Nothing—" I put my hand over my mouth and then straightened, noticing that Kyle pointed toward the front of the store and held up five fingers.

I hurried through the rest of my session and looked around for the clock as I spoke. But the butterflies in my stomach turned to insatiable pterodactyls with each ticking second. I pulled off a calm tone but inside I screamed at myself to stop letting Kyle affect me.

Mr. Carrick checked his notes. "Let's see. You've been here for four weeks, right?"

I nodded.

"Any particularly difficult withdrawal symptoms popping up since the last time we spoke?"

"Just the headaches and maybe sometimes I get a little shaky still."

"What about cravings?" Mr. Carrick gave me time to speak, when all I wanted was to get out of there.

"I guess … sometimes."

"Try to spend a little time meditating or praying when possible, and it should lessen your urges. And try to stick around your guide. It's always better to not be alone during those times."

"Thanks, Mr. Carrick." I truly meant it. Even if I

wanted the session to hurry up and end. "I guess I should go. I have to meet someone." I hurried out the door, but noted his open mouth, as if he had been about to say something, as I bolted for the front of the store.

I rounded the corner of the counter and waved at Dara.

"*Boo.*" Kyle leapt out in front of me as I crossed the threshold.

I almost screamed but thrust my hand over my mouth just in time. "You scared me."

He playfully moved away from me, but he looked a little stiff. The back problem and shoveling were a bad combination. I sucked in his woodsy, wonderful smell.

"It's a good thing *I* came out and not a customer, you know." I wanted to chuckle but refused to encourage him.

"That would have been interesting." Kyle laughed one last time.

"What's up?"

"I came to see if you wanted to go out for a bit. Do you have to go back to work?"

"No, I worked the morning shift so I'm free for a few hours. But I did promise to go with Willa to a quilting class later."

He stroked his chin in a mock-serious gesture. "Joining a quilting bee, I see."

"Ha. I have to learn somehow." That playful mood of his was catching.

The smile left his lips. He looked up to the clear sky and changed the subject. "I think you need one of those funny hats for where I want to take you. We're going to be out for a while."

I grimaced. It wouldn't do to get even more sunburned and be in pain when I had so much work to do each day. I still felt the slight pinkness on my cheeks and nose from working in the garden. "Okay, but I have to go to the boarding house to get it."

He let out a heavy sigh. "Let's go."

"You're the one who suggested it." The playful shove I gave him didn't deter his step even a little, but it made me bounce a couple of feet away. And it made me laugh even harder.

As we walked, Kyle pulled a banana out of his pocket and offered it to me. "Need a snack?"

I raised my chin and an eyebrow. "What about you?"

He pulled another one out of his other pocket and held it up.

"Thanks." As we munched on them, I grew more silent with every block we passed. It was time to stop this magnetic pull between us. But … I couldn't.

I listened to his funny oratory on Bret's most recent fumble at the dock, and pleaded for my tears to stay at bay.

He slowed his pace. "What's wrong?"

"Nothing."

"What is it?"

I twisted my hands. Divert the conversation. "Mr. Carrick had talked about cravings today. I didn't want to talk about it with him. Yet I've noticed that at the most unexpected times, drinking pops into my head, and I can't seem to break away from it. I really don't want it. I just can't stop thinking about it." I gave him a sideways glance. It had all been true, but it wasn't the real issue.

"I do still struggle with it too. That's part of the addiction." He folded up his banana peel and tossed it into a trashcan concealed in a barrel as we walked past the park.

But he didn't seem convinced I'd told him the actual truth. He, too, grew silent.

"Any suggestions?" I slowed as we neared the

boarding house.

"Yeah, try to keep busy and pray. I didn't always believe God would help me, but I've learned I can't do it without Him."

I nodded, then held up my hand. "You wait here. I'll be right back." I ran into the house and up the stairs to my room. Sifting through the closet shelf, I grabbed a straw bonnet and hurried out the door, tying it on as I went.

At the bottom of the porch stairs, I looked down the street. "Where are we off to?"

"Just follow me." He raised his eyebrow as he spoke.

What was he up to? And what was it going to cost me to not have Willa tagging along?

We headed toward the train station, passing gobs of sweet-smelling, sunscreen-lathered tourists. The horse and wagon that had brought me into the historic world passed us with a load of parents and children.

Kyle smiled and waved at them.

Zucchini bread and cider scents from the Daisy Cakes Delicatessen drifted down the sidewalk and made my mouth water. The banana had helped a little, but I needed lunch.

He halted in front of the tea shop as if he'd read my mind. "I'll be right back. Wait here."

He returned with two paper bags.

"What's this?" I eyed them.

"I thought I'd order lunch for us."

I managed to clear the surprise off my face before he noticed. "Is there some of Ms. Daisy's homemade pie in there?"

"Maybe." He smiled and gestured in the direction of the end of town. "Come on."

Oh, boy. I peered down the street. Trouble steamed right for me, but I couldn't get out of the way. "I've never been past the train station."

Kyle smirked. "You've been here a month and haven't seen the farm or anything over there? I'm surprised Willa hasn't at least brought you to the hotel to see her workplace. See it there?" He pointed across the street at a two-story building with columns across the front.

As we passed the hotel, Willa came out of the main entrance. I tried to pull my huge hat down to hide my face. The last thing I wanted was another onslaught of jokes and insinuations from her.

Too late. Willa pranced over to us. She waved at Kyle but kept her attention on me. "Hey, what are you doing?"

"Um, well…"

Kyle rescued me. "Aren't you supposed to be in there folding sheets or something?"

"It's my break." She put her nose in the air. "Ya'll going to the farm?"

"Maybe. But there isn't enough time for you to join us." Kyle challenged her with his cerulean blue eyes.

"Well, I'm Brooke's guide, so I say she can't go without me." She crossed her arms.

"We're all adults here, so you don't need to treat her like she's thirteen. Now go back to work and I'll make sure she stays out of trouble."

Willa narrowed her eyes.

The tug of war between them almost became physical. They both tightened their arms and leaned in. My chest wanted to explode with a pent-up breath. "Listen, you two. I'm going to do what I want, when I want." I took a step away from Willa and Kyle. "It's a nice afternoon. Let's not ruin it arguing. Besides, I bet the farmer will chaperone us."

They both turned to me. Kyle's mouth quirked to one side and he brushed the hair out of his eyes with a shake of his head.

"Now, I'm going with Kyle, and I'll be back in time to get you for the quilting class. What time do you get off, four, like usual?"

"Yeah." Willa's arms were still crossed but her lips pooched out.

"Willa, I'm sure there's someone around to chaperone us." I eyed her pointedly.

Kyle looked away for a split second and then returned his gaze to Willa, a broad smile covering his face. "Bye. Have a nice break."

The irritation didn't clear from Willa's face, but she accepted defeat and returned to the front porch of the hotel. "*Don't* be late."

I fell into step beside Kyle and squared my shoulders. It was time Willa recognized that I didn't need to be controlled—even if it was her job.

27
Brooke

There was nothing right with what I was about to do. My hands began to sweat—and not because the heat seared everything, including the grass. I wiped them on my skirt. Why hadn't I stopped the challenge between Kyle and Willa and stayed with my guide? I gave Kyle a hesitant glance.

He did a good job of evading the awkwardness between us. "What did Carrick have to say about the necklace?"

I toyed with the edge of my hat ribbon. "He said that it probably wouldn't get claimed, but he put it in the lost and found. I can have it if no one has come for it in a month."

"Yeah, tourists leave things here all the time."

But why had it seemed familiar if it belonged to a tourist?

We followed Robin Lane out of town. The road narrowed, and trees dotted the landscape along a fence line close to the edge of the road. As we meandered along, we passed a few families who were heading back to town. I might pull off the at-ease thing, but a war marched around my insides and fought a strong battle.

"It's so beautiful here." I gazed up into the sky, holding onto my bonnet as a breeze threatened to steal it.

Kyle stared left and right, then jumped over the fence. "Come on." He waited for me to step onto the fence, his hand poised to help me over the side. The farm wasn't at the end of the lane?

I glanced in the direction he had and floundered between running back to town and following him. We *were* alone. Not with said promised chaperone at the farm. "What?"

He shrugged, and I threw off the apprehension that had been eating me the whole walk there. I scurried over the rough fence and held on a moment too long to the warmth of his hand as he grasped mine. *Just friends, that's all.*

Kyle quirked one side of his mouth.

He knew. I saw it on his face. *I better start following my own orders or it could get embarrassing.*

"Come on, I'm getting hungry." He headed up the hill, walking at a clip as he went.

Was that the only reason he was moving so fast? The bleating of sheep in the distance stopped me. They weren't usually dangerous, were they? "Why are you in such a hurry?"

"I'm not," he answered in mock offense.

"Oh, really?" I stopped.

He glanced around once again, and then beckoned me to follow. "Come on."

"Are we in danger?" I lifted the hem of my skirts and sprinted toward him. As I caught up to him, he grabbed my elbow and helped me over a log near the edge of the stand of trees at the crest of the hill.

"No…" Kyle avoided my glare.

"Kyle, I'm not going another step until you tell me what's going on." I sat down and stretched out on a branch strewn across the ground, as if I had all the leisure time in the world.

He grabbed my hand and yanked me forward. I laughed but yielded. We went down the hill.

"Okay, okay. We're kind of going to a place where no one can chaperone us."

Just as I'd feared. "I really don't need to get into any trouble right now."

"No one saw us. And," he lifted his first two fingers in a vow, "I promise to keep you safe and to be a perfect gentleman." He lowered his hand and shifted the bags. "Now, let's hurry."

I relented and continued to follow behind him. I had a sudden urge to run through the fields like I'd seen women do countless times in cheesy ad campaigns for various products. It certainly was a glorious day, so why not enjoy it—and stop hooking ulterior motives to everything Kyle did.

We slowed as we neared a short cliff with a bank that dipped down to a wide creek bed of rocks.

I put a hand to my chest. "Wow, this is amazing."

"I told you, you wouldn't be disappointed." Kyle settled on a large boulder outcropping and gestured for me to join him.

I took one final look over the edge of the small cliff. As I settled on the rock, I straightened my dress around my ankles and glanced at him through my eyelashes. "How many other women have you smuggled back here?"

He smirked. "None. I'm really not that kind of guy."

I laughed. And I could've burst from all the happiness threatening to spill out. "Give me some food. I'm starving."

He dug through the bags and handed me a thick

sandwich. "I hope you like roast beef."

"Yes, it's one of my favorites." I turned away and studied the rippling water, the few feet between us not enough to ward off the thumping of my heart. I scolded myself again as I noted that his blue eyes reflected the color of the sky. The sandwich in my hand looked delicious but my stomach gurgled for all the wrong reasons.

"Eat up. Look what else I brought." He pulled out some potato salad. "And..." He lifted out two white boxes. "Here are those pies you wanted."

I reached for them, flipping the lids open, and sucked in a quick breath, taking both.

"Hey, one of those is mine."

"Really? I thought you got them for me." I laughed and pulled away as he reached for one of them.

He raised his eyebrows. "You can have them, but if you want both, you have to pay the price."

The hairs on the back of my neck stood. "Oh?"

His eyes challenged me.

"Here, you can have them then." I tossed them away from me.

He chuckled, and it dispelled the sudden tension between us. Good old heart-thumping thrills. "I'm just kidding, you know."

He took a bite of his sandwich and leaned back, but the undertone of the conversation lingered.

I finished half of my sandwich and spooned some potato salad onto a paper plate. "How did you come across this place? Do the sheep come out here?"

"When I first got here, I wanted to be alone, so I walked every square inch of this land. It helped to ground me."

I scraped the last of the potato salad off its container

and eyed the pies.

"Please, take whichever one you want." He pushed them toward me.

"Fine, I will." This time he didn't tease me. The aroma of the pies enticed me as I flipped the lid open to one and gazed at the warm fudge pie that lay within it.

Kyle popped the last bite of his sandwich into his mouth and began to talk before he swallowed. "Our garden is starting to look nice." His loose shirt plumed out in the slight breeze as he tugged on the cravat at his neck.

"Yes, I love the way you incorporated the vegetable plants in with the flowers. Maybe when the beans get picked, I can find a recipe for them. Did you see the buds on the bean pole plants?"

"Yeah. It worked out better than I imagined." He studied my face, but then looked up to the sky.

I tossed the empty pie container into the bag and reached into my pocket for the small plant book I kept with me.

As I pulled it out, Kyle sniggered. "Do you always carry that with you? What else is in those pockets?"

I shrugged then opened the book. I rolled onto my stomach and thumbed through it. "How else do you plan on getting the best crops and blooms without studying them?"

"You know those dianthus flowers I planted last week…" Kyle popped up just in front of me, with only his eyes showing between the top of the rock and the bottom of the book.

I squealed. "You like to scare me, don't you?" I laughed at the expression on his face but yelped when he ripped the book from my fingers. "Hey…" As he skittered away from me, I sat up. "You know this lazy girl isn't chasing you." I waved my hand at him and pretended to be bored. "Do what you want with it."

"You sure?" He disappeared around the side of the boulder.

When he didn't come back, I tiptoed to the edge and peered over it into the grass below. I slipped down the side and held in a giggle. He had to be somewhere close. The grass rustled near me and I crouched down with my back to the rock. A strand of hair tickled my neck, but I remained intent on sneaking up on Kyle. The tickle distracted me once more, and I reached up to push at the loose lock of hair. Something brushed the side of my face. A yell squeaked out of my throat before a hand snaked to cover my mouth.

"Shh." Kyle laughed in my ear.

I turned in his grasp, then stopped dead in my tracks. If he was on the rock, what was in the grass? With one leap, I jumped onto the massive rock and started shaking.

My reaction cut off his laugh. "What?"

I pointed at the moving grass, lowering my voice. "I thought that was you, but if you're here, what's that?" My heart was in my throat and I was unaware of how tightly I held onto him until his arm went around my waist. I refused to take my eyes off the grass. Something black poked its head out near the base of the rock and, once again, a blood-curdling scream escaped my lips. This city girl had no qualms screeching like a baby and fainting on the spot. A long snake emerged, big and fat, heading for the spot where we both stood. Dizziness took over. I gulped but couldn't seem to get a breath.

Kyle picked up a rock and tossed it right in front of the snake as I burrowed against his chest. The snake abandoned its original plan to slither towards us and rustled the grass as it turned. "It's going away. Look." He pointed but didn't release me. "See?"

"I can't look. I trust you." Every muscle in my body remained tense. It surprised even me that I hadn't high-tailed it out of there already. As quickly as I'd jumped into his arms, I tried to push away from him. "Sorry." I still had trouble breathing.

He refused to release me. But I wasn't ready to leave the safety of his arms until he proved the snake had left for good.

He tightened his hold on me. Was the snake coming back? I tried not to whimper.

"It's okay. It's just a black snake. They're not poisonous, but they do get big."

My eyes snapped back to his, even more aware of his tight grip. A different alarm settled in the pit of my stomach. I unfurled myself from his grasp. "I'm okay. Thanks."

"Yep." His sharp blue eyes intently studied me.

I cleared my throat and tried to tear my gaze away from him but couldn't. With one final push, I gained several steps between us. "Really, Kyle, we've both worked so hard. Let's not mess up now."

I managed to look away, wanting more from him but knowing it was impossible.

He spoke before I uttered another word. "Brooke, please, hear me out." He pushed at the hair in his eyes. "I understand our positions here. We both have a ways to go before we can get out of here. I aim to do things right. I want you to know how important fixing my life is, but I don't want to do it without you."

28
Brooke

How badly I wanted to fall into Kyle's strong arms. How thoroughly I wanted to love him. But we couldn't... I opened my mouth, and then closed it, speechless. He reached for me, but I stood my ground, wanting to be closer but not daring to.

"Come here." He beckoned with his hand.

Our connection pulled me like an anchor falling to the sea floor. The old part of me wanted to give up, give in. The new person I'd become stopped me—but barely. "I, um..." Everything in me screamed for me to jump into his arms when the hurt in his eyes fell on me so completely it actually wounded me too. "Kyle, I can't do this right now. I ... I need to follow through with my plan. It's the only way I'll ever be free of who I was ... *please*." I looked away. "Besides, you don't know everything about me." *Just plunge in and get it over with.* "I almost killed a kid right before I got here." I blanched. "I ... I never told anyone but Mr. Carrick."

His hands dropped to his sides. "What happened?"

I sat on the rock and pulled up my knees. "I ran a stop sign on a drunken binge. He came out of nowhere. I missed him by inches. *Only inches*." I couldn't breathe.

"If you'd seen his eyes—they were so big."

He sat beside me. "It's okay. You didn't hit him. You could've—but you didn't."

"I know, but I can't get his face out of my mind … my nightmares."

"God used it to make you get sober. You agree?"

God could use something so horrible that I was guilty of to change me? Hmm. I rested my chin on my knees. "I guess?"

His voice softened. "Thank you for telling me. You're right. We need to wait. Our plans are so important." He moved enough for me to see his face. "But someday…" He blew a breath out as if he'd been holding it. "We're getting together."

"Someday…" I relaxed as much as possible, considering one more provocative word from him would staunch my determination and cause me to abandon everything for him.

"Good, I'll consider that a promise." Returning to his earlier playful mood, he tossed my book at me, lying against the boulder's warm surface with his hands behind his head. He closed his eyes, then peeked at me through narrowed lids.

How could he be so casual when I wanted to cry my eyes out? I lay back on the rock and tried to read, but could only concentrate on his promise. Did he really care that much for me? I tapped my lip with my finger and watched him.

Kyle got up and went to the edge of the rock.

"Where are you going?" I stretched my legs across the rock's smooth surface.

"Just to do a little exploring. Want to come?" He jumped down and peered at me over the edge.

"I like the view from here. Go ahead if you want."

"You know that snake is long gone, don't you?"

"I know…"

"Okay, but you're really missing out."

I waved him off, and his head disappeared below the rock as he slid down the cliff to the water. But I really wanted him to come back, lay his head in my lap, and tell me everything was going to be okay.

My eyelids grew heavy. I curled up on the rock. The wind played with my dress and I wrapped it around my legs to keep it from blowing. I'd never breathed such fresh air as out there in the field. My bonnet would make the perfect shade for my face. I pulled it over my eyes and looked through the woven straw for a moment. A tiny bit of peace returned.

The book slipped from my hands, and I left it on the rock beside me. I only wanted to close my eyes for a moment, to relax beside the softly moving waters. Sleep claimed me.

My eyes flew open. Where was I? I blinked and pulled my hat off my face. Kyle lay stretched out a few feet away. I sat up and tried to get my bearings.

"Kyle, wake up." I touched his shoulder. "What time is it?"

He lazily opened his eyes, then stretched out his arms.

"Kyle, what time is it?" I jumped up and grabbed for the bag that held our lunch trash.

"Um…" He rubbed his eyes.

"Kyle, we have to go. What if we get caught? Willa will come looking for me. You know how she is." I grabbed the book and stuffed it into my pocket.

Kyle sat up and pulled out his chained watch. "It's four." He soared off the rock and threw his jacket over one shoulder. "Let's go."

I took the hand he offered me and climbed off the

boulder. "We're going to get into so much trouble. There are going to be questions, and I doubt Willa's going to keep her big mouth closed about us going off without her. And this is so terrible. I can't—"

"Shh, it's all right. We'll figure something out." Kyle hurried to help me up the hill and into the trees.

At the top of the hill, he pulled me down to the ground. "Look, there's Bret."

I twisted the edge of my skirt as the gangly teen rode down the lane with the wagon and horse clomping along the dirt road. He looked up toward us, and I dropped as low as I could get, the hard ground cool under my weight and the scent of fresh dirt encircling me. Bret returned his attention to the road and disappeared around a curve. A good sign he hadn't seen us.

Kyle sighed, and then laughed. "So close…"

"Too close." I buried my face between my folded arms for a moment and then pushed myself off the ground. "Let's go. And you need to come up with something. What are we going to tell Willa?"

"Don't worry. Leave her to me."

But Willa was like a bull. She got her way—or people got hurt. We jogged down the hill and over the fence. He pulled me behind a massive tree trunk as someone else passed, and pressed his hard body against mine to conceal both of us.

I shuddered and gulped and caught the glint in his eye. Perhaps he wouldn't give up as easily as he'd said. When he whispered the coast was clear, he pulled away, but I needed a second to get my legs to work right.

We scurried down the road and into town. I whispered, "You go first. Look, there's Willa. She looks really mad."

He motioned for me to hide along the side of a shop and then walked straight up to Willa. I strained to hear him, but only managed to catch bits and pieces as he spoke a little loud.

"…I don't know. I left her at the orchard hours ago. Maybe she's already at the quilting thing she was supposed to go to." His voice softened, and I lost some of the conversation. Then he said, "See you."

I pressed my hand against my forehead and winced. I'd forgotten to ask Willa where the sewing lesson took place. How was I ever going to get out of this predicament? I peeked around the corner. Willa stomped off toward the boarding house, and I slipped into the shop where I'd been hiding. A minute later, I popped out and yelled for Willa. "Hey, wait up."

Willa turned on her heels. "Where have you been?"

"Um, I just thought I'd check out that store and I got side-tracked." I pointed behind me.

"That store? What did yah need there?" Willa narrowed her eyes.

I turned and noted the sign swinging in the breeze. *Buckaroo's Tack and Horse Accessories.* "Well, you know…" I waved my hand. "Well, anyway, we better get going. Sorry to hold you up."

I traipsed beside Willa. *Thank you, Kyle, for interceding once again.*

Willa crossed her arms, and I waited for the onslaught of rebukes about to sting like an Africanized bee.

We were late to the quilting and sewing lesson, but they hadn't started yet. Willa gathered our supplies and drew me to the only two empty chairs.

As I tried to follow Ms. Ward's advice, I worked my needle in and out of the piece of material Willa had given me. I pulled a wayward stitch loose from the small square for like the third time. No easy feat. My eyes hurt from looking so closely at the tiny hole where the stitch needed to come out of.

"Don't do it that way. Here, watch me." Willa held up her sewing square and put a few stitches into it. "See?"

I squinted at hers then back to my own. "This is harder than it looks." The material between my fingers had stretched and pulled so much the gingham pattern on it was no longer perfect little plaid squares.

Willa raised her hand. "Hey, Ms. Ward, Brooke isn't getting the hang of this. Can you help her?"

Ms. Ward hurried over and knelt beside us. "Let me see." She took my piece and studied it. "It looks good for a first try. Here, hold it like this. See?" As she demonstrated, I followed her direction.

"Now put the needle in this way." Ms. Ward held her own up for me to see. "Good. Now do this."

I turned the material and gingerly pulled the thread. "Thank you. I was missing a step, but I get it now."

"Before you know it, you'll be a seamstress like me." Ms. Ward scurried back to her seat across the room. "I'm here if you need me again."

The small circle of women worked and talked, and I studied them. It wouldn't be long before some of them returned to their real lives, and I had to admit I'd miss their camaraderie. Someday I'd leave this place too. But to go home to what?

29

Brooke

Right when things were going to get better, something always happened.

The hard conversation with Kyle had me shaking. And no way did I want to deal with a return of any other devastating withdrawal symptoms, either. "Please, God, don't let obsessive thoughts of drinking ruin this day even more."

I stood outside the tailor shop, waiting for Willa, but she didn't come. I had to get back to cook dinner. The doorbell tinkled behind me as I reentered the shop. "Willa, Willa … There you are. I really need to go. It's my night to help in the kitchen."

Willa waved me off. "Go on ahead without me. Jen needs my help. I'll be back in time for dinner."

"Okay, bye."

I rushed to the sidewalk, covered in lacy-patterned shade, and slowed for a momentary break from the summer heat, wiping my brow. The sewing class hadn't been so bad. How weird to enjoy something that months earlier I'd have considered old lady work. Life was full of surprises.

Crossing the street, I continued toward Main Street.

Something whooshed behind me. I turned. The lane appeared empty, but I had caught a movement out of the corner of my eye for sure. It was probably one of the cats that lived at the center—or a tourist who hadn't found their way out of the museum at closing time.

I spun around, my back to a fence that circled a small kitchen garden at one of the exhibits, and peered around. No one in sight there, either. "The museum closes at five." No one answered me. Maybe they were lost and needed help finding their way. "I can help you to the exit, if you need."

Still no answer. I looked up and down the street.

The scuff of a shoe brought me up short. Someone definitely had been following me. Willa had to be trying to play a trick on me or something. I hurried around the corner and onto the main road, planting my back against the brick wall of a shop. I wanted to laugh at my nervousness. Of course, it had to be Willa—maybe Kyle—teasing me.

"Boo." I jumped back onto the sidewalk at the corner. No one stood on the sidewalk. I grimaced then shrugged. "Paranoia, my old friend," I sang in a sing-song way.

But I had to take one last look behind me, anyway. It was too quiet for a minute. Too scary movie-ish. I bristled and picked up the pace. Maybe I shouldn't be walking alone after all.

30
Sarge

What luck. Sarge sauntered down the side street just in time to see Brooke ahead of him. Her blonde hair glowed in the waning sun, and she looked so happy, so carefree. Who wouldn't love her? Of course, the *no relationships* rule didn't apply to him. He had managed to keep the last one a secret. Even his nosy roommate hadn't figured it out. He'd keep this one hidden also.

Just as she rounded a corner, his shoe caught on the sidewalk. She stopped to check behind her.

In that split second, he ducked down behind the long wooden fence. He wasn't sure why he had done it, but he knew how it would look. Anyone else would say he was following her, and he didn't want to start any trouble again with Carrick if she said anything.

She continued walking, and he slowly raised himself from his crouched position. He just needed one more look at her.

Once again she turned around and called out. No, he couldn't answer her now. He scrutinized her every move—even the cute face when she jumped out from the corner of the store and said *boo*—until she disappeared from his view.

Soon. He'd forget the pretenses and do what he really wanted to do.

31

Brooke

How could I face Kyle again? He wanted me as much as I wanted him, despite his promise to wait. I chopped celery, fresh lettuce, and some carrots for a salad with such gusto that Anna kept eyeing me.

I set the large wooden bowl on the table a little too hard, and returned to the kitchen to retrieve the oil and vinegar dressing I had made. It had become second nature to look at the food list and go straight to work without having to rely on anyone to tell me what to do or where to find the ingredients. Good thing, because my attention refused to stay on the dinner tasks.

Just stop thinking about him. I knew how to use thought-stopping therapy. *So come on, brain, knock it off.*

I returned to the kitchen and ran into Jade. Despite her usual snarky comments, I dared to assist her anyway. "Can I help you with that?"

"Here, I can't get the sauce right for some reason." She handed me the spoon.

Anna moved to Jade's side. "It looks fine to me."

Our housemother grabbed a box of cornstarch from a shelf overhead. "Here, let's add a little more of this to a bit of the sauce." She scooped out a small bowl-worth of liquid. "Then we can return it to the soup and it'll be perfect."

Jade smirked at us, but did as she was instructed, then removed the pot from the stove a few minutes later.

I didn't know very much about Jade, even though we often did chores together. I had gotten good at avoiding her. But I needed a distraction. "So what brought you here?"

"Want to get all personal, huh? Well, it ain't none of your business." Jade tilted her head and glared at me. She stomped away and left me standing in the kitchen with my mouth open.

What had I expected? Her attitude was like a force field of steel. I abandoned all hope of getting closer to Jade.

Willa pranced into the kitchen and leaned against the counter a mere foot from me.

"What?" I tried to shake off Jade's rejection.

"I've got something you might be interested in."

"Really, what is it?"

Willa held up a letter and smiled with a wicked grin, like an axe murderer about to do their worst.

I put out my hand, but Willa didn't offer it to me.

"I'll give it to you, but you have to tell me what it says."

I grabbed for it but missed.

"Promise." She waited for me to consent.

"Okay, okay, hand it over." It had to be really important for Willa to do that.

Once it was in my hands, I flipped it around. In the middle, my name showed in neat handwriting, but no return address had been written in the left corner. "Where did you get it?"

Willa looked down and played with a fingernail. "Well

… it was in your slot at work. I thought I'd bring it to you."

"You *mean* the mail slot that only *I* have a key for? How in the world did you get it?"

"The corner was sticking out of the slit so I thought I'd just take a look, and it seemed interesting." Willa cleared her throat. "It's not as if I opened it or anything. Now, what does it say?"

I laughed and tore open the envelope. Inside a blank folded piece of paper was a daisy. I frowned, and then remembered seeing some in the field where Kyle and I had been earlier. A smile tugged at my lips. I put the flower up to my nose.

"And … who's it from?"

Shrugging, I turned away from her. If she knew what I'd done this afternoon, I'd pay big time.

"Oh, come on, I know it's from Kyle."

Should I deny it? "Well, it could be, but who knows?"

Willa wasn't fooled. "You still owe me an explanation for being late."

"I told you. I lost track of time at the orchard." I put the flower in my pocket.

"I bet you don't even know where the orchard is." Willa huffed. "You think I don't know about you and Kyle?"

I caught one of the women eyeing us, and pulled Willa out of the kitchen and into the hallway. "Sshh. There's nothing going on," I whispered. "You keep your mouth shut about any notions you *may* have, you hear me?"

"So there is something for me to be suspicious about." Willa gloated.

I squeezed her arm. "I mean it, Willa. We're just friends, and it's going to stay that way."

For now.

"All right, whatever yah say." Willa pulled her arm out of my grasp. "But I'm watching you."

32

Brooke

Late again. I had lost free time because of it. Right when Kyle had planned a lunch date. A platonic one. He'd promised. Maybe it wasn't such a bad thing.

Storm clouds gathered speed overhead. The air tingled with electricity as if lightning might strike close by me. I skipped up the steps onto the porch. At least the rain hadn't started yet. My flower garden would be glad, but I wasn't.

"Hey, you."

I jumped and spun around.

Kyle leaned on the porch railing, a top hat in his hand. "I've been trying to catch you." He grinned at me with those doe eyes of his. "What happened to our lunch date?"

I looked up toward the dark sky and covered my face with my hands. "I got too many demerits and had to work. Sorry. They took my free time. Besides, look at the storm."

Thunder rumbled in the distance as if to prove my point.

"Some of the residents like to get together at the train depot. There's a conference room there with some board games and darts. I'm sure Willa wouldn't mind tagging along."

"Let me go talk to her. I'll be right back." I headed up the stairs and to my room. I'd managed to avoid him most of the past week. Now he seemed like we hadn't even had the conversation on the rock. Hmm. "Willa, you here?"

She answered from the bathroom.

I spoke a little louder. "Kyle wants to go to the train depot. You want to come?"

"Sure."

"We'll be outside waiting for you. Don't forget your hat."

I stopped in the kitchen and took three apples from a bowl, then returned to Kyle. "Here you go."

"Thanks."

What should I do about Kyle's amnesia? Best old practice I had was to pretend too. But he had been sweet to give me the flower. "Thank you."

"For what?" He sat on the top step of the porch and placed his hat on his knee, holding it firmly so the wind wouldn't whip it away.

"The flower you sent me."

He frowned. "I didn't send you anything."

"But I got an envelope with a flower in it, and it was the same type as I saw at the field we went to. A daisy."

"It wasn't me." He paused, then grimaced. "Hey, that's not cool. Someone's trying to get my girl." He stood up theatrically. "It's never going to happen."

His girl? Here we go again. What about the candy bar I'd never managed to thank him for, also?

Kyle raised an eyebrow. "You don't think it's Bret, do you? What if he was trying to send you a message that he saw us?"

That would be very bad. "I got a candy bar a while back." I stooped a little more. "You put that in my mail

151

slot, right?"

"No." He hit his fist into his hand. "He better not say a word to anyone." He began to pace. "Candy, you say? It wasn't me, either. Wish I'd thought of it, though. Whoever sent those things better leave you alone."

Possessiveness at its finest. I tried not to like it.

The candy and the flower. From an unknown source. Whoa. No other person had approached me since I'd been there. Who could it be?

Willa slammed the door behind her and I looked up, hoping she hadn't heard us talking. I gave Kyle a warning look.

"I need to stop at the tea shop." Willa fiddled with her shawl. Good. She hadn't heard.

"We need to pick up dinner there too." I handed her one of the apples. "Here. This should help until we eat."

Willa smiled at me and headed down the stairs.

Just as we reached the depot, huge droplets of rain began to fall all around us. I hurried onto the covered platform. "Come on, you two."

Kyle jumped up beside me. "Over this way."

The huge conference room, with its dark carpet and inviting décor, settled my nerves a little. At least it wasn't some tight back room where everyone had to shuffle around just to move from one end to the other. A bunch of residents already swarmed most of the games. We crowded around a small table with our bags of food.

"I challenge you to a game of darts." Kyle's face lit.

"What's with men and competitions?" I laughed, but I loved a good battle of the wills myself.

"What fun is life without either one?"

I scowled at him but didn't hold it long enough to be convincing. "Sure."

"I bet you a free day of weeding I'll beat you." He

pointed his finger at me in challenge.

"Yeah, you can weed the garden if you win." I sniggered.

"You know what I mean." Kyle sat back and crossed his arms.

Willa interrupted our bantering. "Hey, I can't bet or gamble, so you're not going to do it. You wouldn't want me to backslide, would you?"

"You're already backslidden." He guffawed at her.

"Watch it." Willa narrowed her eyes at him.

"What? I'm just kidding. Fine, we won't bet anything, for your sake."

I watched my two friends. They weren't going to turn to blows, were they? I puffed out a breath when Kyle lightly kicked me under the table and grinned at me.

Three men left the darts in the board and moved on to another game. Kyle jumped up and retrieved them. He beckoned me over to the board. "Here, you take the red ones."

Willa followed, and I took the darts from his hand, grazing his palm with my fingers. He raised his eyebrows and I took a surreptitious step away from him. But I didn't want to.

More people filed into the room and I had to raise my voice for Kyle to hear me. "Just watch and see how it's done."

"I'll give you an extra point for each turn and then I'll guarantee you, I will still win."

"Ha." I scoffed and took my first shot. It landed within the small area around the bullseye.

"Not bad."

We went back and forth, but no matter what I did, I couldn't get ahead of his score.

"Uh hah. I win." Kyle did a funny little dance and then

whispered in my ear, "I get to watch you weed the garden this week."

I jeered at him. "So? Let's finish eating." My own competitive nature got the best of me, but I tried not to be too vocal.

Kyle ushered me over to the table. "Don't worry, I'll give you a chance to redeem yourself at a game of checkers."

If I had to weed all by myself, I'd make sure he had a reason to watch. Then who was the real winner?

33

Brooke

Why did I have to go to group therapy? I hated it. Who wanted to bare their darkest thoughts and worries to a group of people? I examined each person as they entered the building. They had no right to know my weaknesses. ...But they had a past too.

I pushed myself forward but skulked the whole way.

Chairs made a circle at the far end of the therapy room. I sat down and fussed with my hair, crossing my legs and wiggling as my nerves shot into full action.

Minutes later, Jade parked herself beside me. "Hey."

"Hi." I focused on stopping my fidgety movements.

"So you've been here over a month? It seems longer than that."

Jade wanted to talk? I bit off a smart comment and settled for a neutral, "Yep." If I thought I was doing better, then I had another thing coming to me. My bad attitude every time I sat there had to stop. I had to accept that part of therapy.

Mr. Reese, who ran the *Buckaroo's Tack and Horse Accessories* store, got everyone's attention and quieted the group. He messed with his handlebar mustache for a moment. "Hello, everyone. Thank you for being on time."

He took a seat across from me in the circle. "Brooke, want to go first?" He smiled at me. But it didn't set me at ease.

I squirmed in my seat and hunched my shoulders. "Most of these people recognize me."

"You know the routine by now. Go ahead." He waited for my response.

I wanted to melt into the floor as warmth rose up my face. I had to do it. Just start with the simple. "I'm Brooke Hollen and I'm from New York. I … I'm an alcoholic." I refused to look into the eyes of anyone around me.

Each person said their little spiel. I peeked up after the third person spoke.

Mr. Reese started our lesson. "Thank you. Let me read everyone a verse from Psalms. It shows that even King David had some very low points in his life. But he chose to cry out to God and ask Him for help instead of internalizing it."

As he read the Bible verse, I sat a little straighter and listened.

"Can you all relate to this?" Many of them nodded. I wanted to. "Anyone want to tell us where you struggled this week? Are there any issues or problems, relapses you want to talk about?"

I listened, and my shoulders began to lift. Almost everyone in the circle shared about their addiction and struggles. My gaze met with a couple of them, and there was no shame in theirs. Just a genuine need to overcome their own dependencies.

The time had flown by so fast I almost didn't believe Mr. Reese when he closed the session. He waited for the others to step out of the circle before he approached me. "Brooke, please feel free to come and talk to me. I'm here most every weekday, and I have an office back there. I mean it." He pointed toward the door. "Good job tonight."

"Thanks." I gave him a quick smile. "I better get to work."

Group therapy might not be the worst thing after all.

I hurried back to work and checked my mail slot. What did I expect to find there?

But there was an envelope. With Dad's handwriting. I tore it open and scanned its contents. No time to read the whole thing until later. I stuffed it into my pocket. I couldn't wait until lunch break to finish it. He cared—at least enough to write me back.

Mr. Carrick passed me in the hall at the side of the store. "Hello, Brooke. How are you?"

"Fine." I combed my hand through my hair.

"Please stop by my office before you leave work today. I need to talk to you about something." His eyes held no clues.

Oh, no. Vipers bit holes through my stomach lining. I muttered, "Sure."

Had he found out about my unsupervised meeting with Kyle? Why couldn't I follow the rules?

I swept the polished wooden floor, reworked one of the displays, and answered a bunch of questions from tourists. But none of it helped my mind to stop spinning into overdrive. Not even the usual aromatic scents of the general store—hot apple cider, cinnamon sticks, and leather—had their effect on me.

At the end of my shift, I tiptoed to Mr. Carrick's office door. An eternity later, I knocked.

"Come in."

A pile of books occupied my usual seat. I noted his closed expression.

He finished some paperwork, and then looked up at me. "Word is getting around that you and Kyle Reston are seeing each other."

My eyes widened, heart pounding. "No, we're just friends."

"Well, a reliable source told me you and Kyle were seen together on Tuesday without your guide or a chaperone."

"I ... I ..."

He raised his hand. "Look, you know the rules. It's for your protection and good that we have to enforce them. I'm putting you on probation and you'll receive twenty demerits for the infraction. I want you to succeed at this rehabilitation, but it's not going to happen if you cannot abstain from inappropriate behavior with the opposite sex."

"Mr. Carrick ... I ... it's..."

"Please don't argue. Your probation period is for thirty days. Please restrain from being in Mr. Reston's presence in any private setting."

As if he had swung a gavel on his desk, the conversation ended.

I tried to hold in my anger. I might've followed Kyle to that cursed field, but we hadn't done anything. Yet someone must have told Mr. Carrick they'd seen more. I wanted to cry. Now I felt like the woman with the scarlet letter on my chest.

The door of the general store closed behind me with a thud as hot tears stung my cheeks. I melted against the side of the building, my knees drawn up against my chest. *I don't know if I can handle this. I just want to give up. Where's a drink when I need one? I knew we were going to get caught. Why did I trust Kyle?*

With sudden clarity, I lifted my head. Where had those thoughts come from? Shame replaced my anger as I rested my forehead against my arms. *God forgive me. I don't know why I'm thinking about that now. I've been*

158

sober for a while. Help me. The words echoed in my mind over and over.

Mr. Reese had just warned the whole group that relapse was a real monster which attacked at any time, even years later.

I fought to steady my racing pulse. *I can't give up now.* With a cleansing breath, I stood and pushed away from the wall.

Who turned us in? Was it possible that Willa had blabbed to Mr. Carrick? Surely Willa hadn't done it. How would she have found out?

I had to tell Kyle what had happened. I headed down the sidewalk. Then it hit me. He was bound to get the same speech and demerits if he hadn't already seen Mr. Carrick. Where had he said he worked? I stopped and considered past conversations. I vaguely remembered him mentioning law school and the courthouse.

Looking up and down the street, I hurried away, and turned onto Courthouse Row. The large brick façade of the building showed off its austere lines to perfection. A few tourists followed me in, and I searched the large open courtroom for Kyle. "Kyle … Kyle." I checked through a few open doors. There he was.

His smile lighted his eyes when he noticed me. "Hey, what are you doing here? Hold on one second." He turned to the small crowd of people. "I'm going to give a tour in five minutes. Take a seat and get comfortable while you wait."

He started to steer me to one of the empty rooms.

I resisted. "It's better if we stay here by all these people."

He shrugged and studied my face. "What is it?"

"Mr. Carrick pulled me into his office today." I clenched my fists together. "Someone turned us in for inappropriate behavior without a chaperone."

"*What?*"

"He wouldn't even give me a chance to defend myself. And he wouldn't tell me who saw us."

"I can't believe it." He paced. "Who would do that?"

"He gave me thirty days of probation, and if I got it, then you will too." I crossed my arms.

A few of the people watched us with way too much interest.

Kyle lowered his voice. "Let me do some checking around. I think I can avoid Carrick long enough to see who started this." He studied me for a moment. I could tell he wanted to give me a hug, but he didn't. "Look, it's okay. Just let me deal with this."

Right then, I wished he could. "Okay, I better go."

He turned his back to the crowd and laid his hand on mine for a split second then walked away.

I left with the sound of his voice booming through the naturally acoustic room as he started his tour. What a beautiful baritone pitch.

At the boarding house, I searched the first floor and then the second, and then started to pace. Willa should have been back from work. Was she scheduled to help in the kitchen? I rushed down the back stairs, holding my long skirts up as I went. Scanning the schedule on the wall, I found Willa's name. I rested against the doorframe and tried to calm down. Any moment, Willa should be there. Other women and teens started cooking.

I strode to the porch and put my hands on my hips as soon as I saw Willa coming up the stairs. "*We need to talk.*"

"Whoa." Willa took a step back and put up her hands. "I didn't see yah there."

I barely gave her time to change her stride. I pulled her

160

by the arm over to the corner of the porch.

"Look, now…"

"Willa, did you say anything to Mr. Carrick about Kyle and me? Because I just got into a whole bunch of trouble today."

"Of course not." She pulled herself up to her full height, towering over me. "Good grief, who do yah think I am?"

The wheels in my brain began to turn faster than a spinning roller coaster. Who, then?

"What's going on? I want you to tell me everything, but I must get to the kitchen. So start talking." She entered the house.

I recounted the situation with Mr. Carrick. Willa gave a few expletives as I spoke but let me finish my story.

"I can't believe it. I always tease you, but I know you wouldn't do anything of the sort." She paused. "Right?"

I caught her eye. "Of course not. Well…" I pulled her aside and said a quick silent prayer. "We didn't go to the farm or orchard the other day. We actually had a picnic lunch in the field."

Willa's eyes got big as horse wagon wheels. "I knew it."

"I promise, though, nothing happened and we agreed that we were only going to be friends for now." Willa eyed me. "You can read my diary if you don't believe me." I held up my hand as if to pledge on the Bible.

"Come on, let's get to the kitchen. I guess this means I'm going to have a lot less free time now that I have to babysit you more." She heaved a heavy sigh.

It also meant I wouldn't be alone on my walks through the center. My paranoia could take a hike—by itself—for once.

34
Brooke

More trouble. I opened the window by my bed as the last light of day died away. The room smoldered, but the breeze that blew in gave me instant relief. But not answers to my new problem.

I wanted to go to bed so bad, but devotions were way more important. The pastor had told me weeks earlier there was no personal growth without spending time with the Lord. And I needed it after the day I'd had.

I kneeled beside the bed, bowed my head, and clasped my hands. "Dear God, I know I made some bad choices this week, and even though I didn't do anything really inappropriate, I am guilty for breaking the rules." I continued to talk to God as best I could. "Amen."

On the bed, I sat and pulled my Bible from under my pillow. I devoured Second Corinthians.

Willa came out of the bathroom. "Want to read to me? I'm too tired to do it myself."

"Sure." I waited for Willa to settle on her own bed. "I'm reading in Corinthians. It says, 'Do not be unequally yoked together with unbelievers. For what fellowship has righteousness with lawlessness? And what communion has light with darkness?'" I paused. "Huh?"

Willa shifted. "What don't you understand?"

"The part about being unequally yoked. What's a yoke?"

My friend tapped her chin. "Pastor was talking about that a couple months ago. Let me recall what he said." Willa tilted her head back and stared at the ceiling. "Yes, I remember now. It's this thing that they use to hook two cows together so they can plow. Don't you remember seeing one on the cows that Jake was directing through the field last week? What it's saying is don't be hooked together with someone who isn't like-minded."

I pondered that. "Oh … that makes sense."

"Yeah, yah know like, you shouldn't hang out with people who aren't Christians because chances are they'll get you to do things you shouldn't. But that's not to say that we shouldn't be there for the unsaved to share His love. The only way most of the unsaved will ever accept Christ is by our witness to them."

"O-k-a-y." I tried to fully understand Willa. It was a little mind-blowing. I didn't have a single friend outside the center who was a Christian.

"Go talk to Pastor tomorrow. He'll tell you—"

"Just like last time, right?" I giggled.

"Yep. Okay, good night." Willa rolled over.

I put the Bible back and turned the light off before I crawled between the sheets. Before the first sheep got counted, I remembered the letter.

Tiptoeing to the dresser, I shuffled through it and found it. Back in bed, I reached into my pillowcase for my book light. Its coolness radiated in my hand as I turned it on and pointed it at the envelope. When I'd sent Dad a letter, I'd never expected he would write back. I peeled it open and pulled the paper free.

Brooke,

I was very surprised to get a letter from you. Surely, I thought you would text or message me after you disappeared. I figured you'd gone to a friend's house for a while. Until I found the pamphlet for your rehab center and the note you attached to it. Was it necessary to take such drastic measures for a little habit? When are you coming home?

Write me when you get a chance. You need to come home soon. I'm going to call the center and schedule a meeting with them.

Dad

I puffed out my cheeks. A little habit? Is that how he felt about his own addiction? How long had it been before he'd even started looking for me? I knew he hadn't paid attention when I gave him the pamphlet about the center.

I tossed the letter into the trashcan by the desk. I wasn't going home, not for a long time at least. I stared at the ceiling. The center was home, where I was growing and changing and being accepted.

Praying, I took a few calming breaths as I cleared my mind and spoke to God.

Sleep slid over me like a tempestuous ocean wave.

35

Brooke

Pain had a way of teaching me. The needle poked my finger as I pulled it through the square between my fingers. "Ouch."

I yanked my hand away before a small drop of blood touched the needlework, and wiped it on my handkerchief. The pressure I applied made it stop bleeding, but it began to pulse with pain.

Ms. Ward hurried over. "Here's a thimble. Put it on like this and it should help."

I looked at it doubtfully but placed it on my finger. Its cold and bulky form made it hard to sew, but I didn't want to draw blood again. Several dots of dried blood on my fingertips showed from other failed attempts.

I returned to my sewing and studied it for a moment. I'd accomplished so much in the few days I'd worked on it. I traced the small bird and the flowers that lined the material on the border, then focused on the delicate pattern in the center and smiled. Soon the square would be sewn to the other ones I'd finished. I grabbed them from the neat pile in front of me and arranged them in a pattern. The colorful flower in my lap would be the centerpiece. How great would it be to showcase the work—but to whom? My old friends would make fun of me if they saw it.

Ms. Ward returned. "Let me know when you're ready to stitch them together. It's pretty simple. Keep the stitches small." She looked at the pattern of squares on the table. "I really like this. Maybe when you finish, you can start on sewing a skirt. It's a little different but a good challenge."

"I don't know. That sounds too complicated. It would probably turn out all lopsided." I wriggled and bit my lips together.

"Come on. It's worth a try." Ms. Ward patted my shoulder.

I shrugged and lowered my gaze.

"You'll see. It'll be fun to learn."

Ms. Ward went back to the mannequin, which had a half-finished dress on it, and I watched her. It had stunning details. I set down the square of material and ventured over to her.

"That's amazing, how you made that." I lifted the long sleeve and studied the stitching on the hem.

"After you've been doing this as long as I have, it's pretty easy." Ms. Ward grinned at me, and then studied the bodice a moment.

Her attention shifted. She pointed to a wooden box and looked nostalgic. "There's a whole pile of unfinished pieces over there. Go take a look."

I went to it and pulled it from the top of the shelf. Peering in, I rifled through it. "What's all this?"

Ms. Ward returned to her work. "Over the years, women have come and gone … started projects and left. I collected them."

I looked in the box again and sorted through the material. "Why didn't you ever finish them?"

"It's kind of like a testament of their journey here. Sounds so sentimental, I know." She stopped sewing and looked at me."I guess it's time to finish them up. Perhaps you're the perfect person for the job."

"What makes you say that?"

Ms. Ward leveled her gaze on me. "I don't know. I see something in you that tells me maybe you're here to stay, to help others someday. You might as well be the one to finish where they left off."

I wrapped my arms tight around my body. Was it possible for Ms. Ward to have that much faith in me? What if I ruined the whole lot of them? "I don't know. Maybe I should stick to the skirt you mentioned earlier."

Ms. Ward's beautiful blond curls bobbed. "Okay, but that box will be there if you change your mind."

I pushed the container back onto the shelf. My sewing sat abandoned on the table. "I'm going to go."

"Okay.Will I see you tomorrow?"

"Maybe." I threw my squares and small sewing kit into my personal box, and put it under the table among the others.

"Bye." Ms. Ward didn't stop me. Good. No questions asked.

The door closed behind me, and I chewed on a fingernail as I headed toward the park. Because I'd left early, I had to walk alone. It didn't seem possible that someone who barely knew me could believe in me when my own father didn't. A tremor shook my hand as I walked. Where had it come from? I hadn't had tremors in a couple weeks. *Oh, no. Please subside.* Stress was a big trigger for withdrawal symptoms to recur. A few cleansing breaths helped to steady my hands.

As the park came into view, I made a beeline for Kyle's and my garden. Blooms already covered several small bushes, and decorative trellises held pole bean vines. The garden looked better than I'd ever imagined. I sat on the wooden bench Kyle had built and played with a pleat in my long skirt. Why was I so upset over a sewing project? No matter how hard I tried to piece it together, no answer came.

God, help me to understand myself, I pleaded. Was I upset because I didn't want anyone to rely on me? Or was it related to a fear of failure? I closed my eyes. "Please, Lord, tell me." The answer came clearly to the forefront of my mind. I had failed at so many things. With someone else depending on me, great risk of failure existed—a risk I didn't know if I could take.

Lord, I'm such a goof-up. Just when I think I have things under control, I mess up. Do you think I can help others someday without ruining things? Help me to see what I'm supposed to be doing.

Something rustled behind me and my eyes flew open. I scanned the garden. Probably some tourists.

Kyle rounded a large bush. "Hey, how's it going?"

I stood and backed away, lifting my hands. "Kyle, I don't want to get either one of us in more trouble. You know we can't be alone."

He pointed to the big oak tree, where the head gardener stood watching us, shaking his head. "He agreed to chaperone."

"Really? He doesn't look too happy about it again."

"Well, I arranged to do some work for him in exchange." His dazzling smile captured me in its depths. Those full, wonderful lips.

I beamed at him and returned to the bench. "You did a great job on this bench." I pointed at the wood and ran my hand along the smooth surface.

"Thanks. What have you been doing? I've barely seen

Erin Unger

you the past few weeks."

I looked away before he could see the sadness in my eyes. "I've been busy at the tailor shop."

"So busy you can't make time to see me or our poor garden?" He made a face at me.

"It's not like that…" How I wished to run my hands along his jawline. I wanted to tell him how much I'd missed him.

"What's it like, then?" He drew closer.

I shielded my eyes from the sun for a moment. "Look, I can't afford to make any more mistakes."

His jaw dropped. "I'm a mistake?"

"—No, I didn't mean it like that." I grasped for the right words. "It's just that we've both gotten ourselves into a lot of trouble recently, and I can't let that happen."

"Oh, so you don't trust yourself around me." He gave me a smug grin.

"Stop joking." I couldn't keep from laughing.

"Well, you can throw up the white flag of defeat if you want, but I won't." He stepped forward and clasped my hand, squeezing it, then released it just as fast.

I looked around and prayed no one saw. "*Kyle.*"

He smiled deviously at me. "I know how to pay him off, don't worry."

I drew in a sharp breath as heat rose up my face, but he spoke before I had a chance.

"I'm just kidding. What kind of a guy do you take me for? Wait, don't answer that." He gave a hearty chuckle and sank onto the grass several feet from me.

The heat in my cheeks started to subside, and I refused to meet his eyes. I watched the gardener rake at the loose soil around some plants. I studied the new flower petals. Anything but look at Kyle, because he'd know how I really felt if I did.

"Now, back to what I was saying. Do you really need to spend so much time sewing?"

"I'm enjoying it—hard to believe, I know. But I do miss you." I threw a hand over my mouth. I hadn't meant to say it.

"I knew it." He gave a triumphant thrust of his arm. "You love me. Just admit it."

As I grappled for words, I raised my shoulders.

"I'll take that as a yes." He stood and danced a jig.

How did he make me putty in his grasp—every time? I managed to pull my eyes from his. "You're such a jokester all the time. How do you expect anyone to take you serious?"

"They don't need to. Only you do."

"And what am I to take serious about you?"

"That I love you, too, but I'm willing to wait." His gaze cut through me like a chainsaw. Raw edges and all were there for him to peruse.

I was speechless.

He stopped his jig. "I don't take that lightly."

I studied him from the leather of his old-fashioned shoes to the green cravat around his neck, then to his sincere eyes. My heart pounded. "Well, this place will prove the worth of your words, because there'll be no acting on them. Not for a long time anyway."

Kyle straightened as if in response to a challenge. "Touché."

36
Sarge

Sarge only wanted to get a look at her again—to watch her work. She was very efficient. He liked efficiency. But there were way more things that drew him to her. His lungs tightened as she moved around the store.

The shelves held countless bags of old-fashioned candy, but Sarge couldn't make up his mind. Grabbing the closest one, he headed to the cider machine. He didn't want candy. Especially not birch beer.

As he pulled out a cup and filled it, her sheer essence distracted him, and he spilled some of the hot liquid down his hand and onto the counter. He winced as it burned his skin. But it quickly cooled. *Be more careful.*

In the line of customers, he waited his turn to pay as the old familiar pain in his stomach signaled an anxiety attack. If he could just get her alone to talk to her, things would be better. Then he'd show her how much he needed her.

He set the items on the counter and pulled his money out of his breast pocket. "Hi, Brooke, how's it going?"

She blew out a breath. "Hey. Okay I guess. It's been way too busy, today."

Her gaze shifted around the store like a ping pong ball

in a table tennis game as she looked down the aisles with quick darting eyes. Was she okay?

"So I'll see you at the performance tonight?"

She smiled her glorious smile and her face transformed. "Yep."

His heart did a flip-flop. "Great. Bye."

He wanted to beat the air, but then he remembered the last concert at the amphitheater and his stomach jolted again. Too many people had packed it last time. And this one would be no different. How was he ever going to find her? He would have to get there early and keep his eye out for Willa. She followed Brooke everywhere like a little puppy. The way she always did. He hated that woman. Enough to make her disappear if she tested him again.

37

Brooke

The heebie-jeebies cascaded down my arms and back. With the store full of people, why did I keep reacting that way? I pushed a strand of hair back into a hairpin and drew closer to the register beside Dara, unable to shake the mood. Several workers in their colonial garb, including Kyle, looked over the shelves, grabbed snacks and drinks, paid, and greeted me as they left. I liked how they seemed to trust me more every week.

Dara handed me a glass figurine, and I wrapped it with care as I stared down every aisle. Distraction seasoned my voice. "Please come again."

Dara waited for the customer to leave. "I need to talk to you when it slows down a bit."

My stomach sank. *Not again.* What mistake had I made this time?

"Can you check the cider machine and the coffee pot? I'll be right back." Dara left.

At the machines, I cleaned up some spills and set some lids in order. Still the creepy feeling lingered, and I looked over my shoulder several times as I worked. *Stop being silly.*

I spotted Martie and Lauren, the two new residents

who'd entered the center days earlier. It was my job to train them in the store, and I hurried over to them. "Did you get a chance to look through the informational guide Ms. Dara gave you?"

Martie stared off into space and ignored me. I'd bet she was the gum-popping kind of chick. But Lauren nodded.

"The more you put into this, the better your chances of succeeding here. Now, please will you help me straighten that shelf and restock it? I'll get the items for you."

As one of them dallied, I ignore her and hurried to the back room to get the small boxes. They weren't too happy to see me return so fast. "Here you go."

Martie and Lauren set the new merchandise out and turned them to show the labels.

At the cash register, I tapped on the counter with hyperactive fingers and studied every customer. No one seemed to notice me. I shook off the feeling and wrapped a few purchased items. "Please enjoy your visit."

When they'd left, I continued to check every person coming and going. Still nothing seemed out of the ordinary.

A bunch of guys moseyed toward the counter with their hands full of snacks and drinks. But the gorgeous guy from Daisy Cakes Delicatessen strode ahead of them.

Eric? Was that his name? My shoulders relaxed an inch.

"Hi. Eric, right?"

"Yes ma'am."

Ooh, and good manners too.

The group stopped behind him like a cowboy's posse.

If I remembered correctly, Richard was the guy to his right. He slowed his pace but kept quiet and barely looked at me.

With a gesture toward the store, Eric said, "Nice to see you here."

For once, I stopped my nervous scanning of the store. "You too."

They all bantered back and forth, joking with me as they paid.

The store emptied, and I took a deep breath. For a few moments, I looked through my dog-eared manual for a few historical facts and closed my eyes to memorize them. I knew almost the whole book, cover to cover, but I wanted to fine tune a little of the information.

The bell over the door rang for the hundredth time, and my eyes flew open. Willa strode in and waved. "Hey, when do you get off today?"

"In forty-five minutes." I was so glad to see her I almost jumped over the counter to hug her.

"Great. I'll be by to pick you up. Gotta go."

At least I wouldn't have to walk home alone.

Dara returned and took over the counter.

I shuffled through the myriad of junk under the counter for the cleaner and rags. "I think I'll wash the windows."

"Thank you. It was on my to-do list for tomorrow. I was going to ask one of them," she said, pointing to the new women, "but you can definitely do it."

I took the window cleaner from under the counter and hurried to the window beside the main entrance. *Please let cleaning help the time go by.* As I scrubbed and dabbed, small fingerprints disappeared and my nerves began to settle. Before I knew it, all the windows were crystal clear and the door looked great. I clapped my hands together. I could see with pinpoint accuracy whatever had my hair standing up if it came through the front door.

Perched on the ladder, I watched customers come and go as I worked. The clock ticked, and I scooted a little to the left, stretching my arm to get to the far corner of the highest shelf with the rag. Lemon-scented air and old wax filtered through the store from the wax cleaner I used. What had Dara wanted to say to me? I couldn't think of a single thing I'd done wrong. I'd even made it to work early for the past two weeks.

I gave the clock one last look and carefully stepped off the ladder. Closing time. I hurried to change the sign on the door, and then checked the aisles for any remaining customers. As Dara closed out the register, I straightened shelves and placed books back in order on their racks. Lauren began to sweep the floor, but the one with a big attitude perched against the wall, looking at her nails. I shook my head. Was she like me? Did she just need time to realize how good it was to be there to get help?

Dara folded her register tape as she called me. "Come back to the office when you're finished."

I hastened through the rest of my close-out routine, and peeked out the window to see if Willa had arrived. Both Kyle and Willa stood outside, their heads bent together in conversation. Good or bad? I knocked on the window. Too late—a knuckle print marred the perfect surface. They looked at me, and I held up five fingers, and then wiped the mark off with my sleeve.

In the office, I closed the door and cleared my throat.

"I have some good news." Dara looked up and grinned over her steepled fingers. Not unlike Mr. Carrick on the first day I'd arrived. "Ms. Ward came to me and said you've been putting in a lot of time at her shop. She seems to feel you're ready to move on to the next step."

"She said that?" My jaw fell open and I unclenched my hands. Shouldn't it take another month before I began to learn a new trade, especially after the probation and demerits I'd received?

"Mr. Carrick seems to agree. He said you've completed the first several steps. What do you think about it? Of course, you could choose a different allocation. It's up to you. Here's a list of different places to consider."

I wanted to jump up and down as I took the paper. I looked at the list. "Thank you so much."

"Just let me know in the next week."

"I will." I beamed at her and hurried out of the store, waving at the others. "Guess what?" I fairly pranced.

"What?" Kyle and Willa asked in unison.

"Ms. Ward gave me a recommendation to work at the tailor shop."

They both smiled, and Willa punched my arm. "You lucky dog. Not just anyone gets to work there."

"I didn't know that."

"No. It's a specialty shop. Usually you have to complete most of your plan before you're considered for that position. I've been here for four months and I haven't gotten anything like it."

"Well, that's because nobody likes you." Kyle teased her.

She gasped and punched his arm too. "You…"

"Boy, you're always forgetting about the no-violence policy, aren't you?" He rubbed his arm and laughed.

"Leave me alone." Willa abandoned her attack on him. "Brooke, I was going to supervise your play date with Kyle, but maybe not."

"What did he have in mind?" I looked over at Kyle.

"Oh, I don't know, a night in the park, since we have a play in the amphitheater tonight."

I laughed. "Tell her you're sorry, Kyle."

"No."

Willa wouldn't relent. "Okay, then, you can sit with Bret while we have a good time without you."

"All right, I'm sorry."

His sarcastic tone wasn't lost on Willa. "Um, doesn't sound like it to me." She lifted her nose and turned, waiting for his sincerity.

"I formally apologize and take back the truth." He pursed his lips.

I stepped between them as Willa began to retort. "You two, come on. Make up."

Willa shrugged, but Kyle said, "You know I'm just kidding."

I sighed. "That'll have to do. Now let's go." I hooked my arm in Willa's and waited for Kyle to fall into step beside me. "How was your day?"

They both tried to talk over each other, and I laughed harder than I had in a long time. They were the two best people I knew, but they couldn't see eye to eye on anything. And why force them to? I had way more fun watching them spar like Roman soldiers.

38
Brooke

Since when did a Shakespeare play make me giddy? I used to hate old stuff like that.

The amphitheater had filled to the brim. I tried to dodge around a group of people as they planted their folding chairs in the grass. Back and forth I went, holding a pillow in front of me, as I threaded through the crowd.

My toe caught on someone's shoe. I looked up as Richard reached out to steady me. "Thanks."

"Sure thing."

He ran a hand through his hair. "This place is way too full."

I chuckled. "Shows how desperate we are."

His face lit up.

"Well, I better find my friends. See you around." With a wave, I hurried further into the crowd.

Willa and Kyle came into view.

"I can't believe how many people are here tonight." My breaths came out in sharp staccatos. I threw the pillow onto the blanket and dropped down beside Willa.

"Good thing I got here when I did. Otherwise we'd be way back there." Kyle pointed behind him.

"Sorry. I had dish duty, and the cooks made a whole

179

lot more mess tonight. I'm glad you didn't wait for me."
I patted my skirt and smoothed it.

"Here. I knew you wouldn't remember your fan."
Willa handed it to me.

"*Thank you.* I did forget." I opened it and fanned
myself. How nice of her.

Several people meandered across the stage, setting up
microphones and testing the sound system.

Kyle pointed. "See that guy? He's a great actor."

I looked where he pointed, wanting to stare at him and
not the man on the stage.

Willa batted my hand with her pink fan. "What do you
think about the two new ladies? You work with them,
right?"

"Yeah." I scrunched my lips together and pushed a
lock of hair behind my ear. "I hope both of them will stick
with it. But the one with the short black hair … I don't
know about her. Every time I try to show her anything,
she has a bad attitude. But I was like that when I first
came. Let's pray for her." I swung the fan back and forth.

Willa chortled. "Coming from you, that sounds
funny."

"People change, you know." I refused to look at Willa.

Kyle caught my eye and smiled as he threw a piece of
grass at me, almost hitting Willa instead because she was
sitting between us.

I grinned at him, watching his perfect lips. *No,* I
rebuked myself. I looked away but not for long.

He didn't flinch. Still watching me, his playful
expression changed to a look I couldn't quite read.

I blinked and raised my eyebrows as I flipped onto my
stomach and stared him down in an attempt to change the
mood.

Willa noticed our rapt attention on each other. "Really,

what are we, kindergarteners?"

He rolled his eyes and reached down and grabbed a handful of grass to throw at her.

"Are you twenty-eight going on two?" Willa brushed the grass off her dress and turned to ignore him as he mocked her.

Kyle perched his chin on the palm of his hand as he stretched across the blanket. "Brooke, what're your plans for tomorrow?"

"I actually have Saturday off for once, and I'm going to sleep in. But I did volunteer to do clean-up at the tailor shop around nine."

"I'm helping the farrier with some of the horses in the morning. But why not get together after we work?"

"What's a farrier?" I played with a string on my pillow.

"It's someone who trims horses' hooves and shoes them with horseshoes. The bay that pulls the wagon has a loose shoe, so he's going to replace it. Some of the other horses are due to have their hooves filed too. It won't take more than two hours."

"We can meet at Daisy Cakes. Since Ms. Ward put in a good word for me, I don't want to cancel, but three hours should be enough time to help her. Will you be finished by twelve?"

"I should be. I'll meet you there."

Willa flaunted a sappy sweet smile. "Thanks for offering to pay for my lunch, too, you know. Since I have to come along."

"Why not?" He spoke with a dry tone.

The stage filled with performers, and the lead actor began to speak into the microphone. The crowd quieted. I relaxed and took a deep breath.

Willa sat forward and wrapped her arms around her

knees.

Kyle's hand snaked over to mine behind Willa's back. I didn't want to pull away. The warmth of his calloused hands tingled through mine, but I had no choice. I gave it one little squeeze, then let go, noting the smile on his face as he eyed me. I glanced around and tried to concentrate on the play, not Kyle, who refused to stop watching me.

39

Brooke

The sun danced across my face as I stretched and pulled my hands free from the blanket. One eye open, I peered around the room. What time was it? As I reached for my small alarm clock, I turned to my side and pulled it down to eye level. Seven o'clock. What happened to sleeping in? I rolled over and pulled my pillow over my eyes. It was no use. I lay wide awake on a Saturday when I had the right to sleep in for once.

Quiet prevailed in the boarding house. I listened for the others moving around and getting ready. A few muffled voices filtered in, but they remained almost inaudible.

I gave up and climbed out of bed. Maybe a long shower would help me stay in relax mode. I grabbed my favorite blue dress and scampered to the bathroom. I actually had a favorite dress after weeks of hating my clothing.

The water in the shower took a while to heat up. I closed my eyes under its warm stream.

A half hour later, I hummed as I brushed my hair into a bun and pinned it. And it wasn't a heavy metal song but one from church.

I had turned into a morning person after all. I tidied up, wiped away the water on the floor, and grabbed my Bible before I left for the park. The perfect place to read devotions in solitude.

A few birds sang and skittered from one tree to another as I sat on a wooden bench. I watched for a moment and munched on the muffin I'd snagged from the kitchen while Anna cooked. Would I ever think of fast food in the same way? I had grown so used to homemade meals and vegetables. Maybe I didn't need fast food anymore. That meant I'd keep the pounds off when I returned to the real world.

My old life. Hmm. Maybe I wouldn't go back to the real world. Could I stay on at the center? Ms. Ward seemed to think so.

I opened my Bible and flipped through it. The sun warmed my cheeks, and a verse I'd read two days earlier came to mind. *What is man that God is mindful of him?* Who was I that He would even consider sending His Son for me? Why did He love me—as unlovable as I was? I thanked the Lord anyway for it.

The crackle of leaves drew my attention, and I studied the soft ruffle of the flowers as the breeze blew across them. The world was as wonderfully made as the psalmist proclaimed. I read several chapters before closing it and setting it down.

The sheet of paper Dara had handed me stuck out of the front of the book. I pulled it free. Why look at it? I already knew what I wanted to do. I tapped it on my knee. Did I have any ability to learn to sew as well as Ms. Ward?

A weed in the garden caught my eye. I stood and reached down, pulling it. It gave way, and I scanned the garden for more of the miserable things. I yanked out a few others but there weren't very many. Tossing them into a little pile, I bent forward to sniff a zinnia at the edge of the bed. It tickled my nose and I smiled.

I reached for one of the roses on a small bush I'd planted weeks earlier, and just as I touched the petal, something hard brushed against me. I struggled to keep my balance, but toppled into the garden.

"What…" I pushed up and looked around as a retreating form raced away from me. I squealed when I saw my flowers squashed to the ground. "You need to be more careful," I yelled. But the person had disappeared.

Why didn't he stop to apologize? *People are so rude these days.*

No amount of preening the flowers revived them, and I gave up after fussing with them. Tears burned my eyes as I touched the leaves. I'd splurged on the delicate flowers and planted them as a reminder that I'd made it through the first month of rehab. So much work had gone into keeping them alive in the heat of the summer. To see them crushed hurt a lot.

I got up and took one last look at the dent in the ground and wiped my brow. Maybe Kyle knew how to fix it.

My shoes clapped on the path as I headed to breakfast with my head down and my good mood destroyed. I should've paid attention to the crackling leaves. Someone had been there for a few minutes before he hit me.

40
Sarge

Of all the times to fumble. Brooke wouldn't have even noticed Sarge if he'd been more careful. He stood back and watched her leave, hidden behind a large bush framing one of the many gardens in the park. No wonder she looked so miserable. He'd only intended on touching her as he'd passed, but he'd gotten too close. He couldn't afford to slip up. He needed to rein in his emotions, trust his instincts, and wait. There would be time, the perfect time, to convince her of his love, but not yet.

As she disappeared into the boarding house, he turned away, looking right and left. No one else meandered through the park. He moved out of the bush's shadow. A vibrant bloom caught his attention and he broke it free from its stem. Perhaps she'd appreciate another flower to replace the one she broke. He carefully pocketed it and headed toward the train depot, whistling as he went. He knew how to make her happy. And she'd make him happy one day too … or else.

41
Brooke

Pricey material should never be given to newcomers like me to work with. My hands shook as I stretched the delicate pattern paper over the fabric that covered the central table at Ms. Ward's shop. My stomach knotted. If I made a mistake, it would take me weeks to pay for it. I shifted from foot to foot. The paper refused to lie flat no matter what I did to straighten it.

"What's wrong?" The muffled sound of a mouth full of pins trailed across the room.

"I can't do this, Ms. Ward." I pointed at the table.

"First of all, you can call me Ms. Stacey from now on. And second of all, calm down and take it one step at a time. Right now it's like a bunch of puzzle pieces. You just have to look at it in its simplest form. See the rectangle? Lay it there." Stacey pointed at one of the pieces.

"But I know how expensive that material is, and I just can't mess it up, Ms. … uh … Stacey." I put my hands on my hips. I'd fallen in love with the rich purple fabric at the general store.

Stacey left the mannequin and came to my side. "Stop worrying. You can do this."

She handed me her pincushion. "Here, put a pin here... Good. Now, one here. Don't worry about the pattern. Sometimes they won't lie flat but if you eye it, you can tell how it goes." She squinted at it and back at me. "Focus on pinning it. When we're sure it's right, I'll help you cut it."

I didn't want Stacey to leave until every piece was properly pinned. No one had ever expected so much of me before. I wanted to throw the pincushion. I'd thought I'd work on a skirt next, not a whole dress.

Setting the pincushion down instead of spiking it like a football, I took a deep breath to calm my inner storm. I bent forward and carefully placed the pins a hand-width apart, checking the pattern as I went. Funny little symbols marked where folds and pleats went, and I tried to remember what one of them meant as I straightened, holding a small piece of the pattern in my hand.

Once I'd pinned it, I turned back to Stacey. "Okay. Is it right?"

Stacey looked over her shoulder at it. "Do you see that bent arrow? That tells you it has to go on the fold of the material."

"Oh, sorry. I forgot. You told me before, didn't you?"

"It's fine. You're doing great for a first attempt."

My hand shook as I cut the material. I looked down the length of the fold and back at the scissors in my hand. "You're sure this is the way it goes?"

"Yes, Brooke. You did well. You can cut it now." Stacey swept her gaze over my work.

Once the disjointed pieces lay in a stack at the end of the table, I breathed a huge sigh of relief. What time was it? Had I been pinning and cutting for hours? My back ached from bending over the sewing table.

Stacey looked up from her project. "Do you think

you're ready to start sewing?"

I plopped into my seat and shrugged. My stomach growled. I should've eaten more for breakfast, but after the incident with the rose bush, I'd only eaten a piece of toast. I ignored it. "Sure."

Stacey laid out all of the pieces. "Now take a look. What do you think this is?"

Stacey set the pieces out in order. I put my hand on my chin and studied it. "I don't know."

"How about this piece?"

I leaned closer. "Oh, I see it now. That's the front piece, right?" I gestured to my top.

"Yes, it's called the bodice. Now, here's the back of the bodice, see?"

I looked a little closer at all of the pieces, and they began to take shape before my eyes. A few didn't make sense, but I saw the general shape of the dress.

"What are these small pieces?"

Stacey picked them up and placed them along the neckline of the bodice. "It's called the interfacing for the neckline."

I raised my eyebrows. It wasn't going to be as difficult as I'd first thought.

Stacey pointed at the scooped neckline. "Now, we need to baste around the edge to keep it from stretching while we sew the pieces together. Get your needle, and thread it the way I showed you the other day."

I followed her instruction and sewed close to the edge of the bodice top with tiny deliberate stitches. When I looked at the clock, another hour had passed. "How's this?"

Stacey gave me the thumbs-up sign.

"I think I'm finished for today." I stretched and rubbed the lower part of my back for a moment, before folding the pattern pieces.

Stacey leaned against the table and crossed her arms. "So, am I right to believe you're taking the position here?"

I avoided her eyes for a moment. "Yes, but I don't think you realize how little I can do."

"How's that?" Stacey shifted her head to one side.

"Well, I just don't know if I can do all of this like you do it."

Stacey smiled at me. "I think you're capable of so much. Look how far you've come. I bet a month ago you would've thrown that pincushion."

I looked away. She had noticed.

Stacey straightened. "Whatever you were before, you're a new person now. I can see such a difference in you, and I want you to recognize it. Don't limit yourself by old standards. You can reach for the stars if you want."

I bit my lip and nodded. Maybe.

"Then it's settled, and you can start here as soon as possible. Let me talk to Ms. Dara. Maybe by next Wednesday you can transfer here. She has those two new ladies to replace your work load in the general store."

I put away the fabric and grinned. "I guess I'll see you soon."

Amazing Grace jumped to my lips. *Better hurry to meet Kyle and Willa.* Too bad Willa hadn't agreed to meet me at the shop. I breathed in slow and steady. Or at least tried. Mr. Carrick had promised paranoia was normal. But I had gone way past the allotted timeframe for withdrawal symptoms.

I tiptoed to the edge of the shop. "Just start walking."

Too many weird coincidences had proved I wasn't dealing with paranoia anymore. Something was going on. And I didn't like it.

42
Brooke

I couldn't think of a better thing to do than eat homemade ice cream with my two best buds on such a hot day.

"Hey, guess what?" Kyle stared at me.

"What?" I said through a mouthful of strawberry ice cream.

"I can start going to town once a week."

"What do you mean?"

"Once you reach certain goals, you get more leeway. I thought I'd check it out next Tuesday. It's my day off."

I shrugged. "Sounds fun."

"Too bad you can't go too."

"It's okay. I like staying right here."

"Well, I'll be glad to get a glimpse of something different." Kyle dipped his spoon into my bowl of ice cream.

Willa smacked his spoon with her fork.

"Hey, that is not your ice cream, so leave me alone." Kyle glared at her and took another spoonful. I didn't mind.

Willa clanked her fork against the edge of her plate as she set it down. "Whatever. About town. I've been doing that for a while. Trust me, it's nothing special."

"Yeah, no casino. That would definitely make it not your kind of place."

Willa blustered at his words. "You…"

"I'm sorry. That was terrible."

Willa crossed her arms and glared at him. "I haven't brought up *your* past. How dare you say that about mine?"

"Please forgive me. It slipped out, and it was wrong." Kyle squinted.

Willa huffed and looked away.

I grasped for anything to break the accumulated tension. "Guys, please don't start World War Three."

Kyle put his hands together as if to pray—or beg forgiveness. "I'm sorry. Look, I'll buy you some of your favorite pie if you forgive me."

Willa narrowed her eyes for a brief second. "Okay."

I tried to steer the conversation back to Kyle's trip. "So what's the first thing you're going to do?"

"I heard there was a great hiking trail along some waterfalls. I'm going to check it out."

"Waterfalls? Here in Connecticut?" Cool. "Now I'm interested."

"I saw a pamphlet down at the train depot. Looks good." Kyle pushed back his chair. "Okay, Willa, about that pie. What kind do you want?"

"Key lime."

Kyle headed to the counter.

I placed my hand on Willa's arm. "I'm sure he didn't mean anything by what he said. You two just can't get along, can you?"

Willa pursed her lips then threw her hands up in the air. "Well, I don't care as long as you're happy."

"What do you mean?"

"Come on. It's obvious you two have something going

on, something more than friendship."

I drew closer to Willa and lowered my voice. "Please don't say anything to anyone. I know the rules, and I plan to keep them until I'm out of here."

"Yeah, I believe yah. You've become such a little angel." Her words dripped with sarcasm.

"It's true." I sat back and dropped my bowl on the table.

"Oh, I believe you." Willa played with the corner of her napkin. "I just mean you've turned into such a respectable person so quick, and it's hard for most people to keep it up at first."

"I will." I meant it.

Kyle returned and dropped the pie in front of Willa. "There you go." He pushed past her to get into his seat. His blond hair brushed his eyebrows, creating a slight wave to one side.

"Please finish this for me." I gave the remainder of the ice cream to him.

He scooped some onto his spoon. "So what are we doing this afternoon?"

"I have to work. Someone at the hotel called in sick, so I have to cover her shift." Willa took a bite of her pie.

"Great. Now we have to come up with another chaperone."

I couldn't think of anyone other than the gardener, and I doubted he'd do it again, even if he was working on a Saturday. I tossed my hair over my shoulder and sat back. Even if I did think of anyone else, I didn't want to take the chance someone would catch on to the feelings I tried to hide. Best policy … keep things simple. "Well, I guess we'll spend the day apart."

Kyle raised his hands and scowled at Willa. "What time do you have to work?"

Willa looked for the hand-wound clock on the wall of the tea shop. "In about forty-five minutes. But I need to run home first, so I have to leave here in a half hour."

"Then let's go. I was hoping we could spend some time at the farm, especially since Brooke hasn't…"

I kicked him under the table. Had he forgotten we never made it to the farm when we'd told Willa we were going there?

He winced. "She hasn't seen the new piglets."

Good recovery. I took a deep breath and smiled. "That would've been fun." I sounded a little unsure to my own ears, making the comment almost a question.

"Well, I'm not going there. It's nasty." Willa moved away from the table, allowing Kyle to shift from his tight spot. "So where are we off to, then?"

"What about the pond behind the blacksmith's shop?" Kyle pushed his hands into his pockets.

"Sure." Nature had become my favorite thing.

Willa didn't mind either.

We left the tea shop. Kyle stopped in midstride and waited for me to catch up to him. "Have you ever been there?"

"No."

"Well, you're going to love it. You'll get a chance to see the log cabin too. It's on the way."

"What log cabin?"

"We've been working on a new exhibit. It's a pioneer cabin fashioned after the ones built around seventeen-forty."

"All that you do never ceases to amaze me. How long have you been working on it?" I studied his profile.

"A few months now, but I don't get out there as often as I'd like. The extra volunteer hours helped to work off those demerits you gave me." He teased me.

I rolled my eyes.

We rounded a corner, and I stopped. Up on a slight hill, surrounded by trees on three sides, a little log cabin sat in harmony with the landscape. We approached it.

Kyle leaned into the doorway. "Just think, an entire family lived in this space with as many as eight children."

My mouth fell open. I studied the interior, not much larger than my room at home. I peered through the wide cracks between the logs at Willa, who lounged on one of the tree stumps in front of the cabin. "Wow. It shows you how blessed we are with our comfortable homes."

"In two weeks, we can start working on chinking between the logs, but the center is still researching the best and most authentic way to do it."

I rubbed one of the shaved logs.

"We better get going." Kyle stepped through the doorway.

We left the cabin and climbed the hill, following the dirt path. Ducks quacked somewhere close by. The sheer number of them astounded me as they littered the side of the pond. They squabbled with each other in their tight quarters.

"See that bench over there?" Kyle directed us to it.

I sat down and looked around the pond and beyond to the fields in the distance. A good portion of the center showed from there. "Look at the view." A breeze blew the trees around the pond, cooling the air. "Every time you show me a new place, I love it there even more."

"Yeah, the Massey family had a piece of paradise, didn't they? I would've held on to this land instead of donating it." Kyle looked up into the trees.

Willa meandered to the edge of the pond, out of earshot. For once, she didn't hang over us and watch our every move. Did she believe me about the conversation we'd had while Kyle was getting her pie? Did she trust me more?

"Kyle, you know every nook and cranny of this place."

"I told you, I like to explore, to be alone … well, at least until you arrived." His expression changed, became unreadable.

"Is it a good change for you?"

"Not wanting to be alone? Uh huh." He didn't look at me.

Goose bumps prickled my arms. He was saying one thing, but his body language another. Why had he shut down all of a sudden? I peered over the pond. A small amount of water filtered out and flowed under a bridge near Willa. When I returned my gaze to him, his intent stare made me gulp. "What?"

He furrowed his brows. "Nothing. There's just been something—" He stopped in midsentence. "Never mind."

"What are you thinking about? You can tell me." I played with a tendril of hair and waited, giving him time to process his thoughts.

"Do you really think I'm going to tell you all of my deep, dark secrets?" Kyle's smile didn't reach his eyes, and his attempt at lightening the air between us fell flat.

"I hope you want to."

He looked down at the ducks. "Someday."

He left the bench in one swift movement. It caught me off guard. "We better get Willa back to work."

I stood up. What had just happened? "Okay." I laid my hand on his arm. "What is it, Kyle?"

His serious expression bothered me.

"I don't want to talk about it, okay?" His tone stopped me.

We crossed the bridge and I paused for a brief second, not taking in the view. Unease infiltrated my thoughts.

Something I couldn't quite put my finger on tried to click in the back of my mind.

"Come on, ladies." Kyle ushered us back to the trail.

What had I said to upset him? It hurt that he didn't want to share with me.

Willa walked in front of us as I grabbed his arm and halted him. "Really, what's going on?"

He bent down and pulled a tall piece of grass free from its root, running it across his palm. "It's nothing. I just have a lot on my mind right now. I thought we would have more time, but it's a long story and I don't want to go into it now. You're complicating things for me…"

"Okay." I wasn't about to keep at him when he didn't want to. Yet a little more hurt creeped in.

We walked back to town in silence. His normal light mood didn't return.

At the train depot, Kyle waved to us. His long strides ate up the ground as he hurried away from me. "See you tomorrow at church."

"See you later." My farewell didn't reach him as he disappeared around the corner.

I fell into step beside Willa. "Hey, do you need help with anything before you go to work?"

"Nah, I'll see you later." Willa didn't give me a chance to respond.

I stood uncertain for a moment and raised my hands. So much for a day of relaxation with my friends. And, unlike Kyle, I didn't want to be alone right then.

43

Brooke

The azure stone in my hand glistened, but it still didn't seem right for me to have it. But why? It was the bluest of blues, and I loved it. "Thank you so much, Mr. Carrick. I'm sure someone is missing it."

"Well, I gave them plenty of time to retrieve it. With all the tourists who visit every day, it's no wonder it wasn't claimed." He set a folder down on his desk and turned to push the window open more. "Let's talk about your week."

It gnawed at me to have to keep Kyle a secret. He'd become such a big part of my life, and the deceit of leaving him out of my conversations with Mr. Carrick rankled. But what choice did I have? My new job was a much safer topic to discuss. "I'm getting ready to start working at the tailor shop." I smiled but crossed my arms.

"Am I detecting some apprehension?"

I looked down at my feet. "I don't know. I want to do it, but…"

When I didn't continue, he shifted in his seat. "Do you feel unworthy of the position?"

Wow, he'd understood immediately. I shrugged. "Well, you know how hard it is when so much is expected of you. I don't know if I can do it."

"Is it possible that your fear is related to past experiences with your father?"

The question stopped me in mid-thought. As I tilted my head to the side, I stayed silent for a moment. I wanted to draw up my knees against my chest. "You think that's why I'm scared?"

"Your relationship with him has formed a lot of your decision-making. It's important you don't base your emotions on his views of you anymore. I believe you can do this."

The tears that stung my eyes threatened to spill down my face. "Thanks, Mr. Carrick."

His voice grew a little quieter. "Remember, it's God's strength you're depending on."

"I want to do that ... but I don't know how."

"Let go of all the things you're trying to do on your own. Give it to the Lord. Ask Him to make you who He wants you to be."

I had been on my own for so long, leaning on God remained a difficult concept to grasp. I took a deep breath. "I'll try."

When I left, a quiet settled within me. It would be nice to get rid of the load of worry that plagued me about the new job. *God, help me.* I had only six days left until I switched from the general store to the shop.

I clocked into work and went to clean the fresh beverage area.

Dara called me. "Hey, can you show Martie and Lauren how to give those drink machines a deep cleaning tonight after the store closes?"

"Who?"

"The two new women." Dara didn't look at me as she folded an apron and returned it to a shelf.

"Oh, sure." Would they listen?

The store wasn't busy. I had the entire place sparkling by closing. It took extra time to disassemble the machines and show Martie and Lauren the way to clean them, but I enjoyed teaching the women.

The fresh air blew in my face as I returned to the boarding house. Like the day at the pond. Kyle had flipped from happy to moody so fast I hadn't known what to think that day. Why had he acted so out of character, and why had he avoided me since that day? It hurt a little that he didn't trust me enough to talk about whatever bothered him.

Anna worked at her usual spot in the kitchen. I put on an apron and gathered the list of ingredients for dinner.

Maybe I should corner him. I had to know if I'd offended him somehow.

Willa pranced into the kitchen. "Hey, I'm here."

I hated to ask her once again to spend her free time babysitting, but I knew of no other way. Would it put her in a bad mood too? "Can I talk to you for a minute?"

"Sure."

I turned to Anna. "I promise we'll be right back."

Willa followed me to the living room.

"Let me guess, you need me to go with you and Kyle somewhere. You know it's getting old always watching you two, especially when I don't have anyone I can sneak around with."

As soon as Willa laughed, I thanked the Lord. "I'm sorry, but I can't rely on anyone but you. I'll make it up to you. Kyle hasn't talked to me for three days, and I'm worried about him. Please, can you help?"

"I guess. There's nothing else to do around here anyway. When are yah going to go out?"

"After dinner. We can try the park first, but…" I

stopped speaking for a moment and winced. "…we might have to go to the farm to find him."

Willa grumbled. "If I step in one pile of dung—"

I'd pay dearly. Was it worth the chance?

44
Brooke

*M*en. Women were supposed to be the moody ones, not them. Kyle had to tell me what had been troubling him. I didn't wait to see if Willa kept up or not as I checked the park for Kyle.

Willa looked around the park. "You know I don't want to go to the farm."

"I know, but Kyle likes to work there when he's upset. He's not here at the park, so he has to be there."

At the end of town, we turned down Robin Lane to the farm, and I walked slower to stay with Willa, who dragged her feet. "Come on, Willa."

"Hey, if I'm going down there, you have to do it at my pace."

Argh. Why couldn't anyone do it my way for once?

Over a hill, a large group of trees set in neat rows led off the main road.

"Oh, look, the orchard you saw with him." Willa's words dripped with sarcasm.

I bit my lips together. She knew me too well, but I wasn't about to confirm her suspicions.

As we rounded the bend at the edge of the orchard, the farm came into view. The old farmhouse, with many

Erin Unger

additions, progressed in age from left to right. The perfect pastoral scene. No wonder Kyle found peace there. Sheep were huddled together in a small fenced area by the barn. A cow mooed as it hung its head over a paddock gate. The city girl part of me disappeared a little more each day. Country had so many advantages to a peaceful state of mind.

"Wait here and I'll check the house." I left Willa by the front gate and tramped up the steps. The kitchen looked much like the one at the boarding house, but I didn't have time to ponder the history of it.

"Kyle, are you in here?" No answer. I returned to the front porch. Several outbuildings dotted the yard, and I looked through them one by one. Not there.

I held a finger up to Willa. "I'll be right back. Let me check the barn."

"Don't worry. I'll come and get you if I see anyone coming," Willa called after me.

I gave a thumbs-up signal and headed to the barn, where I should've looked first.

"Kyle, are you there?" The darkness of the barn enveloped me, and a chill ran through my shoulders. Where had the fear come from all of a sudden? I creeped down the main corridor between the stables. Another section at the other end had a separate entrance somewhere. "Kyle?"

I hesitated at the door and took a timid step. Darkness dropped around me even more. Two horses stuck their heads over the doors of their stalls, and one of them sniffed the air in my direction.

A whisper moved a strand of my hair with the exhaling of the voice. "What?"

I let out a blood-curdling scream that ricocheted off the walls. The horses whinnied and jerked. My heart pounded like a rock band in full swing as I jumped sideways.

"Brooke, it's just me."

Kyle reached for my hand, but I grabbed my chest.

Willa rounded the corner in record speed. "Why are you screamin'?"

Willa's foot landed in a fresh pile of horse dung. She looked down then back at Kyle and me and fumed. "You have got to be kidding. This is *exactly* why I didn't want to come out here with you. Look at my boot." She glared. "Now, tell me what's going on."

"Sorry. Kyle startled me, that's all."

"Don't scare me like that, Brooke." Willa pointed a bony finger at Kyle. "And you, mister, just watch it. You better not be harassing her."

He pressed his hand to his mouth.

"Tell him whatever you need to say, and let's get out of here…" Lifting her skirts, Willa stamped off, wiping her foot as she went. The rest of her remark was lost as she hurried out of the barn.

I would have to pay a dear price for making Willa come to the farm as it was. But at least she hadn't insisted on leaving the very minute after the boot incident.

Kyle's full attention returned to me once Willa disappeared. "What are you doing out here?"

Dive in or take it slow? "I wanted to talk to you."

For the first time, I noticed a leather strap in his hand. "What are you doing?"

His eyes moved down to the strap. "Fixing this. It broke earlier today."

I didn't give him a chance to say more. "Look, I do respect your privacy and I don't want to bother you, but what's going on? I haven't seen you in days. Did I do something wrong?"

Kyle buckled under my scrutiny. As he tossed his hair out of his eyes, he stepped closer to me. "I missed you, too, and no, you didn't. It's just…" He paused. "I've been working on something, and I didn't want to get you involved."

"What is it?" I leaned against the side of a stall.

He paced, rubbing his hand through the back of his hair. "It's something I need to deal with on my own."

Interesting. "Okay, but you can talk to me about it."

"Brooke…" Kyle raised a hand then lowered it. He didn't seem to know what he wanted to say, but then he looked me hard in the eyes. "No other man around here is talking to you or bothering you, are they?"

"What's that supposed to mean? You know I have guy friends here."

He looked around, then drew dangerously close to me. "Stay away from them, okay?"

I backed up and tightened my shoulders. "Why? I don't like the aggressive way you're acting. I've never shown partiality to anyone but you, so calm down."

"I'm sorry." His shoulders hunched. "It's just… Forgive me?"

I kept my distance. "Of course."

"Promise me you'll listen."

"You know I can't be alone with the opposite gender, so you have nothing to worry about." What was he being so possessive about all the sudden?

I changed the subject fast. Why aggravate his temper again? The necklace Mr. Carrick had returned to me warmed in my palm as I held it out to him. "Look, I got the necklace."

"Yeah, that's nice." He didn't look at it but focused on the strap in his hand.

Ouch. He didn't care. "Well, I guess I better go."

"Let me put everything away, and I'll walk you home."

The sudden need for distance from him became tangible. I backed away and pointed behind me. "It's okay. Willa's just outside the barn."

"It's fine. Just give me a minute." His tone was back to its normal pitch. He wound the strap around his arm. "Could you grab that toolbox for me?"

"Sure, here you go." In the back room, he took the box from me and set it on a shelf.

The smell of oil reached my nostrils, reminding me of the mechanic shop down the street from my childhood home.

Kyle pulled the door closed but left the window open.

Willa came out of nowhere. "The farmer's on his way over."

Another worker I'd never met entered the barn. The farmer's smile didn't show any signs of suspicion. "Hey, how's it going?"

"I finished fixing that lead rope for you." Kyle talked with him for a moment, then caught up to me and Willa as we meandered in the direction of town.

"So what are we doing tonight?"

The tone in his voice lightened, but I sensed his edginess still. "We could go to the train depot to play some darts."

"Sounds good to me." Kyle's gait matched my own.

His split personality act hit me hard in the stomach. What was changing him?

45
Brooke

Every time something good happened to me, two bad things drop-kicked me a second later. Like Kyle and his personality alteration. Like dealing with the letter Dad had sent. Three months of rehab had been like a yo-yo. It mirrored my sewing at the shop that day. For every two stitches I jabbed into the material, I had to fix one of them. I couldn't concentrate. I sulked, hunching my back. "I *cannot* get this right."

Stacey came to my rescue. "Maybe you should save that project for another time. Here, let's work on this." She handed me a pile of stockings and socks. "It doesn't really matter if the stitches are even on these."

She demonstrated how to keep the material from bunching too much at the toe, and I went to work on them.

As the pile of darned socks grew, I thanked God I worked there. I wouldn't trade a bad day at the tailor shop for a good day at the store. I set the last stocking in my lap and looked around the sunny yellow room. It'd been weeks since I'd begun working with Stacey, and I grew to love her—and the job—more each day.

I glanced at the mannequin with the deep purple dress I'd started weeks earlier. The hem needed to be sewn. But we were waiting for special lace to arrive for the final touches. What an accomplishment to see it almost finished. All the seams hung straight and were double-stitched for sturdiness. Whoever had ordered it would love it. If only I didn't have to hand it over. I really wanted it.

"Wow. You're done with those already?" Stacey joined me. The pile of socks began to topple as she grabbed it.

The chair squeaked as I stood and stretched.

Shoving the socks into a basket, Stacey tossed it onto the corner of a shelf. "The lace for that dress arrives at the general store tomorrow."

Awesome. "I was just thinking about that."

Stacey shuffled around the shop. "The gown looks great. See, I knew you were meant to do this."

I turned away to hide my warm cheeks.

"Why don't you take a quick break? You can work on some handkerchiefs when you get back."

I closed the door behind me a moment later and sauntered over to a bench. Dad's letter. It lay abandoned in my desk drawer since a while ago, but I needed to write him too. Mr. Carrick would agree I needed to. Besides, wasn't the point of therapy to accept what we couldn't change? To forgive those who'd hurt us? Not responding had been on purpose. I had stayed angry at him. But I needed to let it all go.

Yes, I'd write him. He needed to know about a lot of things. Mr. Carrick had reminded me at our last session that I needed to repair my past mistakes. But did I really want to tell Dad about all of the times I had stolen from him? What about all the nights of defiance I'd spent staying out until dawn? I had to ask forgiveness for all of it. A lump formed in my stomach—hard and painful. It had to be done. And family sessions had to start soon … if Dad and the grandparents made an effort to come.

I took a quick walk around the block to the small garden behind one of the historical homes while I considered what to say. There were always people everywhere. As I passed a few guys I often saw around, they slowed.

"Hey, how's it going?"

Eric.

"Umm, fine. And you?"

He nodded and smiled. "Good."

I got a couple waves from the other guys. Sam from Daisy Cakes fiddled with some type of tool I didn't recognize and made a comment I couldn't hear to one of the others in the group. Richard seemed distracted and didn't say a word to me. Oh, well. He might be having a bad day.

Eric passed me, spun around, and took a few backward steps. His mouth quirked to the side. "See you around."

Dare I say how much I was beginning to like getting to know more of the residents?

Back at the shop, I closed the door, my back resting against it. "Ms. Stacey, do you mind if I leave a little early today? I only have thirty minutes left before quitting time anyway."

Stacey looked at the clock. "Sure, but tomorrow you might have to stay a little longer."

"Thanks." I put away my sewing supplies and left.

I waved at Mr. Carrick, who lounged at one of the café tables outside the tea shop, but kept walking. My mind worked over what to write. Hard stuff, for sure. Maybe it would be easier if I wasn't alone. But that time of day, Willa worked or sat in therapy.

The door to the boarding house swung open as three

women hurried out, deep in conversation, and I caught it before it slammed shut. No one stopped me as I glided up the stairs to my room.

At my desk, I looked through the drawers for some paper and a pen, and began to write.

The sight of my sins on paper cut like a dull blade. That other person I'd been seemed so distant until I had to put it in words. I looked to the ceiling for a moment. "Thank you, Lord, for changing me."

I sat still and contemplated my future. What came after I left the center? But I didn't want a life outside its walls. Was that part of the fear of returning to the world? One thing remained certain—I wasn't going back to Dad's house, where it would be easy to fall back into my old routine.

I tapped the pen on the desk. I had plenty of time to figure out things. It'd been weeks since I'd decided to pay for rehab by staying to work, and the added time at the center would help decide my future course.

As I folded the papers and stuffed them into an envelope, Anna called me. I put extra stamps on it and dropped it in my pocket.

"I'll be right down," I yelled loud enough for her to hear.

I scuffled down the stairs and wandered into the kitchen, where Anna seemed to live. No housemother. "Ms. Anna?"

"I'm in the sitting room."

That room I had never ventured into before. Its pink floral wallpaper may have been authentic, but its gaudy print revolted me. "Yes?"

Dara sat on the settee. "Hello, please have a seat with us." She smiled and gestured to the chair across from her. A smile showed in her eyes. "I've had a few conversations with Ms. Anna, and I've heard great things about your progress this month."

I returned her smile but with less vigor. Dara seldom came to the boarding house.

"I can see you're wondering why I'm here. Well, I've been talking with Mr. Carrick, and he thinks you're ready to be a guide."

My eyebrows shot up as I sat. "Me?"

Dara nodded and smoothed her red skirt. "So let me tell you about it."

She explained my new role and talked about the requirements for it. "You should be very well versed on it, since you've had Willa these three months. And the best part is you don't need a guide anymore."

I blinked. My best friend would finally be free of me. But did I have the control they seemed sure I possessed? Kyle had remained an unknown to them.

"So, we have a new lady coming in two days. She'll be sharing a room with you."

"Whoa. What about Willa?" There wasn't an extra bed for anyone in our room.

"Her time in rehabilitation is almost finished. She'll be moving into the seniors' boarding house until she's fulfilled her obligations here."

Oh, no. I needed Willa. How would I manage without her? A tear stung my eye. I should be ecstatic, not upset.

Dara watched me closely. "It's okay. This is a good change." She reached for my arm. "Don't worry, we're all here to help you."

I clutched her hand.

"There, there, don't worry." Anna smiled.

I nodded and tried to relax. "Let me know what you need me to do."

When I left, I headed straight back to my room.

Why hadn't I considered that Willa would be leaving the center someday?

I scrunched into a ball on my bed. The tears I'd held in began to spill down my cheeks. But I was acting ridiculous. I'd have more freedom. And Willa still had three months to work—but she wouldn't be there every night for me.

"I'm not ready." Maybe I had a chance that Willa would hear me out and decide to stay there.

I stayed that way for a long time.

Willa flew into the room. "Hi." She stopped in mid-stride when she saw me in my bed. "What happened?"

"I'm sure you already know." Thank goodness the tears had stopped an hour ago.

Willa scratched her head then nodded. "Is this because I'm moving out? I thought you'd be thrilled. No more sarcastic comments, no more griping when you want to stay up at night."

I rolled my eyes and sat up. "Well, there's that."

"So what's the problem?" Willa's hands rested on her hips.

"I just don't think I'm ready for this yet."

"You've been here three months. You're ready." She sat down beside me. "Change is always hard, but you'll be fine. I promise to come over and harass you all the time."

I couldn't help but smile. I had to stop leaning on others for my emotional needs. And didn't the Bible say God would always be there? I wasn't alone.

"Besides, I'll only be down the street from here, like two or three blocks away." Willa looked into my eyes and grinned. "Now I'm starving, so let's go eat." Willa pulled me off my bed. "Later you can help me pack, since you owe me for the barn fiasco."

I laughed. "I knew you would get me back. I'll be right down. Just give me a minute."

With Willa gone, I hurried to straighten my crumpled dress and disheveled hair. They were right. I had to take the next step—on my own. Besides, I had a chance to help someone else.

46

Brooke

How had I gotten lassoed into moving Willa's stuff when I'd rather hogtie her to her old bed?

"What did you put in this box?" I dropped it on the bed of Willa's new room.

"Stop your whining." Willa set down a basket full of toiletries and spun around in the room. "Isn't it great? It's my own little studio apartment."

I eyed the spacious room. "I love it. You have a kitchenette and a bathroom to yourself. You're so lucky." The apartment emulated the historical feel of the center. The quilt on Willa's bed featured a bright red star. I'd like to have one like it. Perhaps Stacey had a pattern for the design.

"And someday, you'll have the same thing." Willa tromped to the tiny kitchen and placed both hands on the butcher-block table. "Although I'll say it's going to be hard getting used to cooking on a real stove. I'll probably just eat at the boarding house most of the time."

We emptied the boxes and hung up her clothes.

Willa placed some items on a shelf over her bed. "When is your new roomy coming?"

"Tomorrow. But she's going to the detox center first.

I have to spend the evening cleaning our… I mean my room before she comes, so I better get going."

I started to cross the room to the door, but Willa stopped me. She pursed her lips. "Look, I'm not very good at saying the right things, but I want you to know how great you are. You've been the bestest friend I've ever had."

Was she going to cry? Not Willa. I gave her a big hug and flashed a cheesy grin. "Ditto, friend. Here's to a new life for both of us. Got to go. Kyle's supposed to meet me at the tea shop for dinner."

I sauntered down the sidewalk, pulling at my bonnet ribbons, which lay limp against my shoulders. Kyle. Was he becoming jealous of my other friends? He hadn't liked Willa since I met them.

Fried chicken filled the room with its welcoming scent. I studied the menu on the wall. Why even bother to look at it? I ate there often enough to have it memorized.

I jumped when someone patted on my shoulder.

"Hey." Kyle stood too close, as usual.

"You've got to stop scaring me like that," I snapped. Oops. If I didn't like his mood swings, I'd better cut it out myself.

"Sorry." He moved away and put his hands in his pockets. "I didn't mean to. I thought the bell over the door would have clued you in that I was here."

"Sorry—for overreacting." I winced. "Forgive me? I must've been concentrating too hard to hear it."

"It's okay. Want me to get us a table?"

"Yes."

Kyle's retreating form gave me pause.

"Ms. Daisy, would you mind being our chaperone while we're here?" I asked the tea shop lady.

"Of course not." Ms. Daisy was in her typical cheery

mood.

"Thanks." My voice sounded dull and flat to my own ears.

At the table, Kyle studied me. "What's up with the glum mood?"

"Oh, I don't know." That wasn't true. Maybe it was safer to turn my apprehension to a different subject. "I helped Willa move into her new apartment and … it's hard to think she'll be gone soon."

It wouldn't be long before Kyle moved on too. I hung my head.

"What now?"

"It's going to be you soon, too, isn't it?"

He leaned back, watching me for a moment. "I'm not going anywhere without you. Besides, my roommate back home already rented out my room. And there's plenty of work here at the center. I still have to pay off my debt to this place. So I'll be around."

I looked sideways.

"What else is bothering you?" He stared at me, but I refused to look into his eyes. "You're upset about something else, aren't you?"

I shrugged.

"It's about the conversation at the barn, isn't it?"

Now I looked at him. Would he start making excuses? "You haven't been yourself lately."

"I know." He braced his hands against the table. "I told you I was sorry. Can we just let it go, please? I promise I won't start stalking you because of your male friends."

His attempt at a joke only managed to unsettle me more. Stalking? It wasn't a word to use loosely.

The touch of his hand brought my eyes up to his. I searched for Daisy to see if the gesture had gone unnoticed. I spoke through gritted teeth. "Kyle, don't get me in trouble."

"I'll stop when you say everything's okay."

I wanted his playful mood and apology to make things right again. But could it? I sighed. "Fine."

When he removed his hand from mine, he sat forward. "It's going to be okay. I'll make it up to you."

"And how will you do that?" My heart skipped a beat at the intent look in his eyes.

"You'll see."

I tried to lower the level of emotion streaming through me. The quickening of my heart contradicted my common sense. What a hold he had on me.

What did he have in mind?

The waitress brought our dinner, but I wasn't hungry anymore. I took a few bites of chicken and pushed my potatoes around with my fork.

Kyle's knife and fork clanked against the plate as he set them down and crossed his arms. "What can I do to cheer you up? I can't stand seeing you like this. We could go back to my favorite spot."

"No way."

He laughed. "Right, right." He made me squirm under his scrutiny. "Why don't we work in the garden? I think some of the beans are ready to be picked."

"If only I had the time."

"You can always make time. What's more important than spending the evening with me?" His quirky smile melted my bad mood some.

I contemplated it. I hadn't told him about my new assignment. "Guess what? Ms. Dara asked me to guide the new lady who's arriving tomorrow. I need to clean my room and write a list of all the things I have to show her." Willa had created most of the mess in our room when she started throwing her unwanted papers and belongings off her bed and onto the floor earlier that afternoon. "You wouldn't believe the mess Willa left."

"Good for you. That's not going to take long. I'll help you with the list. Hold on, I'll be right back." He jumped up and returned with an empty paper bag in his hands. He whipped a pen out of his waistcoat pocket. "Now, what to do first?"

I grinned. "Kitchen duty."

Kyle printed on the bag.

"Help with her new clothes." I grimaced at the sour memory of my first attempt to dress in the primitive clothing.

He looked at me for a moment then wrote 'help with clothes'.

"And laundry schedules."

"Yeah, the dreaded laundry day." He shook his head.

As we finished the list, I sipped my cup of tea. "Thank you for helping me."

"Hey, if I do this now, you'll spend the extra time with me."

Always plotting. Tsk, tsk. "Always an ulterior motive with you."

"So back to my original question. What do you want to do?" Kyle handed me the paper.

I remembered the book on my desktop. Would he enjoy it as much as me? Most guys, in my experience, didn't like reading. "Well, I want to start this new book. We can read it together."

"What's it about?"

"Well … it's a suspense novel." True statement … kind of.

He didn't seem so keen on the idea.

"Well, it's also a romance. But it was recommended to me by some of the women here."

"No. I heard about that book." He crossed his arms and glared at me.

"Fine." I crossed my arms too. "You shouldn't be so judgmental about something you've never done."

"I don't even read instruction manuals when I have to assemble things." He challenged me with his eyes.

"Come on, please." I begged.

He lifted his chin.

"I'll read the first chapter to you. Then, if you don't like it, I'll put it away, and you'll never hear another word about it."

Kyle moved his head side to side, as if weighing his options. "Well, it'd be easier to get a chaperone."

"Yeah, we can read at the train depot. There're always lots of people there."

"The ticket master might watch us since he won't have to do anything but keep an eye from his station."

"Great." I jumped up from the table. "I'll be right back with the book. I'll meet you over there."

One more downside to not having a guide anymore … walking alone.

47

Sarge

For once, none of Sarge's work crew had irked him all day. And no one had forced him to fake happiness or interest. He whistled as he headed toward the train station. And he'd had a nice dinner too.

The beauty on the train loading dock caught his eye and he stopped in his tracks. The day just got even better. There she was. Every time he saw Brooke, her beauty astounded him. She searched the crowd right at the edge of the platform, which rose several feet above the ground. He checked around, and then dared to touch the hem of her long skirt. So soft.

She walked into the crowd.

He sighed, moved closer to the station's entrance, and advanced to the edge of the platform, where she stayed in view. She bent to wipe off some of the seats lined along the center of the station, and then planted herself in one of them.

He smiled at her earnest study of the busyness around her. Her awareness of others mirrored yet another similarity she shared with him. When he got near her, he became a different man. His reticent personality morphed into the person he really wanted to be.

Erin Unger

The lowering sun shone through her hair and illuminated the edges of it. Almost as if she wore a halo. Very fitting. Maybe she'd be the one to save him from himself.

48
Brooke

Where was Kyle? The buzz of workers loading and unloading boxes of inventory and supplies for the center hummed around me as I waited for him.

I dusted the seats once more. The volume around there hit a record high. We might have to pick another place, or Kyle wouldn't be able to hear me over it. One particular cart squealed as its wheels turned, but the worker didn't seem to notice its objection to the heavy weight on it.

"Okay, let's get this over."

I startled at the sound of his voice. Jumpiness. Another withdrawal symptom which didn't want to go away.

"I wish you'd stop being so edgy." He sat down and motioned toward a man at the ticket booth, who raised his hand at us.

I nodded in his direction, and then held the book up for Kyle to see the cover. "See. It really looks good."

Kyle slouched down in the chair.

When I looked up, I caught the ticket master's movement. He motioned with his fingers, and I jabbed Kyle in the ribs to get his attention. "Look."

Kyle watched the guy for a moment. With a pouty face, he scooted a foot further away from me and waited to see if the change in his position was satisfactory.

The man gave a thumbs-up sign and turned away from us.

I opened the book and rubbed the binding in the center. "Can you hear me over all the noise?" As if on cue, one of the wagons pulled away and the depot grew quieter. "That's better."

"We're going to do something else if I hate it, okay?" Kyle played with the edges of his waistcoat.

"Fine. But I can't be out too long." I began to read.

As I neared the end of the chapter, I glanced over at Kyle, who seemed to be hanging on every word. The dramatic first pages drew me into the story also. I read the last sentence and set the book in my lap, my thumb marking my place. "So … what did you think?"

"Hmm, it's okay."

"Just okay? You're engulfed in the story line already. Want to keep going or should I put it away?"

"No, read a little more."

He looked like he was trying to hide his interest. But not good enough. I smirked. "Okay, but tell me when to stop."

As the story unfolded, Kyle spread out his legs. He relaxed and listened. But the whole time he watched me. I tried not to squirm.

When he touched the edge of my dress, which covered part of the seat between us, running the soft material between his fingers, I lost my place a few times. The clearing of my throat stopped his movement. "It's really hard to concentrate when you do that."

"What? I'm over here, and you're *way* over there."

I had to admit a sufficient distance lay between us, but it didn't make it any easier to think. I cleared my throat again. "I know, but it's distracting me."

That was the least it did to me.

He raised his eyebrows as he folded his hands behind his head. "Okay, keep reading."

I looked from the book, to him, and back to the book. It took me a moment to find my place and continue, but I managed to regain my earlier momentum.

The quiet and the darkness of the depot made me pause in midsentence. "What time is it?"

Kyle sat up and lowered his feet to the ground. "Umm, it's eight-thirty."

"I'd better head home. I'm going to miss devotions if I don't hurry."

I glanced at the book. "The story's good, isn't it?"

"I have to admit, as hard as it is for me," he joked, "it's interesting. You want to meet back here tomorrow night to get in a few more chapters?"

I laughed. "I'd love to, but it's going to take a few weeks before I can leave the new lady alone, so I don't know when we'll do it."

"Bring her along."

I paused. "Well, I don't think it would be a very good testimony to her if we do that."

"We can look like we're just friends. We have to do it for everyone else around us."

"We better not. Besides, we *are* just friends."

His eyes flashed. "Let me walk you back. We'll have to come up with a plan."

Kyle signaled to the ticket master as we left.

Workers meandered around, cleaning the storefronts and roadways on the way to the boarding house.

"I'll watch you till you get to your door." Kyle stopped a block from the boarding house and squeezed my shoulder as I turned to him.

"See you soon." I really didn't want to leave him

standing there. If only I had another hour to sit with him and bask in the comfort he created by being close.

His eyes held mine. I squirmed under the intensity of his expression. "See you."

I walked to the boarding house door and took a deep breath of the humid night air. Peace and contentment filled my veins. And I didn't need to take any drug to get them.

49
Brooke

Rehab stripped you of your dignity at the door. For good reason. To stop contraband from making its way into the center. But my new charge had pulled off the impossible for sure. She was high on something. *God, give me the strength to deal with her.* I sat across from the newcomer, whose stringy hair fell across one eye. When was the last time the woman had had a bath? "Here's a list of the chores, Autumn. Everyone has to help clean and cook. You'll have a schedule of your own."

"So tell me where you keep your secret stash." The pop of the woman's gum accentuated her words.

I looked at the young woman in grimy jeans, and raised an eyebrow. "Let me guess. You didn't come here on your own accord?"

"You know how it goes. I wanted to make someone happy, get them off my back about stuff, so I'm here."

"Well, there are no hiding places here."

Autumn looked at me and stammered.

"Oh, and by the way, you need to go get your uniforms from the tailor shop. Here's a map." I handed her a paper from the stack in my lap.

"Yeah, they said something about that. Please tell me

they're not like the one you're wearing."

I wanted to be offended and to laugh at the same time. It wasn't that long ago I'd had the same attitude. "Look, I've been in your shoes, and I know how hard this is, but you have to want this. It can't be for someone else. It has to be for you."

"Heard that one too." Autumn rolled her eyes and fidgeted.

"Why don't you get your clothes, and we'll finish talking later." I needed a break from the sarcastic ball of energy in front of me. It was pretty evident what addiction had brought Autumn to the center. Guiding turned out to be even harder than I'd anticipated. I reconsidered leaving her on her own. "I better go with you."

We headed to Stacey's tailor shop. Autumn fidgeted the whole way. "Got a smoke?"

"No, you know we can't smoke here."

She grew more agitated with each step. She fished in her pockets and over her clothes, but came up empty-handed. "I can't do this."

I studied her for a moment. The poor woman. I might not have been as desperate as her, but I understood the obsessive nature of addiction. One had fed off me for years. "I can see you're already getting shaky. You need to go to the clinic and take your meds as soon as we're done. It'll get better. Trust me."

Autumn shrugged but was silent.

I pulled the door open and waited for her to go in. "Hello, Ms. Stacey."

"Hello, ladies." She set her scissors down. "Boy, Brooke, I've missed you today. Can't wait until you get back."

A smile lit up her face, and I returned it. She needed me? "Autumn, this is my boss, Ms. Stacey. She tailors all of the uniforms we wear, and she makes clothing for the general store to sell."

"What's up?" Autumn nodded at my boss, her hands pressed firmly into her pockets. She shook her head to get a wayward strand of hair off her cheek, and then blew at it.

"It's really good to have you, Autumn. Let me get your dresses." Stacey headed to the small storage room where she hung up all finished pieces, and returned with her arms full.

Just like my first day out of detox.

"You're quite small, but these should work." She held up one to her. "I can always alter anything that doesn't fit."

"No way. You can't expect me to wear those." She crossed her arms.

"Well, it's policy, and I know you've been told by Mr. Carrick that in order to be here, you must wear them. It seems so strange right now, but you'll get used to it. Ask Brooke."

I took the clothing when Autumn refused to uncross her skinny limbs. It was all payback for my own attitude in the beginning—and I didn't like it one bit. "Let's walk back to our room. You need to get changed."

Autumn skulked out of the shop and followed at a distance.

I looked back to make sure she hadn't run away. When I passed Mr. Carrick along the road, he quirked his mouth. I wanted to laugh. Yeah, I got it.

Autumn hid in the bathroom. When she came out, I almost cackled out loud. She looked like an old plastic life-sized doll wearing a granny dress. Autumn held out the corset and looked at me with narrowed eyes, daring me to force her to wear it.

"Um, well, I guess you can put that in your dresser over there."

She threw it into one of the drawers.

I groaned but laughter bubbled to the surface. "You can stay in here until dinner if you want, but I have to go to work. Be in the kitchen by five." I paused at the door. "Oh, and don't leave the boarding house without me. At least not this first week."

I hurried to the general store, thanks to a note I found on my desk. My lace and some new material had arrived.

The brown paper that covered the bundles in my arms rustled as I headed down Main Street. Stacey would be glad to see that the material she'd ordered the previous week had come in. The load I carried shifted in my hands. It grew heavier as I went. Once on the side street, I stopped for a break. "This is ridiculous."

With all the work I'd grown accustomed to, why was I already out of breath? Maybe the unwieldy nature of the fabric bolts made me off-balance.

A high volume of tourists descended upon the center, trying to get their last vacation in before school started. Their bustle had become such a normal part of life that I barely noticed them anymore. But the quiet of the street was what drew my attention as I leaned against the fence. Activity everywhere else but here made me smile. A butterfly bumped into my cheek, and its soft flutter tickled.

I better get going. Once I redistributed the weight in my arms, I continued.

Out of the corner of my eye, a tall blond figure dashed away. How odd. Like he didn't want me to know he was there. "Hey, is that you, Kyle?"

No response.

I turned down the next street as fast as possible. One

of the smaller packages tumbled to the ground. "Kyle, what are you doing?"

He slowed and turned to me. "Oh, hey, how are you?"

I wasn't buying his nonchalant attitude. "I know you were watching me. Spill it. What are you up to? Why were you following me?"

He wouldn't look at me as he picked up the package on the ground. "It's just … well, I wanted to make sure you were safe."

"Safe from what?"

"Umm, that didn't come out right. I was just checking on you."

Red flags raised high. "Possessive boyfriends do that kind of thing, not rational men. And if you were only checking on me, why did you run?"

"It's not like that. I knew what you'd think if you saw me, and I was right." His hand went into his pocket. "I didn't mean any harm, I promise."

I took a deep breath. Hadn't I been afraid to walk alone for a long time? "Why wouldn't I be safe?"

As he drew closer to me, Kyle opened and shut his mouth.

I shook my head. "I can't trust you the way I used to, and I hate it."

"Please don't say that. If you only knew … with what happened to Jordan—"

"What are you talking about? What do you know?" The hair on the back of my neck stood up.

He raised his palms. "Don't get suspicious on me. You're taking everything I say out of context."

I pulled myself up straight. Well, as much as possible considering all the packages. "You started it."

"Well, I'm sorry." He stopped. "Boy, I've said that way too many times the past few weeks."

I smirked and bobbled the merchandise again.

Kyle took a few of the biggest bundles off the top and continued. "What do you want me to do? I'm just trying to look out for you and not in a weird crazy way. Please believe me."

"Okay. But you can make it up to me by going to the tailor shop with me." I let him off the hook. "What do you mean about Jordan?" Ice formed in my veins.

"Nothing. You know she left. Who knows what happened to her…"

"So you want to make sure it doesn't happen to me?" The conversation didn't sit well with me. Was he going to stonewall me again?

"You could say that."

Yep. He refused to answer no matter how hard I pushed. And I didn't dare try again.

50
Brooke

My roommate made sure I paid for her hard adjustment—in many ways—especially at night. I wanted to boot her myself. But then she wouldn't get the help she needed almost more than she needed to breathe. But my anger started eating at me the more tired I got.

If I thought I'd gotten a decent handle on it, everything with Autumn proved I hadn't completely received victory over it. Had I even figured out the root in all those talks with Mr. Carrick? "Why, God, do I get upset so easy?"

Mom leaving me. Dad not wanting me. Those were obvious. But what about all the times my many nannies had called me a horrible child and abandoned me? I had failed myself and them. And everyone left because of me. Anger stemmed from it all.

I'd never put the nannies into the equation. But they'd played a huge role in why I had grown into an angry person. I pressed my fingers over my eyes. "Thank you for revealing that to me, God. Help me to forgive them. Help me to stop being angry."

Exhaustion claimed my limbs. I sat at the garden and tried to finish my work there. The bench in the garden looked so inviting. I took a pan of beans I'd picked, headed toward it, and wiped my damp brow. Two weeks had passed since Autumn had arrived, and every night rang out with the girl's moans and cries. When she grew quiet for a few hours, it was short-lived. She'd wake me with screams from her night terrors. I almost fell asleep several times at work, and had a difficult time finishing a solid day's work.

Lord, please help Autumn. I dared not close my eyes during the prayer. God's mercy had brought me through. It could help her.

Perhaps I needed to go to Anna and see if they could do more for Autumn. I didn't want her to give up and leave before she had a chance to see her need for God. My eyes fluttered closed and I couldn't seem to open them in that brief moment. I prayed again before forcing myself to stand.

Someone's voice filtered into my mind. Had I fallen asleep? As I jerked my eyes open, the pan fell to the ground, spilling beans across the path. "Hmm?" I drew out the words in a half-asleep tone, but my bleary eyes refused to focus.

"Come on. Don't you have kitchen duty?" Willa's voice pulled me the rest of the way out of sleep.

"Hi. Boy, am I glad to see you." I wiped my eyes and willed my muscles to coordinate enough to pick up the beans.

Willa stooped and helped. "You look like death warmed over. Are you okay?"

"I don't think I've ever been this tired before. Not even when I first got here."

"Why? What's going on?"

I scooped up a handful of beans. "That new girl is a nightmare. I think I'm going to talk to Ms. Anna about moving her to her own room, at least for a little bit."

Willa patted my arm. "Let me help you in the kitchen tonight."

I was not about to argue. "Thanks."

We went to the kitchen, washed up the beans, and helped prepare dinner, but I worked very slow. Anna watched me.

She patted my back when I handed her the beans. "I can see the toll the new one is taking on you."

"Do you mind keeping an eye on her this evening for a bit? I need a little sleep, and then I think I can deal better." I didn't want to ask too much of her just yet.

"Sure. Why don't you go after you eat? Ms. Dara won't mind if you miss one devotional. I'll make sure."

"Do you think so? I can skip dinner and go as soon as the cooking is finished."

Anna nodded. "Where is Autumn now?"

"I think she had therapy after work and then an appointment for her withdrawal medication, but my brain won't let me remember." I wiped my eyes.

"Not to worry, I'll take care of things. Hurry so you can go."

I wanted to throw my arms around her. I placed a kiss on her soft cheek. "Thank you so much, Ms. Anna."

Hours later, I woke to the sound of someone shuffling through my dresser. My eyes flew open. The small silhouette of my roommate hunched over an open drawer. "What are you doing?"

Autumn tried to hide something behind her back. "Um, I was looking…"

"In my dresser?" I shot out of bed. "What did you take?"

"It ain't nothing of yours."

Huh? "If it was in my dresser, then it has to be mine."

She pushed past me, the object clutched in her hand.

"Give it to me now." At Autumn's refusal, I reached for the girl's arm and the small object fell to the ground. I snatched it before she stopped me. "*You put this in my stuff?*"

"Well, I didn't want to get caught with it."

"How dare you?"

Before Autumn said another word, I stormed out the door and down the stairs. "Ms. Anna, Ms. Anna, where are you?" I looked in the kitchen, and then headed to the formal sitting room.

"What's the matter, Brooke?" Anna hurried to the door.

"Autumn put this in my dresser so she wouldn't be caught with it." I dropped the small object into her hand.

Autumn ran into the room. "Don't listen to her. I didn't do nothin' wrong."

Within minutes, Mr. Carrick and Dara perched in the sitting room listening to my story.

"I can't believe this." I squeezed my nails into the flesh on my hand.

Mr. Carrick looked from Autumn to me. "I think it's time for a bigger intervention. Thank you, Brooke. You can go now. We'll talk to you later."

I nodded and left the room. No worries about falling asleep that night. The situation had been as good as five cups of coffee.

Was it too late to talk to Willa? I searched for a clock. I had a little time before curfew. I walked to Willa's new apartment and knocked on the door. "Are you in there?"

When Willa pulled the door open, I rushed past her.

"What happened?"

I pounded my fist on the counter as I relayed the story. "Can you believe it?"

Willa relaxed on her small couch. "It's amazing the

lengths people will go to when they're addicted."

"I know." I thought back to all the tricks I'd pulled on Dad. "What do you think they'll do?"

Willa leaned against the couch cushions around her. "There's a treatment center on the other side of town. They'll probably send her there for a few weeks." She raised her hands. "Then, who knows?"

I rubbed my temples. "I'm surprised she hasn't left on her own already. Maybe that place can help her more than we can right now." I sat down across from Willa. "Why does it have to be so hard?"

"There will always be consequences for our actions. Thankfully, we have God."

I agreed. I couldn't have done it without Him.

I wanted to change the subject and talk about something good and positive for once. "What are you doing tomorrow?"

"I have the day off, so I'm going to town." Willa didn't look me in the eye.

"I thought you said you didn't care about going there."

"Well, I changed my mind. I need some new scenery. What about you?" As she tilted her head, Willa glanced up.

"Work, work, work. Ms. Stacey has this huge order for a dress show at some big historical plantation, and I agreed to help her finish the outfits for it. It's been a lot of fun."

"I didn't know I created a monster when I took you to that shop to work on a quilt square." Willa laughed.

"Well, I love it there." I got up to leave. "I better get home. It's almost time for curfew."

Willa walked me to the door and waved goodbye. "I'll see you later."

I peered through the darkness to the shadowy corners

on my way home. Fall wasn't too far away, and the sun faded earlier each night.

Something rustled to my right. I crossed the street. Why take a chance?

51
Sarge

It wasn't funny to scare the woman he loved. When Brooke dashed to the other side of the street, though, Sarge started to cackle but threw his hand over his mouth. He waited for her to disappear into the boarding house.

The near darkness made it hard to finish his work. He lifted the last box onto the green wagon and hurried to the cabin. The deadline loomed, and he had to put in a few extra hours to meet it.

As much as he'd enjoyed working on the cabin, and mastering old carpentry skills, he wanted to start a new job. Perhaps he would reroof the barn at the farm. It had a few leaks, and the farmer had talked to him about replacing the wooden shakes. The work should be finished before winter bore down on the center. At least that job meant no tourists asking the most ridiculous questions.

He slowed the horse and jumped down from the wagon on the dirt road in front of the cabin. Sarge stared at it with its new chimney and white chinking completed. Some of the others had built a hand-hewn log hearth for it. Sarge could see it through the open door. His hand rubbed across the coarse chinking that filled the gaps between the logs. The perfect little solitary home for someone like him who didn't need much. What if he used his new-found skills to build one out on the prairie land in the Midwest where he grew up?

Brooke wasn't like the others. After knowing her, he'd realized he hadn't really loved them... Maybe she'd go with him—work at his side. Perhaps he wouldn't have to kill anyone else if she was there to stop him.

52

Brooke

God had to be smiling down on me. I jiggled my knee and beamed the goofiest grin.

"Can you believe it?" I sat across from Kyle. I barely sat still.

"She asked you to go with her to the show?" Kyle sat forward, his hand a millimeter from mine.

My hand tingled even though we weren't touching. "Yes. I helped her design a few of the dresses, and she wants me to get some exposure to the historical design world."

"That's great. When do you leave?"

"In two weeks. We'll only be gone for three days." I hated to pull my hand away, but I'd better. I unloosed my hair down and redid my bun.

"I just got you back after all that trouble with Autumn."

"I know, but it's only a few days."

Kyle relaxed and draped his arm across the back of the chair at the tea shop. "Besides, I'm dying to find out what's going to happen in that book."

"We can meet before devotions."

"At the train depot then, seven o'clock sharp." Kyle

stood up and straightened his waistcoat.

I grabbed our plates and headed to the trashcan.

"I could've gotten that," he protested.

"It's fine. I'll see you tonight."

He waved as he closed the door behind him.

His tall, lanky figure and shiny blond hair made my heart patter too fast. No guy like him had ever liked me. I watched him go and crushed the conflicting emotions inside.

I better get back to work. I hurried to the shop.

"Ms. Stacey, I'm back." I took my seat by the table and pulled out my needle and thread. Stacey had promised to show me a few new decorative stitches in the afternoon. I searched for some scrap material and she joined me, a pattern in her hand.

"I've been thinking about your work. You should consider going to design school." Stacey set the pattern in front of me.

"I don't know." I studied my needle a little too hard. "You can teach me everything I need to know."

"Think of the possibilities." Stacey put her hands on her hips.

"I kind of like it here."

Stacey sat down and studied me. "It feels safe here. But there will come a time when you have to go back to the real world."

"I know." I continued to look away. *Don't think about it.* Did I have to go back? Couldn't I make a life here, working at the center? I didn't have the answers, and I just wanted to change the subject. "So how's the muslin dress going?" I moved away from Stacey.

Stacey stood. "It's going very well."

The bell tinkled as a tourist entered the tailor's shop. "Hello."

Stacey showered a magnanimous smile on the woman and welcomed her. She gave the tourist an animated speech on tailoring in the eighteenth century.

I concentrated hard enough to block my doubts.

Ten minutes later, Stacey returned to my side, and we worked on the delicate embroidery stitches from the pattern until I grew comfortable practicing them on my own.

What about design school? It was way out of my league … but still … I'd skipped school enough to make the worst student in my class jealous. I'd slept through most of my high school years. The only reason I had managed to graduate was because the principal didn't want to see my drunken face ever again. And it would be almost impossible to recount anything I'd learned.

No, nothing was impossible anymore. But how hard would it be?

The cool rain poured from the heavens in a torrent, throwing leaves to the ground prematurely, as I headed back to my room. I watched from the porch of the boarding house, feeling the drops as they cascaded sideways onto me. I needed time to think, to be alone, and the cool air of the rainy day cleared my head. I didn't want to assume Kyle had followed me again. He cared for me, right? But what if he was the one who'd touched me and knocked me into the garden? No. Not possible. He'd explained why he had trailed me. But something didn't seem right.

A figure hurried up the street and turned at the walkway to the boarding house. Who dared to be out in the storm? But as the figure drew closer, Kyle's wet mop glowed in a flash of nearby lightning. In an instant, I went into alert mode as I hurried to the door. I yelled over the storm. "Why are you here? It's pouring."

He carried a storm of his own on his face. Kyle wiped the raindrops from his brow. "I have to see you tonight."

"Why? Are you all right?" I relinquished my hold on the doorknob as he guided me away from the door and windows. On instinct, my hand grasped his arm. When I realized what I'd done, I retracted, tingles in my fingers still spreading to my belly from the touch.

"I'm fine. Listen, I need you to stay with Willa or one of the other women at all times for a while. I don't want you to go anywhere alone. Do you remember what I told you before?"

"You mean about guys?" My ire went up.

He waved his hand. "Yeah, that."

My temper flared for a brief moment. Nobody bossed me. But when I looked into his eyes, my anger deflated. "Please tell me what's happened."

"Have you noticed anyone following you, or watching you?"

"Only you—why?"

"I'll tell you later. I'll be back to get you after dinner. Please, get Willa, and we'll talk." He paused and looked around for a moment. "Somewhere private. Just go in the house for now. I promise I'll be back." Kyle looked at me, and then hugged me tight. He left as quick as he'd come.

I scurried through the doorway and watched him disappear into the storm, my body humming. Why had he taken the chance of getting caught? I tried to rationalize his questions and his responses as I shook the angst out of my limbs. At least I would have Willa there when he returned.

I pushed the door closed, but an arm jutted through it. I screamed and jumped back, ready to make a retreat into the kitchen. My legs turned to jelly.

"What are you doing?" Willa squirmed through the

entrance, her cloak soaked from head to toe.

I grabbed my chest, and my knees threatened to buckle under me as a few of the other women and teens rushed into the hallway to see what had caused the ruckus. I pressed my back against the wall.

"What? It's just me." Willa's tone sent the others scurrying back to their chores. She took one look at me and squinted. "You look like you just saw the ghost of my dead grandmother."

"You're grandmother's dead?" My nerves had addled my brain. What did Willa mean?

"Of course not, silly. I was being sarcastic. It's just a saying. What is going on around here?"

I took a few deep breaths and gestured for her to follow me to my bedroom.

"Just start talking, will you, please."

"No, come on," I said through gritted teeth.

Willa followed me up the stairs.

I looked around the hallway and closed the bedroom door. "Kyle says he has to see both of us tonight. Something's going on and he won't tell me what it is." Should I tell her my fears about Kyle?

"I'm not going out in *that* storm just because he said to." She crossed her arms and stomped her foot.

"Willa, it has to be something terrible. He told me not to go anywhere unless I was with you or one of the other women. And he wanted to know if I've noticed anyone following me."

Willa raised her eyebrows at that. "There *are* some creepy people around here."

I had her full attention. "Have you noticed anything out of the ordinary?"

"Nope."

I wasn't too surprised. Willa thought of herself and

nobody else.

"So he wants me to babysit you again?" she whined.

"You're not concerned at all, not even a little bit?"

"You do know how to be melodramatic. Are yah sure you don't want to go to acting school?" She waved off my concern. "He's probably making a big deal about nothin'."

I grabbed her arms. "Do I usually react like this?"

Willa shook her head.

"Then listen to me. I have a bad feeling about this. Let's at least go and hear him out."

"Okay. But you better hope the rain stops."

I sighed. Willa was a tough woman.

"Now, let's go downstairs and eat. What time did you tell him we'd be there? And where are we going?"

As we headed down the stairs, I lowered my voice and explained what he'd said.

The rain fell at an alarming rate throughout dinner, but the wind died down some. I rushed to the front window and watched the street for any sign of Kyle as soon as I'd finished eating.

Willa's hushed voice sounded in my ear. "What's taking him so long? Do you see him yet?"

I didn't want to state the obvious. "He'll be here."

Even though she didn't believe Kyle, Willa sounded anxious.

Then his tall form ascended the stairs, and we rushed out the door before anyone could notice us leaving.

"Where are we going?" Willa held onto my cloak.

"What about your apartment?"

"Are you kidding me? No, we can't go to my place. I'm not about to lose my apartment because I had a guy in it." She clipped her words as she spoke.

"Look, it's the safest place to talk. And it's the

closest." He kept peering up and down the street.

I looked from one to the other. "No one's really watching us in this downpour. Besides, you want to be in on his scheme, don't you, Willa?"

"Fine." Willa marched off the porch.

The whole bizarre day haunted me. The way Kyle had been acting. The sudden flight into reality that the center wasn't a cocoon of safety. What next? Chills rippled through me.

As we crossed the street, the water ran in torrents along the edges. Kyle wrapped my hand around his elbow to help me across. I followed him and held tight even though we'd been at odds for a while. If only I trusted him again.

53
Brooke

Danger plinked in my mind like the intense raindrops battering me on my way to Willa's apartment. We dashed under the small porch at the grand entrance to the old meetinghouse turned apartment complex. Willa used her key to open the main door. She ushered us in and scurried to the stairs, looking all around her as if Mr. Carrick had mind-melding powers and knew what we were up to. She whispered, "Hurry up."

As we entered her apartment, I released my hold on Kyle.

"Please leave your cloaks over there. I don't want any puddles on the rug." Willa pointed to a coat rack and held her own out for me to take. She went to the windows and pulled all the blinds and drapes closed with a decided yank.

"You're welcome." I took the limp cloak in my hands and scowled at her.

"Oh … thank you." Willa was lost in thought. She turned to Kyle and pursed her lips. "Tell us what's going on, and don't waste time on details."

"Someone here is using this place to hide his sadistic activities."

Willa looked annoyed. "Okay, give us the details."

Kyle took a seat on the couch and beckoned for me and Willa to follow him.

Willa plunked into one of the chairs across from him, and I took a seat beside him.

"Do you two remember when Jordan left?" We both nodded. "I didn't know her well, but I just had a feeling that she wasn't the type of girl to leave without signing out of the program."

"Continue." Willa poised on the edge of her seat.

"A couple of teens in the area went missing a few months before she did, and they had similar physical traits as her. It doesn't seem like a coincidence to me."

"They all had red hair?" Willa leaned in closer.

"One of them did, but it was her small stature and age that matched with the others."

Goose bumps climbed up my arms. I didn't want to think about anything he was saying. Not there. Not where people were supposed to get better and have a new chance at life.

"You think they're linked? Why?" Willa pressed Kyle.

"When I had lunch at the diner in town, I overheard a conversation between the waitress and one of the customers. He had a poster of someone, and the waitress said that the girl on it looked like her friend who'd disappeared. He asked her if he could hang the poster on the back bulletin. After he left, I looked at it. At first it seemed like a coincidence, but then I got curious. I went to the library and checked their newspaper archives. And … I don't think they were runaways."

"So you're saying we could have a serial killer here? Whoa, that's creepy." With her cheeks puffed out, Willa looked like she wanted to desert the center so fast she'd leave smoke in her wake.

My skin prickled. I'd seen enough reality cop shows to want to skip town myself. I shifted my weight and stared at Kyle. "You think Jordan had the same profile as the other women?"

"Well, she had come here for some type of addiction, and the other two were involved in drugs and were suspected runaways. It's the perfect cover-up for their disappearance."

"I wish I had seen the article." My hands began to shake and my mouth grew dry. My fingers tingled when I realized I hadn't taken a breath for several seconds. I sucked air into my lungs and tried to calm down. So much for the theory that good things were happening around me.

Kyle pulled a paper out of his pocket. He gave it to me, and Willa moved closer. "I kept a copy for Carrick to see."

"Read it to us," Willa said.

I unfolded the papers. "Melissa Hack was last seen on Interstate fifty-three, just miles from her home. Her whereabouts are unknown. The police consider her a possible runaway. If you have any information about her disappearance, please contact the Kent police."

I read the young woman's description and then looked up at Kyle. "Where's that road?"

"It's the road between this center and town."

"So is that part of the connection you see too?"

He grimaced. "Yes."

Willa took the second article out of my hand and read it.

My stomach turned. "Kyle, how does this involve us?" My hand shook. "Is this why you've been acting crazy?"

"You're so small, and your hair is a light color." He

crushed my fingers in his and dared Willa to say anything with a mean stare.

His words hit me square in the chest as if a horse had kicked me. I blinked. *Please don't let it be true.* "You think this could happen to me? But there are other girls here who match the description too."

Kyle's fingers grasped mine a little tighter. "Tell me you haven't noticed anything out of the ordinary."

"Wait a minute." I gulped. "I think someone's been following me. I thought I was being paranoid until now, but…" I played with one of the pleats on my dress and looked from one pair of eyes to the other. "There was that time someone knocked me into the garden, do you remember? And several times when I walked home from the tailor shop."

"You never did see who it was, did you?" Kyle prodded.

"No, you're right." I closed my eyes. "There have been too many times that I felt uneasy to even count, but Mr. Carrick had warned me my mind could play tricks on me while detoxing."

Kyle stood up and went to the window, pulled back the blind, and peered out of the corner of it. "I don't want to wait until tomorrow, but Mr. Carrick's in a meeting with a police detective tonight. I can't go to him now. I don't think he'll be back for several hours."

Willa handed him the article she'd taken from me. Her unusual quiet gave me pause.

Kyle folded it up and pushed it into his waistcoat pocket. He returned to the couch. "Please trust me, Brooke. I want you to be safe. I wanted to tell you before, but I had to be sure."

Willa rolled her eyes. "Don't worry about me. I don't fit that description at all, and nobody would dare cross me."

I managed to smile at her. Willa's lanky tall figure and her attitude would be a deterrent to anyone. "Who do you think it is, Kyle?"

He laid his head back for a moment and rubbed his eyes. "Carrick and the detective are going to work on a profile of the person." His hands rested on his lap once again, limp and tired-looking. "But I have a few suspicions about a couple of the guys around here. It's so hard to point your finger at anyone without proof, though."

"Is this what you were keeping from me?"

He opened his eyes and looked down at me. "Yes." His response sounded as if there was more he wanted to say. "Trust me, if I had suspected then what I do now, I would have never let you out of my sight."

"Blah, blah, blah." Willa sounded sick to her stomach, and she refused to look at the two of us. "Look, Brooke, you better get back to the boarding house for devotions. It's late."

What had upset Willa more? Did she not believe Kyle?

"As soon as I hear anything, I'll find you, and we'll go to Carrick and talk to him." He stood up and pulled me to my feet, then seized our cloaks.

I cupped my hand at Willa's ear and whispered, "Are you okay?"

"Um, I'm just thinking."

"Tell me what's bothering you."

"Let's talk about it tomorrow." Willa eyed Kyle, and I got the message.

"Willa, you should walk me home too. I have a funny feeling I can't get rid of."

"I don't know. I don't want to be in that torrent of rain. But … just go. You'll be fine with Kyle, right?" The tone of her voice did not encourage me. Willa seemed to shake herself.

"Okay. Meet me at the boarding house for breakfast." I left her standing in the middle of the room. Willa twisted her hands together, her brows furrowed, and she looked like she wanted to barf. What was that all about? Did Willa suspect Kyle? I shivered and eyed him.

After we threw on our wet cloaks, we hurried to put on our shoes and returned to the torrent of rain that refused to slow.

A headache began to form behind my eyes. Everything made me jump or buckle on our way home. Kyle had wrapped my hand around his elbow again, but he held it a little tighter than the first time. Was I in as much danger with him at my side as if I'd been alone? The squeeze of his hand over mine did not diffuse my raging imagination. He stopped under a tree and pulled me behind it.

Oh, no. What was happening? My silent protest as I tried to pull away didn't stop him. "Kyle."

When he refused to release me, I struggled even more. Earlier, had his display of concern been a guise for something very terrible? I tried to free myself from his desperate hold. My voice rose a pitch. "What has gotten into you?"

"You need to know how important you are to me. Look, I know I messed up when I didn't see you, but I knew you would insist on following me. It wouldn't have gone over well if we'd both been caught alone, watching people. It was something I needed to do on my own. I love you." He bent his head close to mine.

My body froze as stiff as a wooden plank in the sidewalk. "Please let me go."

"I'm just trying to apologize." His eyes darkened for a brief moment. He blinked.

"Behind a tree? You know we'll get kicked out if anyone sees us." I disguised the real reason I wanted him to let go. Had it worked? He was scaring me to the point of panic.

"Sorry. It's just with all this going on, I want to hold onto you." His muscles relaxed and his grip softened.

I exhaled and inched away from the man I had thought I loved. "Tomorrow. We can sort things out, okay?" I tried to slow my breathing, to keep him from suspecting my true thoughts. But my mind yelled danger over and over again.

Before I could stop him, his lips grazed my forehead. "It's going to be okay. I promise." Kyle scanned the road and then pulled me out from behind our hiding place. "Let's go."

My knees threatened to buckle. "To the boarding house?"

"Of course." He tilted his head and frowned.

I nodded, looking for the light of the front porch in the distance. *Please, God, let me get home safely. Please, don't let it be him. Why did Willa let me go out alone with him if she suspected what I suspect?* With each step, I willed him to stay on the path toward home.

He left me at the door and disappeared into the dark night, trying to remain unseen.

My knees shook as I shut the door behind me. I had to brace myself against it to not topple over. *Not Kyle. Please, not him.*

54
Brooke

If Kyle turned out to be the killer, I'd give up—plain and simple. I might as well be in a backyard butt whoopin' with all the bullies kicking me. And I was about to stay down for good.

"Dear Lord, I'm scared, and I don't know what to do." The tissue in my lap lay wet and limp. I had given up trying to keep the tears at bay. In the dark of my room, I knelt by the bed and whispered, "What should I do? Give me clarity about the truth, precious Savoir."

Maybe I should leave. As soon as the thought entered my mind, I rejected it. I wiped my eyes with the tissue and threw it into the wastebasket beside the bed.

Once more, I looked up at the dark, starless sky. "I don't want it to be Kyle. Please, Lord, tell me if it is. Show me. I love him, but now I don't know what to believe."

Blue lights began to bounce off the ceiling. *What?*

Anna's voice sounded loud at the end of the hall. "Ladies, stay in your rooms for the remainder of the night. We have some guests that need to check out a few things. Don't worry, everything is fine."

I peered out my door at the mounting number of faces that peeked out of theirs toward Anna. Had the police come to reinvestigate Jordan's room again?

I ignored the growing murmurs in the hall and closed my door, and then rested my back against it, hands splayed on each side.

At the window, I crouched and pulled the corner of the curtain up to watch outside.

The lights created patterns on the nearby trees and buildings as they flashed blue and white. I turned as heavy footsteps landed on the stairs going to the third floor.

My hands went clammy. Would they notice that someone other than themselves had been in the room? When Willa had talked me into searching through Jordan's things, I'd had no idea the police might return. No one had seen us, but what if we'd left something of ours up there by accident? Fingerprints? DNA?

Anna would've already cleaned the room too. It had been months.

I grabbed my blankets and climbed into bed, pulling them up to my chin. I'd never heard sounds from above in the past and I still didn't hear a thing, even with their heavy footfalls. The house gave up no clues as to what went on upstairs.

Hours later, I tried to shut my eyes, but they refused to close. The police had left awhile ago, but I lay twisted in my sheets, praying still. The thrumming of my pulse in my ears refused to subside, and I rolled over for the tenth time. Should I get up and make sure no one lurked outside the door? I'd already done that twice.

A heavy sigh escaped my lips as I played with the stone on my necklace.

How terrible that the one place where Jordan should've been safe from her old life, she had walked into the most danger. I recounted all the times I'd seen Jordan at the garden or at the dining room table and couldn't recall any detail that warranted concern. Come to think of it, I barely remembered what Jordan looked like. I didn't have any information to give the police, no matter how much I wanted to help. And believe me, I wanted to help. Because the love of my life might be guilty.

55
Brooke

A killer hid amongst us. The law enforcement camped at the center created panic, not calm. Well, more like pure dread.

A detective with his badge clipped to the side of his black suit jacket stood waiting for all of us to settle down and be quiet. "Ladies, I'm Detective Schubert. I need to talk to you. And I'll answer all the questions I can when I finish."

The room hushed, and he uncrossed his arms. "As you are all aware, we were here last night. There has been a possible incidence here and in Kent, involving women between the ages of eighteen and twenty-five."

Jade began to wave her hand to get his attention. "What's going on? I heard someone say they think someone killed Jordan."

The room filled with murmurings, and the detective raised his hand to silence us. "It is a possibility, but there is no definite proof leading in that direction."

"Is it true what they're saying in the papers about other girls in town and a serial killer?" Jade gnawed at her fingers as she waited for his answer, but her comment created an upheaval in the room.

A serial killer? My stomach clenched.

He motioned once again for us to be quiet. "We don't know of any positive connection between them and Jordan Magnus. But we urge you all to take extra precautions over the next few weeks. Don't go out alone. And always let someone know where you are at all times."

I noticed he hadn't answered Jade's question. It had to be true.

"Does anyone have any information about Jordan and her last days here?" Several women shot their hands into the air. "Come see me. And I'll be down at the general store for most of the day. You may come at any time to talk to me. Anything you tell us is kept in the utmost confidence. We need all the information we can to find Jordan, and I'm sure that's what you all want, as well … to find her." Detective Schubert folded his hands in front of him. "Also, we are interested in knowing if any of you have experienced anything unusual here. Have any of you noticed someone watching you? Have any of your personal belongings gone missing which you can't account for?"

My skin crawled as his gaze fell on me. Did he know who I was? I looked down at the floor for a moment, and when I looked up he no longer watched me.

"As I said, I'll be down at the store, and you can come in and talk to me or one of my officers any time." He nodded at us and waited to see if anyone wanted to talk.

The women huddled together. A few went to him.

As soon as I had a chance, I'd go talk to him, but I didn't want anyone to know. I fiddled with a pleat in my dress and continued the mantra I'd started last night about Kyle not being the killer.

He motioned for us to listen one last time. "Not to raise

any alarm, but there'll be officers stationed around the center to provide extra safety. Please let them know if you notice anything out of the ordinary. Have a good day."

He sent one last glance in my direction. I nodded at him then turned and headed to the kitchen to finish serving breakfast. My stomach growled, yet I wouldn't be able to eat. Besides, Willa was supposed to be there already. Where was she?

Five minutes later, I peeked out of the kitchen at the slam of the front door. "There you are." My hand fluttered to my chest. "Come on."

Willa and I hurried up the stairs. "Willa, I was so frightened last night."

"Why? What happened?"

I motioned her into my room. Once inside with the door closed, I dropped onto my bed. "It's Kyle—"

"What is Kyle?"

"If you'd let me finish my sentence, you'd know."

Willa nodded and rolled her hand in an attempt to hurry me along.

"He's scaring me. When we left, he pulled me behind a tree and I didn't know what he was going to do." The quilt bunched under my fisted hands.

"So … you're not thinking it's him, are you? That he's the killer?"

I swallowed hard. "I don't know. I don't want it to be true, but what if it is?"

Willa took a seat beside me and stared at the floor. "Don't think I'm not a little worried, too. He seems to know a lot about the other girls." She gave me a sideways glance. "So what happened behind the tree?"

"He kissed me. On the forehead."

"And you think it's him after that?" We both stared anywhere but at each other.

"It was the way he grabbed me—the way he looked at me."

"Oh." Willa grimaced. "Don't worry. We're going to figure this out."

"Leave it to you to be so calm at a time like this." I wanted to shout at her.

"The truth, that's what I desire." No one was as level-headed as Willa.

"Well, while you're looking for it, can you keep an eye out for me?"

"I'll do my best."

I believed her. But we were only two women. What chance did we have against a killer?

56
Sarge

The police crawled over Sarge's turf like a disturbed ant hill. Sarge stood against the back wall of his boarding house and punched the air. He should've left when he had the chance.

He returned to the kitchen. Apples littered the butcher block, and he grabbed a knife. *Keep busy.* That made it easier for the worry to not eat at his stomach. He tried to sound nonchalant, but even to his own ears his voice shook. "What's going on? I see police out there."

Ryan avoided meeting his eyes. "Don't know."

The mentor of the boarding house walked through the front door, a stranger close behind him. His voice boomed. "Everyone, get down to the meeting room. We have a guest."

Sarge set the knife down beside the apples he had started to cut. He waited for the others to file into the room and stood behind them, out of the direct line of the guest wearing a badge and a gun at his hip.

"This is Detective Schubert. He needs to talk to you." The mentor sauntered out of the way.

"Good morning. I wanted to let you all know that there has been some question as to the whereabouts of Jordan

Magnus. We are looking for any information that will help us find her." He talked for a while, and then told them where he was going to be. "Please come see me if you know anything or have seen anything pertaining to her."

The blood drained from Sarge's face and he brushed the hair off his forehead. He'd known they'd come someday, but they wouldn't find her.

He ducked his head down and struggled to keep his face blank. Wait, what if... Maybe he should go talk to the detective. The racing of his heart made him feel light-headed, but he struggled to maintain control of it. What better person to direct the police than the only one who knew where she really was? The worry lines between his brows softened as a grin split across his face.

"Not one of these backwoods cops is as smart as me." He laughed. He was too smooth for those jokers to figure it out.

57
Brooke

I wanted the whole sordid serial killer situation to disappear and let me get back to my sanity and recovery.

Main Street buzzed with activity that masked the undercurrent of alarm filtering through the center. My mind bounced between every emotion in the book as I hurried to the tailor shop with Willa beside me.

"Did you talk to the detective yet?" Willa waited for me to respond.

"I wanted to get some work done first."

"You're so good at avoiding things."

"I will, but I can't shirk my responsibilities. I promise I'll go as soon as I can." I meant it.

"You know Kyle's going to be looking for you. Who knows, maybe one of the cops stopped him."

I shrugged. "We could be wrong about this whole thing."

Willa looked at me through squinted eyes.

"I know that you two don't get along, but come on, we have no proof it's him." I refused to look her in the face.

"Whatever. I'll catch up to you later." Willa pointed at the police officer down the street and crossed the road, leaving me on the corner.

So much for not going anywhere alone. No one would dare try to take me in the middle of the day with the police everywhere, would they? I tried to remain positive and turned down the side street.

"Hello, Ms. Stacey, how are you?" I popped in the door.

Stacey leaned out of the closet a moment later. Another perfect coif showed off her golden locks. "Good, but I could do without all the hubbub outside."

I pressed a hand to my stomach. "Scary, isn't it?"

Stacey had turned her attention to a cloak in her hands, but then looked back at me. "It's easy to let ourselves be afraid, but we just have to remember what God says about it."

"What's that?"

"He says to not be afraid of what man can do to you."

"Hmm." I crossed my arms. Easy to say but hard to do. I moved into the room and gathered my sewing basket out of the cubby. "Do you mind if I take a long lunch?"

"May I ask why?"

Did I want anyone to know why? But Stacey deserved an answer if I wanted her to give me the time off. "Well … I need to go see Mr. Carrick about something."

With a bunch of material gathered in her hands, Stacey went to the mannequin. "That's fine."

"I don't mind staying late." I pulled my scissors free from the bundle of knotted threads.

"Not tonight, but maybe tomorrow you may make up the time. Here, take this and work on it. It needs a new button. And look at the hem." She pointed at a small tear in the fabric on the cloak. "That needs to be patched."

"Sure." I reached for it. A few bowls of buttons held a close match, so I set to work.

I watched the clock way too much. My stomach might as well have been the ball of knotted thread in my basket. Would the detective believe my claims? Maybe not. And if he did, then I had a new problem to face. Either way, I lost.

At last, I put the sewing basket back on the shelf. "Ms. Stacey, I'll be back. The cloak is in the closet. And don't worry, I'll set the mannequin in the corner."

I ran my hand over the fine cotton of the red dress which hung on the mannequin after I set it out of the way. I had to finish tailoring it with Stacey's help later. Then we'd sew the fine beading on the collar. The best part of the work. The details made each outfit unique.

I peered out the door and searched for an officer in the near vicinity. Only tourists strolled along the street. How much would the center be impacted if the tourists got wind of what had happened and stopped coming?

A moment later, a uniformed man waited at a corner up a block. I'd better hurry. I didn't want to waste too much time and have to stay too late the next night. I hurried toward the general store and studied the main street with the policeman at my side. It buzzed with activity. Way more than a normal weekday in the school season.

"Hello, Ms. Dara. Is Mr. Carrick available?"

"Let me check." Dara disappeared down the hall.

I looked around and smiled. The coolness of the large room and the wonderful smell of brewing cider and tea reminded me of where I'd started and how far I'd come. I rubbed my hand on the waxed counter, where light reflected off its surface. Maybe later I'd grab a cup of cider on my way to lunch.

A few minutes later, Dara returned and beckoned me to follow her. Her warm smile lessened my misgivings.

"Thanks."

"Hello." I closed the door and looked around the room. As he'd promised, the detective sat in my usual seat.

"Brooke, this is Detective Schubert." The detective nodded.

Mr. Carrick might seem relaxed, but he couldn't hide the energy pouring off him. "We've heard some things. Would you care to elaborate? From what we understand, there's been some unusual situations happening to you, is that correct?"

Who had blabbered to them? I began to tell them what all I'd noticed over the past months.

Detective Schubert stopped me in midsentence. "So you felt threatened when someone pushed you into the garden, but you didn't bring it to anyone's attention?"

My hands began to tremble. Law enforcement never believed druggies. I was sure that was how he saw me. "Well, I ... I didn't understand the importance at the time."

He leaned closer, and I wanted to back up, but there was nowhere to go in the small office.

"So you felt apprehensive and you thought someone may be following you. What days?" He looked down at the pad of paper in front of him, pen poised.

When had it happened? Brain fog still blocked lots of little details. I narrowed my eyes and tried to put a date to the events. "Umm, I can't quite remember."

He knew how to make me nervous with his penetrating eyes. I squirmed. "I guess it all started a few weeks after I got here."

He raised his eyebrows. "And when was that?"

"In the end of May."

"So you arrived in May or you noticed you were being followed then?"

"I arrived at the center in the end of May."

"You're saying that for months you've been stalked, and you didn't tell Mr. Carrick or any other authority?"

"Yes, sir. I mean no. I never said someone stalked me. But you're right, I didn't go to anyone." A heavy breath escaped my lips. A stalker? Where did that come from?

He raised his eyebrows once more, and then nailed me with the police glare, as I liked to call it. I wanted to run out the door and hide. He nodded an eternity later and wrote a few notes on the paper.

"Has anyone made any direct contact or threats to confirm your feelings?"

"No." *But what about last night with Kyle?*

His eyes were on me like a bird of prey. He sat forward and linked his fingers, watching my every move. "Do you have any information about Jordan Magnus?"

"I barely knew her. She worked in the gardens around the boarding house, but she was very quiet."

He scribbled on his pad. "And did you notice anything out of the norm on the day she disappeared?"

"No."

"So let's talk about the day you were pushed."

I nodded, trying to keep up with his line of thinking.

"What were you doing alone in the garden that early in the morning?"

I bristled. "It isn't against the rules to be out in the morning. I was doing my devotions."

"When you fell, you didn't see their face? They escaped so fast that you couldn't see them?"

"There were bushes and trees all around me. I didn't see who did it." My skin crawled.

He nodded and wrote again.

I thought back to the day I'd received the flower in my mailbox. "Now that I think of it, someone sent me a candy bar and a flower. I thought it was…" I stopped before I blurted out Kyle's name. "…it was from a friend, but when I asked, the person said they weren't from them. At the time, I thought it was a joke, but now I wonder who left them."

The detective turned to Mr. Carrick. "So he could be leaving tokens." He turned back to me. "Is there anything else you want to tell us?"

How was he going to believe me when I had no proof—no concrete evidence? I should mention Kyle's strange behavior, but even with my new paranoia about him, I couldn't do it. What if he was innocent? "I can't think of anything else."

"If you notice anything, please go straight to someone in charge, and please don't go out alone. It's better to take extra precautions than to take a chance." He studied me once more.

Mr. Carrick stood. "Please don't wait so long next time to tell us what is going on. I'm here, and so is Ms. Dara, whenever you need us."

"I will, I promise."

Detective Schubert smiled, but it didn't reach his eyes. "Be safe."

It took a minute for me to gain my composure before leaving the hall. Mr. Carrick's door flew open and I jerked back.

Mr. Carrick filled the opening. "The detective thinks it'd be a good idea to have a patrol officer with you for a couple days."

Oh, great. It must be bad. I tried to keep my knees from beginning to shake. "Okay."

"Just wait with Ms. Dara while he calls one to meet you. Should I call anyone for you?"

"No—" Dad might try to show up and look like super

dad in front of everyone.

"Please check in every day for the rest of the week on your way home from work."

"Sure." A police officer of my own? I groaned even though I had to admit having my own cop might be nice.

If all of this had happened months ago at home, I would've laughed and texted all my friends about how cool the whole situation was. I wouldn't have taken it seriously. But now life was so different, and the danger clung to me like saran wrap to a bowl.

I'd better hurry and get back to the tailor shop.

The tinkle of the doorbell brought me out of my reverie, and a police officer looked around as he entered.

"Hi, I'm Brooke. I guess you'll be following me for a few days. Sorry about that." He had to have other, more important duties.

"Not a problem, just part of the job." He adjusted the thick belt at his waist as he spoke. His gun holster and other gadgets lining it sat in perfect symmetry.

"I need some lunch. Have you had any?"

"Yes, ma'am." Calling me ma'am seemed incongruent, considering he looked almost as young as me.

"Okay." I pursed my lips. He followed me. Some people turned to watch us, but I ignored the stares. With him around, I'd remain the most conspicuous person in the center. A good thing for sure.

58
Brooke

All the stares and whispers because of my new best friend in the police suit got old real fast.

The police officer stood outside the door of the boarding house, hands together in front of him. I ignored him as Willa barreled toward me.

"What is going on? Is he for you?" Willa stared.

"Yep. He's been following me all day."

Willa laughed. "You love all the attention, don't yah?"

My glare shut her up. "Not today, Willa."

"Sorry."

"It's been a long day." I pushed the small strands of hair away from my face. "So you want to help me with dinner?"

"Let's get it done."

Good. She wasn't going to push my buttons tonight.

As we poured batter into cupcake pans, Willa questioned me. "You're going to tell me what happened later, right? What do you want to do tonight during free time?"

"Yes, I'll tell you later, and I don't know what I want to do."

"We can go down to the depot and play some games

or something. It's too wet in the park to play quoits or hoop trundling."

"Okay, but what if Kyle's there? I haven't seen him all day."

Willa didn't give her usual smart remark. "Maybe we can outright ask him if he did it. Get it off our chests. What's the worst that could happen? He attacks us both and drags us to our death?"

She never knew when to quit. "Stop. That's not funny."

"Well, you have to deal with this. Those officers won't be around forever, and they might not catch the guy they're looking for."

"And how do you suppose I do that? You want me to tell the police my suspicions?" I grappled with my words.

"I guess."

"I can't." What was stopping me? The idea that I could be very wrong? The fact that I still loved him?

Willa changed the subject as she donned an apron. "I can't be out too late. I have some exit paperwork to do for Mr. Carrick."

I raised my eyebrows.

"Don't even think about getting upset. You'll have to do it too when you're near the end of your plan. It's part of the process. So stop getting weepy on me."

"You mean those reports everyone has to do close to the end of their stay?"

"Yep." She rolled her eyes.

I swallowed hard and concentrated on scraping the batter out of the bowl.

"Hey, I know what we can do tonight. There's a special meeting at the church. A group is performing a play or *something* out there."

"That's right. I forgot about it." Kyle should be there.

271

"I'm glad you remembered."

"I'm relieved you got the police officer. It gets dark earlier now."

She was just saying that. She wasn't scared of anything.

59
Brooke

I could have suffocated in the overcrowded sanctuary, stuffed as tight as a can of Vienna sausages. The shimmery glow of candles filtered through the room, and I fanned myself as the heat of the crowded room pressed me to near faintness. I pulled at my corset. Why hadn't I gotten Willa to loosen it before we left the boarding house?

In the church, the women sat on one side and the men on the other, like on a Sunday morning, as the play began.

But it was worth the discomfort. Kyle eyed me from across the room. By the time the play ended, I needed to decide what to do about him.

The play unfolded on the small stage, and I watched the crew scurry around to change scenes. My police officer got replaced by another one. I looked over my shoulder at him for a brief moment. He stayed as stern and quiet as the first.

Willa elbowed me. "Sit still," she whispered. "There isn't enough room for you to keep moving."

My smirk went unnoticed as Willa strained to watch the characters move to their new locations on the stage. The amateur group did an excellent job portraying the life of Christ. But once again my mind wandered to the serial killer. And Kyle.

I studied every face in the church as best as possible with the dim lights. A monster sat among us, but all I saw were the ordinary faces I'd looked at every day. It could be someone who didn't belong at the center, like a local tourist, or supply truck driver. Not Kyle.

As the play ended, I pointed for Willa to follow me out the back door to the restroom. Willa nodded, but the crowd stopped her from keeping up with me. Her delay gave me a chance to talk to my officer. "Sir, I need to do something. I'll be right back."

"No, ma'am, I can't leave you."

"I'll be fine. See my friend over there?" I pointed at Willa. "She'll keep an eye on me and I'll only be a minute in the ladies' room."

"Okay, but stay on the premises, please."

"Yes, sir." I hurried to the back door. My throat burned with acid. I should've gone to the bathroom before we got there.

The mass of people didn't allow much movement, but I pushed through them. Where was the powder room? A door near the stage gave way with a creak. Not a bathroom or room at all.

Someone in the crowd pushed me through the door. I turned with relief. "Willa, what happened? I thought you saw me gesturing, but it took forever for you to come."

The person towered over me. Too tall to be Willa.

I flinched.

Shadows covered his face.

"What's going on?" My heart caught in my throat.

He whispered my name and moved so close I smelled his muskiness.

I shuddered. "I'm sorry. I thought you were someone

274

else. Excuse me." My voice hit near hysteria as I tried to brush past him, but he seized my arm, a gentle but firm pressure holding me in place.

"What are you…?" The air rushed out of my lungs before I finished my question as he pulled me against him.

"Sshh. I just needed to see you. *You* motioned for me to come out here with you, so I did." An unfamiliar voice.

My mind whirled. Who was he? What was he doing holding onto me? "*Please.*" His face became clearer as my eyes adjusted. I pulled back and my brain screamed danger even louder. His hard stare darkened his beautiful face. One I'd seen around the center many times. Eric Sarcon?

"Please what? I've been waiting for you."

Terror strangled me as I began to struggle. The growl that emanated from his throat warned me as he tightened his grip and pulled me so close his rough shirt material scraped my cheek. I recoiled, and the blue medallion of my necklace freed itself from my blouse as I resisted.

He looked down and growled. "Where did you get that?"

"What?" Why hadn't anyone come to my rescue? Where was my officer? Willa?

"It doesn't belong to you. It's *hers*, and you should've never touched it." Eric grasped both of my wrists in one hand and reached for the necklace.

"Let me go," I screamed. Someone had to be out front in earshot. I struggled to push away from him and kicked at his shin. I went full-force street gang on him. I wasn't going down without kicking some serious buttooty.

But he began to pull me down the hill. I screamed and octopused my way out of his grip.

Too fast, he tackled me and almost fell to the ground on top of me, but caught his balance. "Shut *your* mouth."

He pulled me farther away from the church. I bit and clawed until his hands pinned my arms to my side. We tumbled down the hill toward a stand of trees in the distance.

"No. Don't—please."

He gave me one harsh wrench, so strong it took my breath. I shut my mouth. *No, no, no.* I had to get away. *God, save me.*

The door flew open as I twisted again.

"Brooke?"

I went limp as a noodle. The guy lost his grip, giving me a chance to shriek at the top of my lungs.

Kyle paused for a millisecond, and then ran and steamrolled the guy so hard I bounced away and fell as he jumped on him like a spider on its prey.

My assailant knocked Kyle off him and sprinted down the hill, cursing as he went.

Kyle lifted me off the ground and pulled me to his chest.

"He grabbed me." My breath came out in short gasps. I could've died that night. My heart throbbed, and a cold sweat broke out on my brow. Kyle had been true to me the whole time. How could I have ever doubted him?

The door clinked open again. "Ma'am?"

I grimaced. How must the scene look?

"Sir, remove yourself at once." The officer pushed Kyle off me and shoved him to the wall. He spoke into his walkie-talkie. "I need back-up at the white chapel on Church Street."

I pointed down the hill. "That's the guy you need to catch."

"Ma'am, let me handle this. Now, don't you move." He directed the last comment at Kyle, and then turned to listen to the response on his walkie-talkie.

"Sir, he's *down there*. You need to stop that guy."

He followed the pointing of my finger. "You had two assailants?"

He got back on his two-way radio.

"No, this is my friend. Can you let him go? The other guy tried to abduct me. It's Eric Sarcon."

He nodded as he answered the dispatch from his radio and released Kyle.

Kyle looked down the hill in the direction of the fleeing figure. "Tell me what he looked like."

"He was taller than you. Blond hair. He worked at the train depot when I arrived."

Kyle took off down the hill and the officer followed suit.

"Ma'am, you go inside and stay with the group. I'll send someone." He called after Kyle. "Sir, do you know who it is?" But his answer carried away in the wind.

I threw the door open and shot into the church. "Willa, Willa."

Willa pushed past one last person. "What is it?"

"You were supposed to meet me by that door. But you didn't follow, and someone almost abducted me. Now Kyle is chasing him."

Willa's eyes bugged. "You don't think…" Her words trailed off. "Not—"

I panted. "Yes."

Willa put her arm around me. Her voice shook as she spoke. "I shouldn't have let you get ahead of me."

"He grabbed me, and I thought it was you, only it wasn't, and then he said some crazy things about this necklace and how he'd been watching me. And then Kyle burst through the door. And the officer thought it was Kyle who attacked me. But it wasn't. And now Kyle could be in trouble. Oh, Willa, that man must be the killer they're looking for. What if he has a weapon? Kyle might get hurt."

"Sit down. You're hyperventilating." Willa directed me to a pew. "Do yah have asthma or something?"

"No." I bent low with my elbows on my knees.

An officer entered the room. "Ms. Hollen?"

Willa waved at him. "She's over here."

His radio went off before he reached us. "All units report to Main and Blossom for emergency 190."

60
Brooke

Screaming echoed from an invisible source as I dashed out the door of the church. It carried on the wind up the hill. Such a frightening sound. At first, I didn't understand what made the noise. Was it a horse?

The officer's radio continued to squawk in a coded language I didn't understand as he stood beside me. Then flashing lights bounced off the buildings and trees way down at Main Street.

Willa gripped my arm.

"Willa…" I couldn't pull my eyes from the lights.

"It's okay, it's probably the police apprehending that guy."

"I don't think so." I moved away from the officer, down the hill.

"Stop, Brooke," Willa called, losing her grip on me.

"Ma'am, we should stay up here for now."

I continued forward and ignored him as I picked up speed.

"Ma'am." The officer's voice echoed behind me as I moved closer to the lights and noise—and the awful sound of the horse's whinnies.

The officer grabbed my arm, and I whipped around

and glared at him.

"Look, I'll see what's going on. You stay here."

I shook my head as he disappeared around the corner of the depot.

"Brooke, he said to stay here." Willa had caught up to me. She clutched my arm with a stranglehold.

"Let go. I have to see—"

"No."

I yanked so hard I was sure I'd find nail marks. As I rounded the corner of the street, lights illuminated the tangled scene in front of me. Everything came to a stop as my eyes focused on an overturned wagon and a figure under it. Did I see Kyle's blond hair? Or Eric's?

I reached out and screamed. It sounded too far away to belong to me. I tumbled to the cool hard ground, my dress billowing around me. My breath whooshed from my lungs. My mind shut down. And there was nothing I could do to stop the black from taking hold of me as I drifted out of consciousness.

What had happened? Why were voices floating around me? And how had I gotten on the ground? My head hurt, and my stomach gave in to violent convulsions. Someone turned me on my side.

"Brooke," Willa yelled.

I couldn't control the pangs that brought my dinner up.

The full impact of the horrific scene came to me in little strands until it poured over me at lightning speed.

The old green wagon lay twisted on its side, the horse between the shafts, kicking its legs as someone tried to free its harness from the wreckage. EMS workers surrounded one section of the wagon, but Kyle's hand and his golden blond hair protruded from under the mass of wagon, cargo, and horse.

EMS workers tried to lift the heavy vehicle off him as

I tried to stand on wobbly legs. I needed to reach him, but my body wouldn't cooperate. The officer came out of nowhere and tried to tell me something, but I didn't understand.

My words slurred. "Let me go. Kyle needs me."

"You have to stay here. You're in shock. They're helping him, okay? If we get in the way, he won't get what he needs." The officer prevented me from moving forward.

He supported me as he spoke. Was it a sick nightmare? A drunken stupor? No, I hadn't had a drink in months. For sure. I pointed. "What...?"

Haziness threatened me once more. I caught movement beside Kyle. He wasn't the only person trapped.

"Let's sit her down over there." Willa helped the officer move me.

Tears began to pour down my face in torrents, and I suddenly knew it wasn't a dream. A woman in an EMS uniform approached. I heard them talking around me, but I stayed trained on the sliver of golden hair under the wagon.

When the woman bent down in front of me, I had no choice but to look at her since she blocked my view. "Are you hurt? I hear you hit your head on the road."

I shrugged.

The woman said, more to the others than to me, "She's in shock. We should lay her down and prop up her feet."

I moved as they directed me. When I finally looked at Willa, she reflected the same sorrow on her face. Willa held my hand and her shoulders sagged.

The wrenching sound of old wood and metal reverberated down the street as a tow truck helped to pull the wagon upright. The rush of medical workers increased.

"Is he all right, Willa? What about the other guy?"

"I don't know, sweetie." Willa trained her eyes straight ahead.

The EMS worker at my side said, "I think you should make a trip to the emergency room just to make sure you're okay."

I cried, "I want to get up."

"Just lie still a little longer."

"I need to go with him." I pointed toward Kyle.

"We'll get you there," Willa assured me.

"Please tell me what happened." I pleaded with the officer.

"Apparently, one of the guys spooked the horse when he ran in front of it. The horse reared up and fell back on the wagon, toppling it on both of them. The driver made it out okay, though."

"It's my fault." Tears wracked my body. "He chased that guy because of me." Anguish tore at my chest. "Please take me over there now."

The officer said no and shielded my view as they lifted Kyle onto a stretcher.

When the officer moved, Mr. Carrick appeared beside me. "Brooke, are you hurt?"

"I saw you over there. Tell me if he's okay." The words came out in gasps as I cried.

Mr. Carrick's gaze never left mine. "We don't know anything yet."

I sat up and tried to stand. Once I got my feet to cooperate, I bolted for the ambulance, but it pulled away and sirens pierced the night air. Were sirens a good sign?

I prayed harder than I'd ever prayed before for Kyle.

61
Brooke

Something clenched my arm in a tight hold. I jerked and trembled. *Not again. Not trapped again.*

"*No.*" My head ached, but I struggle to open my eyes and escape.

"Girl, it's me, Willa. Yah hit your head very hard. It's okay, though. We're at the hospital and you're going to be fine." Willa took my hand.

I couldn't quite place something in the sound of her voice. "I hit my head? How?" The blood pressure cuff deflated as I tried to focus on it.

"Well … you fell on the road and they think you have a concussion. One too many hits, you know?"

"What are you talking about?"

"Mr. Carrick's here. He's been beside himself with worry over you, but you don't need to think about anything right now. Just stay still. Do yah remember the last time you came to? You were spouting off all kinds of weird stuff."

"No, not really." I released Willa's hand. "Something happened, right? I can't seem to grasp what it was, but I know something happened."

"Let's not worry about it until later."

I definitely heard the inflection in Willa's voice that time. She refused to look at me and rubbed her arms up and down. I stared at her until she looked me in the eye. "Tell me now."

"Umm, let me get the nurse." Willa moved away from the gurney, but I reached out and grabbed the back of her dress before she could disappear.

"Willa, please…" The memories began to come back in flashes. I grabbed my head as pinpricks of pain shot through it.

"It's going to be okay, I promise." Willa paused but didn't turn. Her voice faltered on her last words.

I watched her leave, but didn't have the strength to do anything about it. Willa didn't believe what she said. I turned as slow as possible to take in the room, thankful for the dim light. A television hummed in quiet tones in the corner. The words 'Breaking News' plastered across the bottom of the screen. What had they discovered this time? The too-low volume kept me from hearing every word.

Flashing lights and old storefronts looked vaguely familiar. I laid back and held my head for a moment, then turned back to the screen. My heart leaped into my chest. It was the center. I fumbled for the nurse call button remote, where the TV volume was located, and turned it up. My body involuntarily shook.

The woman reporter glanced behind her at the upturned wagon. "As you can see, this wagon is responsible for the tragic accident that…"

A maroon-clad nurse bustled in and blocked my view with her ample form. "Hi, I'm Priscilla, and I'll be your nurse for tonight."

Willa followed close behind, and I watched her glance up at the screen, grab the remote when she saw the picture of the wagon, and shut it off. She cleared her throat.

Priscilla continued. "Let me just take a quick look at you." Glancing at the stats on the machine beside me, she leaned in and studied the side of my head. "That's a pretty good cut you've got. Can you tell me what happened?"

The room seemed to shift as I concentrated on the nurse's face. "I'm not sure, but I know I was running and…"

Willa patted my arm. Since when had she become so motherly?

"Just take your time." The nurse checked the computer screen with my stats on it again.

"My friend Kyle…" My eyes flew open. "Where is he?"

"Do you remember anything else that happened?"

Memories rushed back.

Priscilla watched me. "It's normal for things to be a little scattered at this point, but everything should come together for you pretty soon."

"How's Kyle?" I refused to leave the question alone.

The nurse prodded my head. The smell of disinfectant assailed my senses a moment later, followed by a sharp pain on my temple as the nurse wiped at a tender spot. "What's his full name?"

"Kyle Reston."

"Are you related to him?"

"No." Hospitals were funny about sharing information.

"I can't tell you anything. Sorry. HIPAA policy." She adjusted my pillow. "But as for you, the doctor's sending you down for a CAT scan, and then he will be in to see you, so sit tight." The nurse left.

Just great. I closed my eyes. If only the haziness would stop. "Willa, I know you know something. Tell me how

Kyle is. *Now.*"

Willa plopped into the only chair other than the doctor's stool in the room. "It's bad, Brooke."

A tear slid down her face. Willa never cried. My pulse echoed in my ears and heat rose up my neck to my face. I forced myself to ask, "How bad?"

"Really bad. Maybe Mr. Carrick should tell you." Willa stood in one sudden motion.

"Don't you dare. I don't want to hear it from him. You tell me. Is he okay?" Once again the room tilted, and my stomach lurched from the dizziness.

"We're all waiting to hear." She drew out the statement.

"But…"

Willa wilted back onto the chair. She buried her face in her hands. "They were doing CPR on him when they put him in the ambulance."

Tears sprang to my eyes. "Tell me from the start. What happened?"

"We were at the play, and you disappeared. I didn't think anything of it because I knew you had that officer following you everywhere. You see, Kelly had this new purse. I wanted to see it … and now it seems so ridiculous, after all that's happened. I should have just stayed with you." A new bout of tears riddled through her. "When you didn't come back, I went looking for you. You ran into the sanctuary and said someone had tried to take you and Kyle was chasing him. There was this terrible noise down the road, and you ran … but I couldn't keep up with you. And you were on the ground when I reached you. I don't know what happened. Then you insisted on going with the ambulance and you fell and hit your head again."

A flash of the dark figure looming over me stole my breath. I shivered. What about the bad guy? Where had he gone?

"Careful." I held my head when Willa bumped the gurney.

Once the room stopped spinning, I pleaded with her. "Willa, we have to pray now. You…"

Willa bowed her head and started to pray as I clutched her hand. *Please, God, let Kyle be alive.* I echoed the prayer over and over as I tried to concentrate on Willa's words.

Someone's throat cleared behind Willa as she finished.

Another scrub-clad emergency room worker waited at the door. He pointed at his badge for me to see. "I need to take you down to X-ray. I'm with the radiology department."

Willa's voice rose a pitch. "I'll be right here. Besides, I need to let Mr. Carrick know you're awake."

I released her hand as the tech wheeled me out of the room. I closed my eyes as the bed spun around and we crossed the threshold into a much brighter hallway. "Please, tell me what you know about Kyle Reston."

"Let's get this done first, and then I'll have your nurse see if there are any updates on your friend."

"You don't know *anything*?"

"There're special policies to protect patients' rights to privacy. I have to follow protocol. Sorry that I can't tell you more."

I groaned. *Please look out for him, Lord.*

Priscilla came back to check on me once I returned. She set the call box on the bed near my head. "It shouldn't be much longer. The doctor has to look at your scans. And I'll let your friend know you're done. Just call me if you need anything."

Willa swept through the door.

"Have you heard anything?"

"No. Mr. Carrick was relieved to hear your injuries aren't serious." Willa straightened the blanket on my legs. Where had that Willa come from? "Want me to find a show to watch?"

"No, thanks. I don't like television anymore." I grew quiet for a moment. My headache began to lessen. "But you could read to me if you wanted."

"Read to you? I don't know." Willa scanned the room. "I don't see anything in here to read, but I think Mr. Carrick has his Bible. Do you want him to read to you?"

"Can you ask to borrow it? I don't want to bother him right now."

"Sure." Willa obviously didn't want to read, but I needed something to keep my brain from focusing on the worst possible outcome.

When Willa returned, she flipped the Bible open and read, but it didn't bring the calm I'd hoped. "Sorry, Willa. I can't concentrate, but thanks for trying. I think I just need to pray."

Willa closed the book and studied me. "Me, too."

I bargained with God for Kyle's life—begged Him to intercede. When a small knock at the door interrupted me, I opened my eyes.

Willa jumped out of her seat. "Mr. Carrick?"

His voice faltered. "They just told me they revived him on the way to the hospital, but his injuries are very bad. He went too long without oxygen. The weight of the wagon…"

He struggled to maintain control of his voice, and I wailed. "It can't be. It's my fault."

The nurse pushed past Mr. Carrick. "Brooke, can I get you anything? Is there anyone you need to call?"

"No. I don't want to call anyone. But please … let me

see Kyle. *Now.*" Hysteria gripped me to the core. My head throbbed as if it might explode.

The nurse put up her hand. "Okay, listen. The doctor will be here in just a minute. Let him talk to you. Then if he clears you, I'll discharge you, and you can go see your other friend. I brought you some medication to help with the nausea and dizziness, but it'll take a few minutes to work."

I waited for a cue from Mr. Carrick before I took the medication. He nodded. Priscilla gave me the little pill. My tears dripped off my nose and face, but I didn't care. *Let me get out of here. Please. Please. I need to see Kyle.*

"Mr. Carrick, did they get the guy who did this?" I trembled.

"Yeah." Willa raised her fist. "He deserves—"

"He's in custody, but I can't talk about it yet." He moved a few more feet into the room. "I know there's nothing I can do to take away the hurt, but you should know that Kyle alerted us about the guy he was chasing. He didn't have a positive I.D. at the time, but he opened up the investigation. He saved your life and perhaps many others, and he did it selflessly. It's so hard sometimes to understand God's ways, but we need to look to Him now."

Numbness crept through my body with aching slowness and uncontrollable sobs escaped me. "Did I see that guy under the wagon too?"

Mr. Carrick's knuckles were white. He looked away. "He's in surgery."

"How bad?"

The shake of his head told me he wasn't at liberty to say more. "I'd tell you if I had permission."

He didn't deserve to live. But something twitched in my heart. Why did I feel guilty for thinking that?

When the doctor arrived, Mr. Carrick excused himself. "I'll be right down the hall."

Willa didn't move from my side. She handed me a box of tissues.

The doctor took his seat and rolled up to me. "I got your scan back, and you have a concussion, but it's not too bad. You should be back to normal in a week or two. Let me take a look at the cut on your head."

He stood and pulled my hair back as the nurse waited for his instructions. "It doesn't need stitches. Steri-strips, please, Priscilla."

The nurse held out an open packet. After cleaning the area again, the doctor took the strips one at a time and placed them on my abrasion.

I held still and stared at the wall as Willa squeezed my hand a little.

Returning to his seat, the physician typed a few notes in his tablet, and then returned his attention to me. "I'm going to send you home. You can recover there with a little rest. The nurse will give you discharge information about your care, okay?"

I nodded, and he patted my arm before he left. The nurse followed him out the door and then returned. Her voice was soft again. "I can take you back to see Mr. Reston if you want."

"Please." When Nurse Priscilla returned, she pulled a computer on wheels behind her. "Here's all your paperwork." She ran through the care directions on the papers and clicked on the computer screen as she made sure I understood my injuries and limitations over the next several days. "If you follow the doctor's orders, you'll be fine. But if you don't, you'll be in here again, okay?"

"Yes, ma'am."

"Just sign these." Then Nurse Priscilla took the paper from me. "Let me get a wheelchair for you."

I crushed the tissue in my hand. *Hurry up.* Kyle was waiting for me. My nails bit into my skin. The pain didn't matter anymore. I sat up and squeezed my eyes shut. *Why?*

"Are you ready?"

I managed to get in the wheelchair with little trouble. If the nurse didn't hurry, I'd hijack the chair and zoom down the hall on my own.

Willa took over pushing me once we exited the emergency department. As we rolled down the hall, we passed the 'Trauma' sign over the doorway. Every step brought me closer to the truth—to my guilt. Should I turn back? I stared all the way to the end of the hallway as we passed door after door. My peripheral vision blurred until all I saw was the last one. The thumping of my heart left me breathless. I tried not to hyperventilate. "Willa, I never asked how you were?" I sucked in a breath. "Are you okay?"

"I'm fine," she whispered.

And then we stopped in front of the final room. The nurse pushed the door open. Kyle lay so still. Tubes came out of so many parts of his body.

Willa gave a loud gulp. "I'll give you a little time."

When she left, the door closed behind her. I pulled myself up from the chair and moved to the side of the bed with slow deliberate steps. Drawn to his side, yet not wanting to see the damage to his body, I took a sharp intake of air.

"Kyle," I murmured. How could I live with the guilt? My chest throbbed from it. "How did this happen to us— to you? I'm so sorry I didn't believe you. I should have known you were innocent."

For the first time, no one could stop me from touching him, from being close to him. I reached over and gingerly stroked his cheek, noting the matted blood in his fine blonde hair. A tear glided down my face. I drew back at the reality of it, looking at the trauma of what he had suffered, and wailed. What if I'd hurt him by touching him? I used the softest pressure to take his hand in mine.

"Why, God?" His chest seemed to rise and fall so slow it didn't seem conducive to life. The machines did the work for him, though.

Bile rose to my throat, and I swallowed, squeezing my eyes shut. My mind wanted to shut down, to close off all the hurt and pain, but I struggled to maintain control, to stay upright.

Willa knocked on the door. "Need more time?"

I glanced at the clock. Whoa, a half hour had somehow passed. I nodded, and watched the door close behind Willa, but it opened a minute later when a nurse and a couple doctors entered to check over Kyle.

Another hour passed. The ticking of the clock echoed in the room. I had held his hand, rubbed his arm, straightened his blanket ten times.

Nurses came and went.

I'd even tried to check all of his injuries, but chickened out before I got too far. I didn't need to get in trouble with the nursing staff. He had a broken arm. One leg was wrapped at his thigh. A humungous bruise showed just at his collarbone. Scratches and bruises covered the right side of his face, and his eye had almost swollen shut. A bandage on his head hid most of his hair.

The machines beeped and pulsed and registered stats up on a monitor.

More medical staff came and went several times. I asked everyone who'd talk to me if Kyle was going to make it. They maintained their tight-lipped stares.

I talked to him and told him how guilty I felt, and begged him to forgive me. I whispered that I loved him so much over and over. He didn't move. Not even a finger twitched.

One of the nurses returned and checked the IV lines. "A Mr. Carrick asked me to send you out to him."

I wanted to stay all night.

Willa popped her head through the door. "Mr. Carrick wants to go home."

I shrugged. "Give me a minute."

To Kyle, I spoke in a soft whisper and gave him a gentle kiss on his temple. "I promise to come back as soon as I can get a ride. Goodbye."

I abandoned the wheelchair. My legs had steadied.

In the hall, Willa jumped up when she saw me. Dark shadows circled her eyes. "Let's go."

If I staged a coup, would they let me stay until Kyle opened his eyes? Probably not even that would sway Mr. Carrick.

62

Brooke

If it weren't for a debilitating migraine, coupled with broken sleep assaulted with recurrent nightmares, I'd have been down at Mr. Carrick's office demanding a ride to see Kyle before sun-up. The old demons of my past returned to fight hard and I'd lain in bed crying myself to sleep. But I fought back with the word of God. And won.

Anna's voice carried up the stairwell. "Ladies, can you all come down and join me in the living room, please?"

I dragged myself out of bed and threw on my robe. Would the pain in my head ever let up? The sun was too bright, and I squinted. A few stragglers in front of me walked at a snail's pace down the stairs.

Few seats were available by the time I reached the living room. I took a seat in the packed room. Their murmuring and whispers sounded as if they were yelling into microphones.

Anna waited for us to settle down, her eyes red around the edges. Her voice trembled. "I have some very sad news for you. As some of you probably already know, Kyle Reston was injured last night in an accident."

I tensed. Uh oh.

A buzz of shock filtered through the room, and Anna's

294

composure dropped. She sniffed. "He's in a medically induced coma right now."

Several women jostled to be heard. "What happened?"

Crying filled the room. I wanted to wail myself. But at least she hadn't said that he'd died.

"I'm not at liberty to talk about it, but I'm sure we'll all know soon enough. I haven't been apprised of visitation arrangements yet, but I'll let you know as soon as I get any details." She wiped her nose with a linen hanky.

Two of the women near me began to whisper. "I saw the wagon last night. Did you?"

"Yeah," the other one said. "And all the reporters. They were pouring in when the police sent us to our rooms. I heard they caught Eric Sarcon last night. He was the reason the accident happened." One of them pointed in my direction. "She was involved too." They gave me a surreptitious glance.

Eric Sarcon.

"Ladies, ladies." Anna struggled to get our attention again. "If you need to talk to anyone, all of the therapists and staff will be available for you. Please don't deal with this alone. Go see them. They are here to help."

The pounding in my head intensified. I pushed myself out of the chair and headed to the hallway, but Anna stopped me.

"Brooke, I got a doctor's note saying you're to take three days of rest. I've already lined up others to do your chores, so please go to bed and get some sleep. I'll bring you some breakfast in a bit, okay?"

I closed my eyes and put a hand to my temple. "Thank you, Ms. Anna. I really appreciate it. But what I really want is to go see Kyle."

"I'm sorry. I forgot to tell you Mr. Carrick said you

needed to stay inside for the next three days. There's a drove of reporters around, and he wants to protect you from them."

"*I can't.* I have to be there for Kyle."

The older woman hesitated, and squinted before she continued. "Well … I'm sorry … but they are trying to make a story out of your relationship with Kyle."

"*What?*"

"I know, honey, but you must understand how they can be." She laid a comforting hand on my shoulder.

I pursed my lips and patted her arm. "Thanks for the warning. But I'm going to Mr. Carrick's office."

She didn't argue but gave me a tight smile.

I returned to my room and searched for my best dress. It took extra time to get ready with my head pounding as if a drill dug into it. A gasp escaped my lips at my reflection in the mirror. *That can't be me.* The puffiness from crying and the dark bruise, slightly visible on one side, made me look sick and broken. I looked away and concentrated on working the knots out of my hair.

Eric Sarcon had tried to abduct me. Why hadn't I realized who he was last night when he'd first come out of the church? He had been so nice to me before. It didn't make any sense. Yet sometimes he had made me uneasy. Could someone as ordinary as him be responsible for the heinous crimes they accused him of?

A chill shook me. He must've been the one who sent me the flower. And he had to be the one who'd turned me and Kyle in when we'd gone out to the field. I got the heebie-jeebies thinking about him watching Kyle and me tease each other at the rock. What all had he seen? Kyle's proclamation of love must've angered him beyond belief. Maybe Kyle's accident had been calculated, not just a mishap of circumstance.

How dare he? Good thing God had the only right to vengeance, because if it were up to me, Eric would pay ten times over.

When I slid the bedroom door open, the slight breeze that blew in reminded me fall had come. The season no longer held the appeal it once did. I'd forever remember it as the time I'd almost lost everything.

At the bottom of the stairs, I looked both ways and hurried through the hall to the door. The unseasonably cool air flitted through an open window somewhere. I took my cloak off the rack and wrapped it around my shoulders.

Perhaps a trip through the garden on the way to Mr. Carrick's office would calm my nerves. But Mr. Carrick had left staunch directions to stay in the boarding house. I promised to only divert my path for a minute, just long enough to collect my thoughts.

All I wanted was a few minutes outside.

I dashed to the entrance of the park and slowed where the bushes provided privacy. When I saw Kyle's bench, I fought the tears that escaped and sat on it, rubbing the smooth, polished surface. Leaves and dying flower petals blew across the path. I looked away to the clouds that scuttled across the sky. The heavens seemed as if they wanted to weep with me as I gazed up. What a profound moment.

A rustle made me sit straight up and listen with new intentness. I had been alone when I entered the park. I jolted off the bench. Reporters? I jumped as the sound drew closer and I got ready to make a run for it.

Flashing lights blinded me for a moment and I threw my hand up to block my eyes from its harshness.

"Brooke Hollen, did you know you were being stalked by a serial killer?" The reporter inched into my view with his camera and microphone.

"Did you knowingly lead him outside of the church? Did you think the police would catch him, or were you expecting someone different to meet you?" The person came so close I smelled the peppermint on his breath.

Another camera blinked its lights in my face from the other side of the path.

"Brooke, did you know that breaking the regulations of the program by having an intimate relationship with a fellow resident was enough to have you dismissed? Who's protecting you? Who should be held accountable for Kyle Reston's accident? Did you know the serial killer?"

I fell back but caught myself before I tripped on my long skirt. "Where—"

Strong arms pulled me up, cutting off my question. It took a moment to realize Mr. Carrick had come to shield me from the two reporters. "Gentlemen, if you have any questions, you need to direct them to me. I don't have any more information than what Detective Schubert gave you this morning. May I remind you that you are on private property?"

"We are paying customers so we have the right to be here." One of them pointed to the admission sticker on his shirt.

"Please leave her alone."

He put his arm around me and guided me out of the park, back to the boarding house. I cowered in his grasp and shook from the violation of my privacy.

"Brooke, I warned you not to go out. Didn't Ms. Anna tell you to stay in the house?"

I avoided eye contact. "Yes, but I only stopped in the garden for a brief minute. I was on my way to see you about going to the hospital."

"Breaking the rules will endanger you. I'm trying to protect your reputation, but I can't if you don't listen. Don't you remember what happened the last time you ignored them?" He looked at me and crossed his arms. "I'm sorry, I shouldn't have said that … but please, stay here for one more day, okay?"

I studied his austere expression. "How did you know I was there?"

"Jade saw you leave."

So much for my uncanny ability to sneak out of the boarding house. I abandoned the line of questions and switched to desperation mode. "Mr. Carrick, please take me to the hospital."

He rubbed his elbow. "I don't know. It's even worse outside of the center. Reporters are everywhere."

"Please."

He gave in and sighed. "I guess you'll be safer there."

I squealed but shut up fast since it sent a shock of pain into my brain. "I'm ready. Let's go."

He moved to the front entrance and tried to avoid the stares of the women. "Ms. Anna, I'm going to take Brooke to the hospital."

They conversed in private for way too long. I tapped my foot on the handwoven rug and kept peering around the room to see what took him so long. When they finished, he escorted me out the door. "Your father contacted me and said he'd be here tomorrow."

Not now. Shouldn't I be glad he cared enough to come for me? I rubbed my hand across my mouth. "Okay."

"How's your head?"

I didn't want to lie but would he take me if he knew how bad it hurt? I settled for a nonchalant shrug.

He chuckled. "You can have some acetaminophen for your headache before we go."

I blinked. "How—"

"I can see you're in lots of pain."

"No, thanks. I don't want to take any medication ever again. I'll be fine if we can just get to the hospital."

And even better if Kyle lived.

63
Brooke

Maybe I should've accepted the headache medicine from Mr. Carrick. I squinted from the pressure in my head. Hospital odors choked me and worsened my headache as we strode to the ICU. But I had to get to Kyle.

I didn't wait for Mr. Carrick to follow me into Kyle's room. I bolted for his door and screeched to a halt. A man and woman sat beside his bed and held his hands. His parents? "Hello?"

They seemed to startle out of some alternate universe into the horrible reality of the hospital room.

The woman had Kyle's eyes. Such crystal-clear blue.

"Ma'am, I'm Brooke, a close friend of Kyle's."

The woman bit her lip as she focused on me. "Yes … the woman in the news."

I shrank a little. Yikes. They already knew something. And I doubted it had much truth to it. And I had no way of contradicting it since we had no television at the center to explain what they'd heard. "I, um… Its… he's so important to me … to us."

The woman nodded and called over her shoulder, "Tom, this is Brooke. You know…"

"Oh, hello." He studied me the same way as the

woman, through bleary eyes.

I quivered at the sight of Kyle's father, but shook his hand when he offered it to me. "I'm so sorry for all of this."

"Yeah, who would've thought we'd be here, when my son came to this place to change his life around, to get back on course with his future."

"He was doing everything to finish his plan."

Kyle's father looked at me. "Thank you." He cleared his throat as if to stave off tears. "Is it true what they say in the news about you two?"

I took a deep breath. "I don't know what they're saying, but I can tell you we cared deeply for each other. But we'd never let anything get in the way of our recoveries, including a relationship against the rules."

Kyle's mother teared up. She threw her arms around me. "Honey."

I froze.

"You love him, don't you?"

My own tears started to roll down my face. "More than almost anything."

Mr. Carrick entered the room. Good thing he hadn't come until after I admitted how much I cared for Kyle.

Mrs. Reston didn't release me for a minute, and I allowed her to comfort me.

When she let go, Mrs. Reston said, "If you need anything, just let us know." She fished in her purse for a personalized business card and handed it to me. The name of a beauty salon emblazoned the top of the card.

"Thank you." I held back and watched them.

"We'll be staying in Kent for a few more days, so just call, all right?"

The woman squeezed me one more time, and the gesture brought more tears. It wasn't at all what I'd expected. Anger, for sure. Hate? Maybe. Not acceptance.

64

Brooke

Day two. Kyle still slept. But his hand moved when I squeezed it. His mother gave the doctors permission to talk to me. The news remained grim but not hopeless.

I had to return to work at the tailor shop, but at least Mr. Carrick allowed me to spend the evenings at the hospital. The day dragged by until I stopped looking at the clock.

I folded the last re-hemmed dress on a stack of others and put my needle in a pin cushion. "Ms. Stacey, I'm finished for the day."

I got the same sad eyes from her as everyone else who had learned about me and Kyle. Lots of things had been exposed.

She shooed me out the door. I still didn't want to walk alone. Captured killer or not.

At the hotel, I stopped and waited for Willa to come out.

Once more, cameras flashed around me out of nowhere, and I recognized one of the men who'd accosted me in the park. To prevent his view, I turned. What horrible things might he say about me on national television or even the internet? My old friends had to think the whole mess was a riot. "No comment. Leave me alone."

I scurried into the hotel. Where was Willa?

I didn't notice a woman at the reception desk until she spoke.

"Miss, I just want you to know..." She touched my elbow and I reacted like a deer caught in someone's headlights. "We are so thankful, after what he did to our little girl."

What did she mean? "I'm sorry..."

The woman dabbed at some tears. "We saw you on the news. You're Brooke, right? Jordan was our daughter." The woman reached for the shirtfront of the man beside her. "If it wasn't for Kyle, that man would've escaped. I know one's life is a terrible price to pay, but at least no one else will be hurt."

Jordan's mom wiped at her tears as she spoke. Then she looked down at the necklace around my neck. "Where did you get that?"

"Get what?" I looked down too.

"That necklace?"

"I found it in our—the garden." A new onslaught of tears erupted, and I wanted to cry with her. "I turned it in, but no one claimed it."

"May I see it?"

I leaned forward to give her a closer look.

"I think that's Jordan's. You said you found it in a garden?" She took another look.

I hesitated. "Yes."

"You don't think..." The woman put her hand to her mouth and closed her eyes for a moment.

I wore a dead girl's necklace? My stomach lurched.

Jordan's mother opened her eyes. "We need to show it to the police."

I released the clasp on it, but it seemed to cling to my skin. I struggled to remove it. "Please take it."

"I bought it for her just before she left home for rehab." The mother raised her hand but paused, as if she were afraid of it.

Jordan's father put his arm around his wife. "They'll need you to show them where you got it."

"Here." I dropped it into her hand. It was almost too much to bear to realize I'd been wearing Jordan's necklace the whole time. Had it been lost in Jordan's last struggle against her killer? Did it have anything to do with why he'd chosen me next? He had said something about the necklace when he grabbed me.

"Thank you." The woman stared at the piece of jewelry.

"If you take it to Mr. Carrick, he'll know what to do." I wanted to run and never look back, to escape the horror of the last two days.

The flash of a few cameras reflected off the piece of jewelry as the woman held it up then placed it in her purse. The corners of her mouth drew down as her eyes swelled with more tears. "I'm so sorry you have to go through this."

They left me standing there in total shock. What next?

The flash of another camera caught my attention, and suddenly someone stood in front of me.

"Brooke Hollen, tell us why you were allowed to have an open relationship with another resident when it is strictly against policy here at the Carrick Living Museum. And do you take responsibility for Kyle Reston's accident and his involvement in the capture of the Rehab Serial Killer?"

My breath caught as my fists balled at my sides.

Willa raced down the grand staircase and yanked me

behind her. "She has nothing to say to you. How dare you accuse her of something so heinous?" She balled her fists. "Now, back off."

My good old bulldog friend. At that moment, I loved her so much for protecting me.

The reporter tried again. "But…"

"I said back off and leave her alone." Willa stood with her hands on her hips between the newsmen and me.

The reporter dropped the big microphone to his side and harrumphed.

When Willa turned to me, she winced. And whispered. "Not to give you more bad news, but your father is here. Mr. Carrick wanted me to bring him to you."

I hurried away from the reporters to the window and spotted him climbing the stairs at a slower pace. What should I say to him? But … he had come. A good sign. I dabbed at my puffy eyes. Better get out of the hotel and meet him.

Willa stayed as close as a stitch on material.

I straightened my back and ran a hand through my hair.

"Brooke, there you are." He covered the distance between us with his arms extended.

"Dad." I stepped into his embrace. I'd better be careful not to get any tears on his starched dress shirt, devoid of the usual tie. He wouldn't be happy.

"I'm so sorry about your friend."

Kyle was more than a friend. He was my future.

"Let me take you home. Your grandparents and I are worried about you." His wavy hair with its streaks of silver-white at the temples didn't even ruffle in the wind. The heavy ironed pleat down his pants bent in perfect lines with each step. But it was only a façade to a corruptness I knew well.

I'd known he'd say that. "No."

"But…"

I cut him off before he continued. "I need to be here … now more than ever."

"No, you don't."

"I do, Dad." We walked into town with Willa close behind, and I avoided the sympathetic glances of the people on the sidewalks. I wanted to run to my room and stay there forever, to sleep the weeks away until the pain disappeared.

"You're not being reasonable."

"I have something I need to do in a bit, but we can sit down and eat first. Want to get dinner?" Could I manage to put a bite in my mouth? I doubted it, but anything to distract him had to do.

"Here?" Her father looked around the center.

"Yes. There's a nice restaurant in town."

Willa squeezed my arm. "I'm going to leave you two alone."

I raised my hand to stop her, but she moved away too fast. The last thing I needed was to be alone with Dad. He'd spend the whole mealtime trying to convince me to go home.

At the tea shop, I ushered Dad into the cozy restaurant. Boxes of food lined the counter, and I waited for Daisy to take our order.

"Hello, Brooke." She reached out and squeezed my hand. "What can I get for you?"

"Ms. Daisy, this is my father, Dallas Hollen."

"It's nice to meet the father of this fine lady." She smiled at him then at me. "I want you two to order whatever you want. It's on the house today."

The kind gesture made my throat tighten. I tried to swallow. "Thank you, that's really nice. Are you sure?"

"Yes, ma'am. I tried a new recipe with those cupcakes. You should try one."

My father and I ordered, and then moved away from the counter. The seats in the back of the restaurant were empty, and I guided him to my usual spot. But when I got there, I backed away. Too many memories of Kyle invaded me. Turning on my heel, I hurried to the front and picked one of the small tables. "Here's a good place."

Dad sat across from me. "Listen, it's all over the news about your secret relationship with some guy. They said that kind of thing is forbidden here. And they said he was protecting you when he got trampled. I need some answers."

"That guy's *name* is Kyle, Dad." I avoided his watchful eye. "I don't want to talk about it right now."

He shrugged and looked around the store. "Tell me about this place. It's different than I imagined."

"Well, it's a living museum. The design of this rehab center is to have the residents work while they get treatment for their addiction. And let me tell you, we work very hard, but it's worth it. It gives you a reason to want to quit, you know. A goal."

"Hmm."

"You're a workaholic. You'd like it here." I treaded on thin ice.

"We're not talking about me."

I raised my shoulders and dropped them.

He redirected the conversation. "I heard this place might be shut down for not investigating that killer when he got here."

That took me aback. "Really? We don't have television so I didn't know."

"Yeah. And there's probably going to be lawsuits involved as well. It's going to get messy. That's another reason why I don't want you here."

"Dad, I'm twenty-two. I can handle it." I gave him my best no-nonsense look, which usually worked when I was a kid.

Ms. Daisy brought platters of food.

Dad put the thick linen napkin across his right leg. "Wow, she's really generous."

The food on my plate held no appeal. I stirred it around but didn't eat.

"Come on, you need some nourishment. When was the last time you had a full meal? Look how skinny you've gotten."

I looked at him, eyebrows raised.

"Okay, I get the message. Butt out."

"Where are you staying? In town?" I hung my arms at my sides.

"Yes."

"How long will you stay?"

"Just tonight. I have this deal that has to be closed in two days, and I figured one day was plenty of time to get you out of here." He raised his hand as I started to protest. "I get it, I get it. You're staying. Let me say this though … you can come home whenever you want."

A nice gesture. It'd been a long time since I'd seen concern on his face. Then I remembered the empty space on my twelve-step plan sheet. I'd evaded it for far too long. And it seemed like the worst time to bring it up, but any more avoidance hindered my rehab. I did need closure before he left. "Dad, we have these plans we have to work, and part of it is dealing with things from our past." I paused for a moment and tried to collect my thoughts. "You know, we don't have a very good history together."

He started to protest.

"Please hear me out. I always felt like such a burden to you, as if you don't really love me. And all your drinking—"

"Brooke—"

"No, listen. I took a lot of money from you, and I stayed out to make you mad. And sometimes I fought with you just to get your attention." It all rushed out before I lost my nerve. "I'm sorry."

"Honey, there's no need to say that."

"Yes, there is. Do you forgive me?"

He waved his hand. "It's all in the past."

"But I still need to ask you."

"They make you?" He furrowed his eyebrows.

"They don't make us do anything. They help us to fix the past so we can move forward. It's very necessary."

He looked down at his plate. "I know I was never good at showing my love. And … the drinking, that's something adults do. I never considered you in all of it."

I hadn't expected him to get the point that his drinking was the catalyst to many things, but how nice if he did see it. "That's why I'm here—to change everything in my life. I was doing the same thing you were, coping in the same way, but now I see there's a better way."

He held his hands up once again, but I continued before he said more. "I'm not forcing you to do anything. I need you to know, though, there is a way to stop."

"Can we talk about something else?" He avoided my regard with pointed distraction.

I picked up my fork. "There's one more thing I need to tell you, and then I promise to talk about something else."

He raised his eyebrows. "You're really nailing me today, aren't you?"

My stomach churned. "I got saved when I first arrived

311

here."

"Saved? What's that?"

I told him, but why was it harder to talk about that than about my addiction? I forced down my fears. "Dad, you can have the same peace I have."

"That's good for you, but I'm fine. Now, can we *change* the subject?"

I wanted to cry, to beg him to hear me. I forced a bite between my teeth and worked to swallow it. Maybe he'd have to see the changes in me over time to start his own.

Mr. Carrick pushed the door open. He headed straight for us. "Mr. Hollen, it's nice to have you here." He turned to me. "I don't mean to impose on your dinner, but Detective Schubert is here to speak to you about the necklace."

I rose and dropped my napkin beside my plate. "Dad, I'll see you later."

He wiped his mouth with the napkin in his lap and sat forward. "What's going on? You're meeting with a cop?"

"It's okay. I'll explain it to you later."

"You didn't do anything, did you?"

"No." I glared at him. "I told you, I'll explain it later."

I couldn't thank Mr. Carrick enough for rescuing me from Dad. And the necklace? It provided one more bit of closure for the terrible events of the past few days.

But how could I stand on the ground where Jordan had lost her necklace and her life, and show it to the police?

65
Brooke

I'd really appreciate it if people stopped asking me how I was doing. Someone had tried to abduct me. The love of my life lay in a hospital bed in a coma. And I wanted to scream.

Mr. Carrick ushered me down the street. "I'm here if you need some extra sessions."

I managed a shrug. Anything else would draw more tears. Dad's rejection of Christ, on top of Kyle playing the role of sleeping beauty, hit so hard I almost buckled under the pressure.

"I wish I didn't have to do this to you right now, but I do. The searchers are still looking for Jordan. Anything we can do to speed that up is of utmost importance."

"He refuses to tell you what he did with her?" *How terrible!*

He cleared his throat. "Sarcon isn't telling anyone anything."

"Of course not."

"We'll know more when…" His words trailed off.

"I understand." I studied the boards of the sidewalk as we marched over them and changed the subject. "Thanks for letting Willa stay with me."

"I don't want you to be alone right now at such a difficult time."

I sighed. "I know, but don't worry. I'm not planning to return to any old habits."

He raised his eyebrows. "That's very reassuring."

At the general store, he led me back to his office, where the detective waited.

Detective Schubert stood. "Thanks for coming. I know you have a visitor, but this shouldn't take too long."

I took the seat next to him and tried not to let his steely gaze shock me into sheer silence.

The detective got to the point. "We need to know about the necklace. Where did you find it?"

"In the garden." I gestured toward the general direction of the park, and then sat forward. "I'll show you."

"Okay. Let's go." Schubert put his notepad in a back pocket as he rose from the seat.

We stood moments later on the path beside the garden. "Right there." I pointed at the very spot where I'd picked it up out of the dirt. "The flowerbed wasn't here at the time. We were digging up the grass when I found it."

"We?" Schubert questioned.

"Yes. Kyle Reston and I." I bit my lip.

He nodded. "I think we're going to have to dig this all up. More evidence might be here."

I put a hand over my mouth. "Please, no, it's all I have left of…" I didn't finish my sentence and didn't stop the new set of tears that spilled down my face.

"Sorry, but we have to. Was it the only thing you found? Were there any footprints? Blood?" Schubert studied the flowerbed.

"No," I yelled. I couldn't stop myself from running away. I sprinted fast, without regard to where I went. As long as it was away from them.

Mr. Carrick called after me, but I refused to stop.

"Don't worry. We'll find her if we need more answers." The detective's voice boomed.

My breath came in sharp gasps as I hit the edge of town and headed down the lane to the field by the farm.

When I ceased my wild dash, I was at the rock overlooking the creek. The sharp edge of the stone pressed into me as I landed against it and sat in a tight ball, head buried in my knees. My body shook, wracked with crying. The sun receded as I sat. Nobody would find me out there. I didn't care about anything except Kyle anymore.

When the tears finally stopped, I lay against the rock and rested my head on my arm.

I heaved a sigh and pulled myself up, rubbing my eyes. If I didn't go back, I'd miss my chance to see Kyle that night.

Eric Sarcon should rot in prison the rest of his life for doing this to me and all those women. I tried not to get skittish, but apprehension grew as I headed over the hill and back down the other side. Every time I thought about my brush with death, it became so fresh. The perp lay in a hospital bed with guards watching him. But an irrational paranoia stirred me into a frenzy. When I reached the road, I looked both ways and hurried into town.

On Main Street, my heavy tread echoed across the wooden sidewalk, but the sound of other footsteps pressed in my direction, and I stopped in mid-stride. Had I been followed? I plastered my back against the building, waited, and then slid to the ground in a ball of tears. The center stayed quiet. I tried to get up, but my body didn't obey. I took a deep breath. *Stop being a baby.* Two men appeared, and I let out a shrill screech and buried my face in my arms.

One of them called to me. "Hey, Brooke, you okay?"

The sound of Bret's voice made me look up. "You scared me."

"Sorry. Do you need help with something?" He kept his distance while his friend watched in silence.

"No, I'm fine." Yeah, I'd bet I looked like a two-year-old in the middle of a tantrum. I lied but I just wanted them to leave. Not a good reason to be dishonest.

"Whatever." He turned back to his friend and they walked away.

As they disappeared, I shuddered and stood with slow deliberation. Maybe it was time to talk to Mr. Carrick. I didn't want to be out of control like that. He might be able to help me get rid of the unreasonable fears that had started to debilitate me from out of the blue. We had a twenty-minute car ride to talk about it. And I'd see if Mr. Carrick had a few extra minutes to stop at Dad's hotel. If Dad had to leave in the morning, I'd better say goodbye. Who knew when I'd see him again? …And I didn't like the way we had left things at the tea shop.

66
Brooke

It would take a miracle to end the old tug of war between Dad and me. But I wanted to try. I grappled with the right thing to say to him. To let him leave on good terms and not angry words or dirty looks.

At the hotel, I knocked on his door. "Dad, it's me."

He pulled it open and ushered me in, waving at the TV. Even in his room where he'd begun to settle in for the night, he hadn't changed out of his business clothes. So typical of him. Always with an air of propriety that was only skin deep. "You're not going to believe this."

I sat rigid. Another nasty news broadcast. It'd been so long since I'd watched TV—other than the other night in the emergency department.

Dad gestured at the screen. "See? They turned this *event* into a nightmare."

"Wasn't it one already?" I played with my fingers and sat against the back of the chair.

The newscaster's voice with its mock concern ate at my annoyance levels. "Shouldn't the state create a stricter regulation on these kinds of rehabilitation centers?"

The anchorwoman turned to the camera and answered. "It would seem the Carrick Living Museum and Rehab

Center is lacking proper guidelines and screening processes. Will they change their policies on how they select future residents, or should the state step in and close the agency? To allow certain residents, like Brooke Hollen and Kyle Reston, to openly break the rules has led to this tragedy."

I rolled my eyes. "Please turn it off."

He shrugged and hit the power button.

"It's amazing how they twist a place as wonderful as this center into a den of iniquity. And I promise you, we weren't having a *relationship*."

Dad raised his eyebrows.

"Mr. Carrick and Ms. Dara are trying to help people. The newscasters make it sound like they had no idea what was going on there, as if they allowed all kinds of illegal activities to happen. Well, I assure you, if they had known what that killer was capable of, they would've had him arrested long ago."

"They didn't protect you."

"Dad, how do you think they would've known about the guy? They were trying to help him."

"It's their job to know."

I squinted at him.

He sighed and threw the remote on the bed. "Anyway, you were almost a victim like that Jordan girl."

"But God kept me safe."

I replayed the words of the reporter over and over in my mind. There was no doubt the center would take a lot of criticism for its part in the murder of Jordan Magnus.

"How sure are you there aren't more people like him here?" Dad paced the floor.

"It's a rehab center. There're all kinds of people."

"That's my point."

"You can stay here and keep me safe … among other

things."

He wiggled his index finger back and forth. "Nice try."

I exhaled and looked at the clock. "I have to go. Do you want to meet for breakfast?"

"Can't. I have to leave early."

"We can meet around seven."

He stopped in mid-step as his eyes got big. "You'll wake up that early?"

I laughed. "Way earlier than that. People can change in more ways than one."

Dad shrugged and reached for his shoes. "Sorry. Not this time. Come on. I'll walk you to your ride."

"Thanks, Dad." My sense of safety hadn't returned, no matter how brave I tried to be. Ridiculous as it was.

He grew silent as we walked. I didn't want to disturb his thoughts.

At Mr. Carrick's car, Dad gave me a hug. "It's a relief to see the media gone for the night. I don't want them to bother you."

How many hugs had he given me in the last few years? Not many. I breathed in his rich cologne. "I wish I never had to see them again, but I doubt this is the end of their harassment."

When I moved away, he put his hands on my shoulders. "Well, don't speak to them, okay? They don't need to know anything."

"I wish it was that easy." I leaned into the strength of his hands.

"They'll get the hint if you keep quiet."

"I doubt it. Do you remember the arsonist in the news last year? It was months before they dropped the story, and this one is bigger, you know."

"Yeah, a serial killer is big news in this sick world." He put his hands in his pockets and sighed. "But at least try to stay out of the public eye. I'll get my lawyer involved to help if need be."

How did anyone stand the cameras being jammed in their faces and people crowding them, hammering question after question at them?

He stopped at the bottom of the stairs. "Lock your door when you get to your room. I mean it."

"I promise. Goodbye." He swaggered to the sidewalk, and I leaned against the window as he went. He didn't look back. He wouldn't want me to be sentimental or needy. Yet I watched until he vanished behind the glass doors. And I was okay. Really okay about us.

67
Brooke

Kyle refused to open his eyes, as if his dreams were way sweeter than the nightmare we faced. They'd taken him off the medicine to keep him in a coma, but still he slept. I squeezed his hand and begged him to come back to me. His mother worried over him with her trembling hands, which straightened and re-straightened everything within reach. "Please, Kyle."

His bruises had darkened to the worst shade of purple and yellowish green. At least his swollen eye had gone down a little. And there were fewer tubes coming out of him. He'd downgraded from being intubated to a nasal oxygen cannula in his nostrils.

I spent three hours at his bedside. Mr. Carrick sat in the room for a while, but left to get some coffee right before Kyle's parents decided they needed another break too.

The Restons gave me some time alone with him—but not much. I reveled in those moments when I had no one to tell me not to get too close or not to hold his hand and touch his cheek.

But I'd stalled Mr. Carrick long enough. We both needed to go home and rest.

When the Restons returned with soda bottles in their hands, I gave Kyle one more rub on his arm and bid them goodnight.

Mr. Carrick hadn't returned from his coffee break. I'd bet he had gone to the coffee shop on the first floor. I'd save him a trip up the elevator.

Peeking right and left, I headed out of the ICU. Several other visitors passed me in their tight jeans and logoed tee shirts. The time warp my costume created didn't embarrass me as it would've four months ago. In fact, I still didn't know if I wanted to go back to the contemporary world.

I stopped at an intersection of halls. Which way had we come from? The empty corridors echoed my footfall. I hadn't gone too far. Maybe I should go back and start over.

A patient limped from the opposite end, hustling it in my direction. Did he have an idea of how to get to the elevators?

68
Sarge

What guards underestimated someone like him? The police from Kent had no idea who he was to be stupid enough to leave him alone in the bathroom for even a minute. But, his gain.

One chance. That's all he had. Sarge thrust his body against the hospital room door and pulled it open. He scrutinized every doorway in the hall. How hard would it be to get past the nurses' station? He had no option. He hoped they were too busy to see him limp past them. But if he didn't take the chance, he'd never see freedom again.

Sarge limped to the nearest exit. Pain radiated from his knee to his shin.He had to get out of there.

He stopped at the wall just before the station, where he had a view of most of the nurses working at computers. Beeps began to echo from the parallel hall, and the nurses stood in one accord and raced to whatever emergency the bells signaled.

He bolted, and limped so fast he almost crashed into the cold floor, still wet from a mop job.

The rod they'd placed in his leg seared as if it wanted to come out—but he kept going. He only had to worry about one cop. The other one had to be put down. And he'd never get up again. But it was his fault. He shouldn't have tried to stop Sarge. Sarge figured he had about two minutes before that guy woke up and chased him.

Too bad he didn't have time to find Reston and finish him off too.

He clambered out of one unit and through another. A nurse exited a room and checked something on the mobile computer she wheeled. She looked at him and paused.

"I don't need help." He tried not to let his voice rise or shake.

Good thing she was too busy to really care.

He continued to the next intersection. What perfect timing. The halls were empty—except a women in colonial garb.

Wait—Brooke? Thin frame. Blonde hair hanging loose. Red dress to the floor. It couldn't be.

But it was.

As if his heart hadn't pounded enough on the harrowing trip through the halls, it threatened to lodge in his throat at the sight of her.

He pressed against the wall by another exit. Had she seen him? She had looked straight at him, but he had been too far away.

Forget the fierce pain in his leg, he grimaced and took off at a near run. Just as his fingers came into contact with her cloak, she turned.

Too late she stared into his face. He wrapped one arm around her waist and the other around her throat. She tried to flail but he twisted her neck back to the point that she stopped all movement. "Don't scream. Be absolutely silent."

He breathed in her sweet scent.

Carrick had to be somewhere close.

He pressed her to him. "Start walking."

She took hesitant steps one way, but he pulled her in the other direction.

Someone exited a room to their right. He jostled her into the nearest room and waited at the door to see the nurses return to where they'd come from.

Brooke resisted, trying to bite his hand. He crushed his fingers over her mouth so hard a muffled yelp escaped. But she stopped.

They returned to the hall. Ten feet further on, the elevators lined an alcove. He used his elbow to press the down button.

Brooke kicked back at his injured leg. Somehow he managed to move in time. But it set him off balance.

Together they toppled to the floor. She brought her elbow up and cracked down onto his bruised ribs. He groaned. With a twist of his hand he managed to stop a second blow, but he didn't halt the kick she throttled into his surgical site, where bone and metal were meant to fuse. One loud crack sent his mind reeling with more agony than he'd imagined possible.

He released her and tried to breathe. She crawled away from him as alarms began to screech through the whole hospital. Her own screams mingled with the blares.

Brooke turned hazy and everything went black. And then the screeching alarms faded with the darkness.

69
Brooke

My screams might as well be whispers, the way the alarms covered them. I wailed and struggled to the corner.

Eric lay very still.

I tried to get up, but my twisted dress imprisoned me. No cell phone. No way to get help in the endless halls of emptiness.

If I left, he might wake up and escape. If I stayed, no one would find us. I put my hands to my head. "God, what should I do?"

A couple nurses appeared out of nowhere, followed by several more. "We're in lockdown, ma'am—"

"*Help.*"

They looked from me to Eric and raced into action.

"He tried to kidnap me again."

Several of them pushed a button at their lapels and began to talk into the wire connected to it.

Another pulled me up and steered me clear of my captor. "Are you hurt?"

"No." My skirts came loose and billowed around me.

Yet another male nurse reached down and checked Eric's vitals.

The elevators beeped. Mr. Carrick raced out of the farthest one and stopped short. He took in Eric on the floor, and then me. "Brooke?"

"Mr. Carrick?" I let go of the nurse and darted toward him.

He took my hand and pulled me down the hall. "It's okay. I have you now. It's okay."

One of the nurses halted him. "We're on lockdown. You need to go back to the section you came from. I'll send the guards to you. Where will you be?"

He held tight to me and gave them Kyle's room number.

We fled back to the ICU unit and waited for them to beep us in. The skin around my mouth ached from the crush of Eric's hand. I touched it with a gentle finger.

At Kyle's room, we hustled through the door.

"What's all that racket?"

I almost fell over at the sound of Kyle's weak voice. "It took the screaming alarms to wake you up? I could've almost made that much noise myself if I'd known."

I almost toppled onto the bed in my rush to get to his side.

Mr. Carrick made as if to stop me but backed off.

"Kyle. I can't believe you're awake." My voice croaked. The pressure Eric had put on my neck had done some damage.

He put out his hand but closed his eyes again. "Love you."

I tried to catch a glimpse of Mr. Carrick's reaction at the proclamation, but he kept a blank face.

To Kyle, I whispered, "I love you too. Just wait until I tell you what happened."

He fell asleep again. But at least not forever.

70

Brooke

Not a hundred prayers for him to wake stirred Kyle from his sleep the rest of the time I stared at him and prayed. But we all had a new hope for him. His fingers did move in mine. Another very good sign.

Officers sent a nurse to call us out of Kyle's room and down to the family sitting area outside of the ICU. "We've apprehended Eric Sarcon."

Too many questions later, I leaned against the wall, about to pass out from sleep deprivation and pain.

Mr. Carrick had his back to the wall also. "As the Bible says, 'This too shall pass.'"

The infamy in the media? Impending police interviews? The fear I hoped wouldn't turn into a phobia? "I pray that you're right." I shook my head and tried to keep my eyes open. "I have some things to talk to you about when everything settles."

Detective Schubert ambled through the door. A slick of hair stood up on the side of his head. Did I see a red mark on the same side of his face from sleeping? He pulled out his pad. "You just can't get enough drama, huh, Ms. Hollen?"

I was too tired to laugh.

He settled in the stiff plastic couch across from me. "Our man is finally talking this time. It took some strong meds to calm him down first, though. Calls himself Sarge."

"That's an unusual nickname." I fixated my stare on the painting behind his head, where flowers bloomed and a gazebo promised quiet peace. Where life seemed beautiful and happy, not wrought with death and sorrow.

"I'm meeting with the special crimes department tomorrow." His voice softened. "They found Jordan and one of the other girls." His words brought tears to my eyes. "Eric Sarcon has been formally charged. They're going to be recovering their remains."

The tears wet my face. I'd be forever linked to Jordan in a horrible and dark way. Except I'd escaped. I wanted to yell, to say how much Sarcon deserved what he got, but I shut my mouth tight.

"He'll also be charged with attempted kidnapping."

My eyes fixed on his. "Because of me?"

"Yes."

I managed a nod. I wanted to get away, to let out my anger. My clinched fist balled in my lap and my nails bit into my skin. I cleared my throat. "What about the others?"

"The girls who went missing months ago? They may not prove so easy to find."

Did I want to know what Detective Schubert meant?

His hands spread across his thighs.

I twisted my fingers together. "I can't get his face out of my mind. It was so awful to see him like that. I don't know if I'll ever sleep again."

Mr. Carrick stretched, his long jacket shifting to expose the vest underneath. "You will. God can lessen your pain and fear. Remember, prayer and meditation.

And we're all here for you. There's no rush for you to leave the center."

I took a deep breath and gave him a tight smile. They might have to force me out of that place at the end of it all. It was the best home I'd ever had.

With a push away from the wall, Mr. Carrick beckoned for me to follow him. "If that's all, Detective…"

Together, we all traipsed out of the waiting room. Detective Schubert shook our hands. "I'll be in touch."

The ICU doors flew open and almost banged against the wall. Mrs. Reston held one of them open. "I'm so glad you haven't left yet. Kyle's awake, and he insists I have to bring you back to him."

I picked up my skirts and hurried to the doors. "Mr. Carrick?"

Mrs. Reston pressed against the door. "If you don't mind us driving her, we can drop her back at the center later."

He waved me away. "Fine."

Yes. What would I have done if he hadn't understood? I scurried behind Kyle's mother. Was he okay?

As if she read my thoughts, she said, "No worries. He's just so adamant. And after all that he's been through, I'll give him almost anything he wants."

My chest almost exploded when I entered the room and he held his arm out for me to come to his side. I went to the other side of the bed, where his injuries were less severe, and took his hand. "Kyle, they caught the killer. And all because of you."

He tried to focus on my face. "Caught who? What killer?"

My mouth fell open.

Mrs. Reston went to his other side. "They said it's

common for patients who've experienced brain trauma to have some amnesia. It might be temporary ... or not. They won't know for a while."

I blinked hard and tightened my grasp on his hand. At least he knew who we were. That was what counted.

His words slurred a little. "Did I say anything embarrassing earlier? Can't ... remember."

"Well, Mr. Carrick was in the room when you proclaimed your love for me."

He grimaced and then winced as he touched his ribs. "Ouch. Oh, great. We're in trouble."

"But nothing is going to get in the way of our recovery. Right?"

"Mom. Dad. Can we have a moment?"

The Restons hesitated and looked at each other. His mother pursed her lips. "But..."

"It's okay. What am I going to do with half my body broken to pieces?"

They gave us a few moments alone.

He tried to pull closer to me but gave up as pain washed across his face. "I ... I won't let anything get in the way of putting our lives back together. God's gotten us this far. He'll take us the rest of the way. But I want you with me. Stay with me."

I touched his cheek with the back of my hand. "I'll always be here for you."

"Good." His eyes drifted closed. "You probably think I was out of my mind earlier, but I meant what I said. I love you. Forever..."

I leaned close to his face and smiled. His eyes opened and grew big but before he said another word, I pressed a soft kiss on his lips. "I love you so much."

"Good thing I'm in this bed ... or you might not be safe from me right now."

I giggled. "So you already forgot your promise? I see how it is."

He wrapped his good arm around my waist and drew me closer. "Sorry … I'll rehabilitate that thought later. But for now…"

I leaned in, and our lips touched again with the gentlest kiss. Sparks lighted through me all the way to my toes. I loved this man more than anyone. "Last kiss for … seven months."

He groaned. "Hope you can hold me to it."

Epilogue

Who knew I'd find full redemption at a center where I had to go back in history to solve my present misfortunes? But there I was on the one-year anniversary of the beginning of it all at the center. And with the best man I had ever known at my side. And to think I'd survived more than rehab. I'd even come to see my near accident that almost killed a kid as providential.

Kyle grasped a picnic basket full of Ms. Daisy's cooking. He shifted his weight to his good leg and reached for my hand. For the first time in public. "We made it."

I laughed. "Barely. It was tough with you tempting me the whole time."

He pulled me close and kissed my forehead. "Good thing you have the willpower I lack."

Willa hustled out of the hotel. "Guys. Wait up. You're not going without me."

I wanted to stay glued to his side, but not with Willa there ready to tell us off if she felt like it. "I'm so glad your new job let you come for the weekend."

"Me too. Who'd want to miss the ceremony for everyone getting their one-year clean chip." She poked me in my arm. "And you're receiving special recognition for your work at the tailor shop. All thanks to me introducing you to sewing."

"You would take the credit." I elbowed her.

We continued down the dirt lane to the emerald green fields by the farm. I breathed in the honeysuckle-scented air and took in the warm spring sun.

Carrick Living Museum and Rehabilitation Center had hired Kyle and me on extended work programs after we'd finished our rehab and repayment period. But soon we'd be off to college for Kyle to finish his law degree, and for me to major in fashion design and minor in psychology.

Picking up my skirts, I followed Kyle over the fence, and fell into his waiting arms. Willa pushed me away a second later and it made me giggle. "You should be a jail warden. You'd be so good at it."

"Ha ha. You need one."

Up the hill we waded through the wet thick grass. As we followed the slope down the other side, I spotted the rock. Our rock. We moved faster until all three of us climbed over its side and perched on it.

My dress settled around me as I sat on the rock's surface and folded my arms around my legs. I lifted my face to the heavens. *Thank you, Lord, for your abundant mercies and blessings.*

Kyle tried to steal a kiss, but Willa sprang between us and made a face at him. "Not while I'm here."

The last sweet kiss we'd shared had been that night at the hospital. Kyle nailed her with a glare. "We've finished our plans, as promised. This is our first official day of freedom. Can't you look the other way for two minutes?"

Willa narrowed her eyes and pursed her lips, looking from one of us to the other. "Fine." She scooted off the rock and rested against it, facing the other way. "The clock has started."

I stood and looked into Kyle's eyes. "Hurry before she changes her mind."

He closed the space between us and put his hands on my waist. I gulped. I'd waited so long for this day. In one motion, he raised a hand to my neck and pulled me close. I breathed in his essence when he started at my eyelids and dropped butterfly kisses on them. Then my cheeks. My belly burned with his closeness. I waited.

His lips touched mine and I crushed him to me. How I'd longed for this day. Dreamed of it for too many nights to count.

Our fervor exploded in tingles the entire length of my body.

But my senses prickled in a different way a moment later. I opened one eye and jumped back. Kyle came with me but stopped when his eyes flew open.

Willa had her head tilted to the side, right in our faces. She almost fell over laughing. "I knew that'd cool the fire between you two."

"*Girl.* That's just not right."

Kyle lifted his chin. "You won't win this one. I don't care what you do."

He pulled me back into his arms and started to kiss me again, but I pressed my hands against his chest. My breathing remained heavy. "She's right. We better … wait."

"Okay, then. But not for long." He tried to crouch on one knee but his leg stiffened. Then he tried to switch to the other one. What was he doing? "I'll get there. Just give me a second."

Stepping back, I put a hand to my heart. Wait. Was he about to propose? If my blood wasn't zipping through my veins before, it accelerated into high gear even more.

"I'm bungling this." His adam's apple bobbed. He stopped trying to get down on one knee and took my hand.

Willa's jaw dropped, and she plunked down onto the

rock. "This is turning out good. Keep going, Kyle. Don't mess it up."

I gave her the stink eye.

Kyle reached into his brocaded vest and pulled something out of his pocket. With my hand in his, he held it out for me to see. "Will you marry me?"

At our rock? On the most perfect sunlit day? "I will," I squealed like a kindergartner. "I love you."

The ring slid onto my finger and sparkled as if it had its own light source from within.

We fell into each other's arms. I buried my face in his shoulder and cried. "Thank you for your patience and commitment, in more ways than one. I can't wait to spend forever with you."

Made in the USA
Middletown, DE
01 February 2019